PRAISE FOR WILLIAM BERNHARDT AND THE DANIEL PIKE LEGAL THRILLER SERIES

"*Final Verdict* is a must read with a brilliant main character and surprises and twists that keep you turning pages. One of the best novels I've read in a while."

— ALICIA DEAN, AWARD-WINNING AUTHOR
OF *THE NORTHLAND CRIME CHRONICLES*

"*Judge and Jury* is a fast-paced, well-crafted story that challenges each major character to adapt to escalating attacks that threaten the very existence of their unique law firm."

— RICK LUDWIG, AUTHOR OF *PELE'S FIRE*

"I could not put *Trial by Blood* down. The plot is riveting....This book is special."

— NIKKI HANNA, AUTHOR OF *CAPTURE LIFE*

"Once started, it is hard to let [*The Last Chance Lawyer*] go, since the characters are inviting, engaging and complicated....You will enjoy it."

— *CHICAGO DAILY LAW BULLETIN*

"Bernhardt is the undisputed master of the courtroom drama."

LIBRARY JOURNAL

D0907897

FINAL VERDICT

FINAL VERDICT

A Daniel Pike Novel

WILLIAM BERNHARDT

BABYLON
BOOKS

For Harry, Alice, and Ralph—
My final verdict on joy

I have fought the good fight, I have finished the race, I have kept the faith.

— 2 TIMOTHY 4:7

JOY TO THE RIGHTEOUS

CHAPTER ONE

TULIP AWOKE TO THE SOUND OF A GUN CLICKING IN HER EAR.

At first, all she could see was a penetrating bright light, so strong it washed everything else from her field of vision. All she could feel was an intense heat. A fiery heat. So severe she felt as if her skin were cooking.

She couldn't see the gun. But she knew it was there.

She closed her eyes to protect them from the searing whiteness.

What happened? Last thing she remembered, she was in St. Petersburg. Then she left the meeting at the bar and that hideous man grabbed her and she knew she was in danger...but it was all cloudy after that. Indistinct. Like the hazy fuzz following an all-night binge, but she hadn't had anything to drink and she hadn't taken any drugs.

She seemed to be reclining, lying down on something soft. It didn't make sense, nothing made sense, but she couldn't straighten her head out—

The gun. Forget about retracing her steps. She needed to worry about the gun.

Cold steel pressed against her left temple, which somehow managed to burn at the same time that it chilled her to the core.

"Where... am I?" Her voice sounded like the front door of a haunted house, creaky and broken, as if long disused and in desperate need of oil.

She heard a chuckling from somewhere above her. "Your gravesite."

The gun pressed harder into her temple, shoving the side of her face into the...*sand?*

She had grown up around beaches and knew what sand felt like. But this was not beach sand. This was hotter and coarser. More like...desert sand. Which would explain why she felt as if she were baking. But there were no deserts near St. Pete...

"Got any final words, Krakowski?" The man spoke with a thick Central American accent. "Parting requests?"

"Yeah." She licked her dry lips. "Let me go."

He laughed. "That is the one request I cannot grant."

She opened her eyes again, and this time she kept them open, though they watered and the intense light gave her an even more intense headache. She had to pull it together before it was too late. She stretched out her arm, traveling along the length of her body, making sure she was still intact.

Her arms were there, but her t-shirt was torn at the neck. Her slacks were ripped. Her legs were still intact, but exposed from the knees down. Her pockets were empty.

Her brain must be reconnecting, because all at once she felt a powerful surge of hunger. And thirst. Her mouth was parched and dry.

What had happened to her?

She twisted her head around. More cold steel. Another gun? A two-fisted assassin?

Wait a minute. That wasn't a gun.

She squinted, trying to focus.

It was a hammer. He held a gun in one hand and a hammer in the other.

She drew in a deep breath and tried to stifle her mounting fear. "Hot day...for carpentry work."

The man smirked. "The gun is for killing you. The hammer is for making sure that if your body is found, no one recognizes your face."

He moved between her and the glaring sun, a welcome respite. He was only a shadow now, a towering silhouette.

"Can't you...tell me what this is about?"

"Sorry. No."

"You don't have to kill me."

"Not my decision. I have my orders."

"What did you...do to me? My head feels like a steamroller drove over it."

"That's the drugs. So you would sleep. Didn't want any trouble during the trip to Nevada."

Nevada? What the hell was going on? "Long way to travel. Just to get to this garden spot."

"This is no man's land. North of Vegas, south of nothing. A reliable place to dispose of a body. Part of an established pipeline. It has never failed us." He moved in closer. "I do not think anyone will find your shriveled-up carcass. But if they do, it will be unidentifiable. I will hammer out all the recognizable features. I will remove your hands and bash your teeth. Your flesh will boil. Scavengers will pick the meat from your bones."

"You don't have to kill me," she repeated. She could probably think faster if her head weren't throbbing, and she could probably negotiate better if her heart weren't hammering. She was sweating profusely, and not just because of the heat. "I can keep my mouth shut."

"That is not a chance we are willing to take."

"I could be useful to you."

"I have not been asked to extract information. My boss wants you punished and eliminated."

She reached out blindly and found his arm. "I could...be good to you."

He shoved her arm away. "Do not sicken me. You think I want your favors? In Vegas, I can get better than you simply by opening my wallet."

She could feel some of her strength, her muscular coordination, returning. It was just possible she could move, maybe even get to her feet, given half a chance. But he did not appear likely to give her half a chance.

"I have been watching you since we left Florida," the man continued. "Watching you drool and snore and wet yourself. This did not excite me. I drove you from our private airport and dragged your body through the hot sand while you slept. All I want now is to be rid of you."

"Please don't." She tensed her muscles, testing. She felt stiff, broken, as if somehow her brain was disconnected from the limbs it was supposed to control. She needed more time.

She allowed a pleading note to enter into her voice. "Please help me. I'll do anything. Anything you want."

He made a disgusted snorting noise. "So weak. Like all American women. Pampered and useless. You should prepare to die."

"Please!" She screamed, and her voice echoed as if she were at the bottom of a canyon. An abysmal void in the pit of hell. "I'll do anything. Please don't hurt me."

"The first bullet goes to your feet, so you don't run. Then your hands. Your legs. Your arms. Perhaps more...intimate locations. And eventually your head, but only hours later, after the pain has become so excruciating that you cannot feel anything any longer." He smiled. "Then I'll start taking you apart with the hammer."

"I...don't want to die."

"I cannot spare you. But if you do not struggle, I will show mercy. You will die quickly, with one bullet. Rather than slowly. With many."

"I'm a real person. Not just a...disposable body. I've got a name."

"I know your name. Tulip Krakowski. What of it?"

"I mean, I've got a name your boss wants. The one he's been looking for."

The man hesitated. "I do not understand."

"Come close. I...I can barely speak."

He leaned in lower, closer to her...

Her knee jutted upward like a cobra, smashing between his legs. He winced and cried out. At almost the same time, she brought her right arm around and pushed the gun aside. He fired, but the bullet soared over her head. The sound was ear-splitting, but her head already hurt so badly she could barely tell the difference.

The man toppled over. "You...bitch," he grunted. He swung the hammer in the air, barely missing her head. He pushed against the sand, trying to right himself, but she was already on top of him.

She shoved him down hard, then grabbed the gun arm. He fired again but the shot went wild. She pinned down his arms.

He fought hard, trying to regain control. She had leverage for now, but he was stronger than she was. Her hands were slick with sweat. She strained to maintain her grip, her neck tightening. They were locked in a lethal arm-wrestling contest, one she was bound to lose.

His left arm broke free and he brought the hammer around, pounding her in the center of her back. She yelled and growled and drove her knee into his chest. The gun flew off into the sand. He tried to bring the hammer around again, but she grabbed his wrist and twisted his skin in opposite directions.

He screamed and dropped the hammer. She sat up, hoping

to find the gun. He grabbed a fistful of sand and threw it in her face, blinding her. She sputtered and shook her head back and forth, trying to wipe the sand from her eyes and mouth.

He found the gun first—and fired. It missed her, but only by inches. She had to do something fast.

She bent down and bit his hand, driving her teeth into the fleshy part of the palm as if she intended to take a bite. She felt his skin tear. She heard him scream.

He writhed furiously, still holding the gun. His car keys tumbled out of his pants pocket.

He pointed the gun at her head.

She grabbed his car keys and rammed the largest key into his right eye.

Blood and viscous matter spurted everywhere. He shrieked, a high-pitched keening. She wiped the blood away with her elbow. He thrashed on the sand, bellowing, incoherent.

She used the flat of her hand to ram the key in even farther.

His screams reached a fevered pitch. He waved his hands in the air, thrashing at nothing, trying to make the pain go away.

He relaxed his grip for only an instant, but it was an instant that cost him his life. She yanked the gun out of his hand, whirled it around, and pulled the trigger.

He fell backward into the sand, gurgling, blood spewing from his neck.

She stood up and wiped the sand and blood from her face. He appeared to be dead. But could she be sure?

She shot him three more times in the head, just to be certain.

You wanted to kill me, you filthy son-of-a-bitch? You thought you could hurt me because I'm a woman?

Your mistake. It's true what the kids say. Girls get the job done. And she just proved it.

He wasn't coming back. He wasn't going anywhere.

But where was she going?

She stretched to her full height, feeling her bones creaking and popping.

She was in the middle of the desert. She could see a few rock formations, but no signs, no roads, no indications of life.

Where was she? And how would she get back to civilization?

He couldn't have dragged her far. There must be a car somewhere near. But where? How could she find it?

She searched his pockets. Nothing. No map. No identification. She found an iPhone, which might have led her to the car. But it required a passcode.

She pressed the keyless lock button on the keychain, but heard nothing.

The sun beat down on her relentlessly. She was already parched. She would not last long out here. She couldn't assume help would find her.

She would have to find help.

She brushed herself off, then started walking. She kept the gun and the keys and the phone, just in case they proved useful later.

How long could she survive out here? No way of knowing. The man had mentioned Vegas. Surely if she kept moving, eventually she would find some trace of humanity.

Walking was her only hope. A slender hope, but all she had. So she put one foot in front of the other. And walked.

CHAPTER TWO

DAN POSITIONED HIMSELF IN FRONT OF THE POLICEMAN ON THE witness stand, Patrol Officer Thomas Banner. He was a short man, mid-thirties, carrying more weight than he should, which at his height was probably easy to do. Dan had read that the Napoleonic complex was a myth, basically just an excuse to stereotype short people and accuse them of arrogance or over-compensation. But if ever there was an argument to be made for the complex, it was sitting before him at this very moment.

This case was a showdown between two witnesses who told starkly different versions of what happened. According to Banner, the vicious behavior of the defendant's dog required him to seize control of it, and eventually, the defendant. He said the dog was a public health hazard and he wanted it put down, and he charged the defendant with disorderly conduct. But Dan's client, Mandy McKenzie, said the cop was a bully who attacked her dog when she refused to move out of the under-ground storm tunnels. Because she lived there.

Dan scrutinized Officer Banner carefully. Long ago, Dan's favorite law professor taught him the importance of paying attention, watching people, collecting small bits of information that might later add up to something important. His eyes scanned Banner, collecting everything of interest. Buzzcut, slightly uneven sideburns. Immaculately polished shoes. Dirt under the nail on his right forefinger. Clear blue eyes.

"Could you explain what you were doing in the storm tunnels on the day in question?" Dan asked.

Banner cleared his throat, a solemn expression on his face. "It's part of my regular beat. Lots of homeless people down there, unfortunately. So lots of crime."

"Crime by the homeless? Or crime perpetrated against the homeless?"

"Both. It's a bad situation all around."

"And you've tried to address the problem by clearing out all the homeless people, right?"

"No one has a constitutional right to live in the tunnels."

"It's public property, isn't it?"

"Doesn't mean people have a right to squat there."

"Do they have anywhere else to go?"

"That's not the issue."

Of course it was, but he would never get this officer to see it. Homelessness was on the rise in St. Petersburg, as it was in many other parts of the country. The city had run out of space in the shelters, so the police usually looked the other way. But not this guy. There's always one...

Dan's last case had taken him into the tunnels and introduced him to the so-called "Mole People" who lived there. That was when he met Mandy, a tunnel resident for more than five years. He gave her a dog, a little chihuahua mix to replace the one she lost. So in a sense, he was responsible for her being dragged into court today.

"You've spoken with my client, Amanda McKenzie, on many occasions, correct?"

"True."

"What was the reason for the conversation on the day in question?"

"I was trying to help her."

"You were trying to push her out of the tunnels."

"As I said, no one has a right to live there."

"Did you offer her an alternative residence?"

"She didn't want one."

"Please answer the question. Did you offer her a different place to live?"

"Not my job."

"Why did you target her?"

"I didn't. I wanted everyone out of there. It's unsanitary."

"Is that a judgment call for you to make?"

"It's my beat."

Dan shook his head. Monumental arrogance, founded on… well, nothing. He'd known many outstanding cops in his time. His father had been one of them. But this guy was definitely not.

"And when you couldn't get Mandy to leave on her own, you went after her dog."

"That is absolutely untrue." Banner inched forward. "The dog was not on a leash, thereby in violation of the city municipal code. And it was violent."

"Liar, liar, pants on fire!"

He whipped around. Mandy, seated at the defendant's table, was muttering her thoughts in a *sotto voce* stream. Dan's sister, Dinah, sitting beside Mandy, tried to quiet her. Dinah was taking legal assistant classes at the local community college and seemed to have a real interest—and aptitude—for the subject.

Judge Quinn looked unamused. "Mr. Pike, you need to control your client."

Easy to say… "Yes, your honor. I apologize."

"Keep your apologies. What I expect is compliance. If she can't behave, she'll be excused from the courtroom. And I'll issue a fine that I suspect she might find difficult to pay, which will increase her time in jail."

Talk about overkill. Was everyone here determined to treat this poor homeless woman like Hannibal Lector? Judge Quinn was new to the bench, swept in during the recent elections. She probably thought her case docket would have something more glamorous than animal-control disputes.

He walked quietly to the defense table. Mandy was small and wizened, but she hadn't lost her fire. Two teeth missing on the bottom row. Hair looked like it had been in a cyclone. Loose-fitting clothes. "Mandy, you need to be quiet. You're interrupting, and it's pissing off the judge."

"Isn't this my case?"

"In a way…"

"Then I got a right to speak."

"And you'll have your chance. Maybe. But this isn't it."

"Don't let that cop say lies about me. He's mean. I can tell you all about him."

She already had, of course. At length.

"I agree," Dinah whispered. Trim figure. Short brown hair. Brown eyes. His mother's eyes. Dinah had spent some time on the streets herself, till Dan learned to his surprise that he had a half-sister. "He comes on to women. Hassles the ones who won't cooperate."

And he mistreats dogs. That pretty much established him as the worst person to walk the face of the earth. "Try to keep Mandy under control. The next few minutes will be crucial."

"I'll do my best."

Dan bounced up on the toes of his Air Jordans. He'd spent enough time on the preliminaries. It was time to introduce the most important witness. And it wasn't Banner. Or Mandy.

He gestured to his partner Jimmy, who stepped outside, then returned a few moments later holding a pet carrier. The high-pitched yipping announced that the key witness had arrived.

Dan took the carrier, set it down, and slowly removed the pet in question. Mandy's dog. She had named him Dan.

The dog leaped into his arms and started licking his face. Did he remember that Dan was the one who rescued him from the shelter?

Dan had obtained the court's permission to produce the pooch in advance. Judge Quinn didn't like it but, given the importance of the dog to the case, it was hard to say no.

Opposing counsel, Associate DA James Akers, rose to his feet. "Your honor, I know we agreed to the dog's presence in the courtroom, but I see no reason to remove it from its carrier."

Dan pulled a face. "Is my esteemed colleague afraid of a dog?"

Akers seethed, which of course was the whole point of the remark. "No, your honor, I'm not afraid of a chihuahua. It's simply a matter of courtroom decorum. We've already had"— he glanced at Mandy—"sufficient distractions."

"The dog has to be properly identified by the witness," Dan explained, nuzzling the doggie.

Judge Quinn rolled her eyes. "I suppose. But get the dog back in the carrier as soon as possible. We don't want any accidents."

Pity that this case, like most municipal matters, was a bench trial. If he flashed this cute doggie at a jury and told them the mean copper wanted to take him away from Mandy, this case would be a slam dunk.

Dan returned to the witness stand. "Officer Banner, is this the dog in question?"

"Looks like him."

"This is the dog you tried to remove from its owner, correct?"

"He wasn't on a leash."

"Do you normally stop every time you see a dog that isn't on a leash? Or was this just because you were trying to get Mandy out of the tunnels?"

"What difference does it make?" Banner's jaw jutted forward. "It's no different from a traffic cop who pulls someone over for a minor infraction because they suspect a records search will yield something more criminal. You use the tools you have to achieve a greater good."

"Then you acknowledge that you were trying to get Mandy out of the tunnels. Out of her home."

"Do you know how long it's been since she had a bath? She's a health hazard."

"I understand she's allowed to shower at a local shelter once a week."

"She doesn't brush her teeth. She doesn't wash her clothes. Her so-called home, an eight-foot stretch of collected trash, is a dump."

"But you didn't offer her anything better."

"I'm not a social worker. Policing my beat is my job."

"I would've thought taking care of the people on your beat was your job."

"Objection." Akers rose. "Argumentative."

"Sustained." Judge Quinn glanced down at the papers on her desk. "Mr. Pike, I can see where you're going with this. But the issue is whether the canine in question was violent, which required the officer to take it into his custody. If so, it should be put down, not only for your client's safety but for the safety of the public at large."

Dan pressed the dog close to his face. "Your honor...it's a chihuahua." Thank goodness the dog was cooperating. If the mutt took a bite out of his nose, his case was blown.

"I've seen a chihuahua tear a sofa to shreds. I wouldn't want to see what a mean one could do to a person."

Back at the defense table, he heard Mandy start up again. "My precious little doggie wouldn't hurt—"

Dinah slapped a hand across her mouth.

The judge drummed her fingers. "I can't devote my entire day to this."

"Understood." Dan returned to the witness. "You're suggesting that this sweet little doggie was violent?"

"Completely out of control. I had to contain it—"

"Him."

"—whatever. I didn't have a leash or a muzzle, so I grabbed it."

"Did you use excessive force?"

"I didn't shoot it, if that's what you mean. Though the thought crossed my mind."

"Tell me you're joking."

"I had to hold that dog for more than ten minutes, and it fought me the whole time. Could've done some serious damage if I'd let it."

"Did the dog injure you?"

"No."

"Cause you any lingering physical or mental distress?"

"No. I finally got the dog to my car, then took it to the pound. I tried to give your client a citation, but she resisted and caused a scene so I was forced to put her under arrest for disorderly conduct."

Dan nodded. "Mandy was just too much for you to handle, huh?"

"You might be surprised."

"First you were threatened by a toy dog. Then by an elderly homeless woman."

Banner's lips pressed tightly together. "You can be sarcastic all you want, mister, but when you wear this uniform, your job is to keep the peace, and that means your neck is on the line 24/7. Your client might've had a knife or a gun. That dog could've been trained to kill. You can't be too careful."

"Tell me you wouldn't hurt this poor defenseless pooch." He

thrust the dog toward Banner, who instinctively lurched backward.

Bit of an overreaction, Dan thought. Was there something here he was missing?

He heard a *pssst!* behind him.

Dinah curled her finger.

He asked the judge for a moment, then leaned beside his sister. "What?"

"Look at his eyes."

Officer Banner was staring impatiently at them. And...

Dan smiled. It appeared he was not the only one who was a keen observer of people. Must run in the genes.

He returned to the witness stand, still toting the dog. "Officer Banner, I'd like to ask a favor."

The officer looked suspicious, as he had every reason to be. "What?"

"Would you hold this dog for a moment?"

DA Akers was back on his feet. "Your honor, this is ridiculous. Counsel is just wasting time. Trying to humiliate the witness. Making a mockery of the court."

"All that, huh?" Dan said. "Just by asking someone to hold a dog."

"It's completely unnecessary and irrelevant."

"It isn't," Dan said. "The witness claims he took custody of the dog and held him for more than ten minutes and that he suffered no physical distress as a result. I submit that in fact he would never voluntarily hold a dog for anything close to that length of time."

"I'm not afraid of a chihuahua!"

"Let's test that theory, your honor. Let's see if he can hold the dog for five minutes." He looked Banner straight in the eye. "Because I don't think he can. And I don't think he did on the day in question, either."

"That's absurd!" Banner bellowed.

"Then hold the dog."

"Fine." Banner thrust out his arms, then turned his head, as if he were sacrificing himself on an altar.

Dan lowered the dog into his arms. "Now draw him nearer. Like you're restraining him."

Banner brought the dog closer, though not all that close.

"Do you own a dog, Officer Banner?"

"No."

"I thought not. My associate noticed that not long after I brought the dog near you, your eyes, previously clear, became cloudy and red. I think you're allergic to dogs. That's probably why you dislike them, but more importantly, guarantees you would never pick up this dog and hold him for an extended period of time. You wouldn't do anything that made you look weak or vulnerable. Your ego wouldn't allow it."

Banner whipped his head around. "Do I have to listen to this?"

The judge shrugged. "You have to answer his questions. Listening is optional."

Dan continued. "You say you took the dog into custody, but Mandy says you kicked the dog"—Dinah gasped—"more than once and it ran off. Mandy wouldn't stop yelling so you arrested her, figuring no one would believe a homeless woman. The dog later turned up, no thanks to you. You went back later, probably with a friend, found the dog and took it to the pound. But you never personally took control of the dog. You didn't hold it for one minute, much less ten."

"I can't believe you listen to anything that crazy woman says," Banner said, looking increasingly uncomfortable. "Look at her. Look how she behaves."

"Yes, you were counting on that attitude, weren't you? We ignore the bag lady, the beggars, the homeless—all the marginalized members of our society. So the bully cop can get away with anything." He paused. "What you didn't count on was that this homeless lady has a lawyer friend. Who cares about her very much. How are your eyes doing, Officer?"

"Just fine, thank you."

"Getting a little itchy?"

"I told you. Fine."

"They look red and filmy to me. I bet you want to rub them desperately, but you can't because if the judge sees how allergic you are, she'll realize you didn't hold the dog for ten minutes and this whole paranoid story is your overcompensating macho vengeful revisionist history of your failed attempt to bully a homeless woman and a chihuahua."

"Objection!" Akers said.

"Withdrawn." Dan's voice dropped. "But it's true."

"You don't know what you're talking about," Banner said.

"We'll see. You know, some people think chihuahuas are hypoallergenic, but they're not. No breed is 100% hypoallergenic. I mean, chihuahuas are better than big hairy sheepdogs. Less shedding, less dander. But they can still trigger an allergy. How are you doing, officer? Breathing okay?"

"I'm fine." But his eyes were swelling and he was sniffling. His voice sounded congested. "Will you take the dog back now?"

"Not quite yet. Here's the thing—though the allergen usually produced by pets is dander, the cause of the allergen is a protein found in the pet's skin, saliva, and urine. Air filters help, but for people who are extremely allergic, there's no 100% problem-free pet. Which is why you don't have a dog, right, officer? And why you didn't pick up this dog on the day in question, though you lied about it later to cover the fact that you kicked and mistreated the poor puppy due to your pervasive hostility toward animals. And homeless people."

"I'm telling you, I'm not allergic."

"Your eyes are watering."

"That doesn't—"

"Your face is red and puffy."

"I'm not allergic. I—I just don't like—I just—I don't *like*—"

And then he sneezed, possibly the most titanic sneeze Dan had heard in his entire life.

"*Take this mutt away from me!*" Banner bellowed, wiping his nose and eyes with his elbow.

"Gladly." The dog scampered into Dan's arms. "And your honor, I move that all charges against my client—and the dog—be dropped. And someone get this poor man some Benadryl."

CHAPTER THREE

DETECTIVE JAKE KAKAZU TRIED NOT TO GAPE AS HE STEPPED OUT
of the elevator on the penthouse level of SweeTech's downtown
office building. Perhaps because of his Oxford education, he had
a reputation for being urbane and unflappable. Gaping would
not be in keeping with the image. Still...this place was
impressive.

The lobby was richly adorned with mirrors and chandeliers
and more gold than Trump Tower. Kakazu had traveled all
around the world. He'd seen the Taj Mahal, Notre Dame, the
Hagia Sophia, St. Paul's. This didn't have the religious or spiritual aspects of those famous sites. This was more a monument
to capitalism than spiritualism, or perhaps, given the nature of
the man who built it, a gauche monument to ego.

But still impressive.

He turned right. The mirrored walls created an infinity
effect, making it look as if the corridor extended endlessly
toward the vanishing point.

"This way, I think." Sergeant Pemberton pointed to the left.
Pemberton was a young officer who had worked on many of the
cases surrounding St. Pete's most prominent businessman and

philanthropist, Conrad Sweeney. "Are you planning to arrest Sweeney?"

Kakazu shook his head. "So far, we can't prove it didn't happen just as he says."

"The guy fell out Sweeney's window."

"Which is probably not how someone as smart as Sweeney would choose to commit a murder. Defenestration is somewhat difficult to hide."

Kakazu followed his sergeant down the foyer. A few moments later, a tall red-haired woman emerged from a previously indiscernible door.

"Hello, gentlemen. I'm Prudence Hancock. Dr. Sweeney is ready for you."

Kakazu nodded. How generous of the great man to make time for mere policemen investigating a murder that occurred on his property. He was somewhat disappointed she had emerged so quickly. He easily could have spent an hour admiring the artwork.

Without another word, Prudence pivoted and disappeared. He supposed they were intended to follow.

Sweeney's office was about the size of Kakazu's house, and it was just as art-adorned as the elevator lobby. Sculptures poised in the corners. Paintings on the walls.

After a long trek, they came to an immense desk. More art behind it. An original Basquiat, if he wasn't mistaken.

And to the left, a broken window, floor-to-ceiling, currently patched with duct tape and cardboard.

That must be where it happened. The question was, Why? And of course, Who?

Conrad Sweeney sat behind the desk, slightly reclining, his fingers steepled before his face. His nose was bandaged but his expression suggested he hadn't a care in the world, when in fact, Kakazu knew he was experiencing serious financial setbacks and probably on the verge of bankruptcy.

Sweeney was a large man. His perfectly tailored suit made him appear powerful rather than obese. "Detective Kakazu. Thank you for coming." Prudence positioned herself behind Sweeney, as if she were his personal color guard.

"I wanted to see where it happened. Of course, we know where the body landed. But that didn't tell us much. I think most of the action happened up here."

"That is true," Sweeney said, shaking his head. "So regrettable. I still don't understand how that man got in here."

"You didn't know him?"

Sweeney made a slight wincing face. "No. Didn't look like... my kind of person."

"His name was Fabian Fuentes. He's been linked to the Central American cartel we know has operated in Florida for decades."

"I'm not surprised. Why we continue to let these people into our country—" Sweeney stopped short.

Kakazu arched an eyebrow. Had Sweeney suddenly realized he was speaking to an Asian-American? With a British accent?

Sweeney cleared his throat. "I'm sure you've read my report. I called the police immediately after the incident happened. I didn't want any confusion or false accusations."

Or more likely, Kakazu pondered, there was no way to cover up a body flying out of your penthouse office window. So you concocted a story and called the police before they called you.

Sweeney continued. "I suspected a connection to that cartel. They've been out to get me for years. Tried to strongarm me into providing them tech in violation of USMCA. I'd die first."

"You said in your report that the man attacked you?"

Sweeney pressed a hand against his forehead. "Completely without warning. I was just standing behind my desk, thinking. He punched me in the face. Broke my nose. While I was dazed, he threw me against the window and broke it. Miracle I wasn't the one who fell. But I pulled my head together and retrieved the gun I keep in my desk. Unfortunately, a man in my position has to be prepared for the unexpected. I shot him, and the bullet propelled him out the damaged window."

"Sounds like quite the action-packed ordeal."

"You have no idea."

"Mind if I look around?"

Sweeney spread his arms wide. "Of course not. I'd stay away from the window, though. It's a windy day and I can't guarantee that cardboard will hold. I have a man ready to replace the window, but the police asked me to wait until the investigation is completed."

"I'm sure you'll be able to repair it soon." Kakazu approached the window and did his best to see beyond the cardboard and tape. Prudence followed him around, keeping a semi-discreet distance, but matching him step-by-step.

Could a bullet push someone out the window? Granted, it was already weakened. But Kakazu still wasn't sure he bought it. He'd studied the reports on the caliber, load, and bullet. While it wasn't impossible, it didn't seem probable. Nothing about this story did.

Or maybe he was just suspicious because he knew Daniel Pike was convinced this man was in league with the cartel—or had been. A falling-out would be a much more convincing explanation of why Fuentes appeared and a fight-to-the-death ensued.

"Has this been photographed?" Kakazu asked Pemberton.

"Yes. Before it was patched."

Kakazu turned back to Sweeney. "And you have no idea why this man wanted to kill you?"

"None."

"How did he get past your security?"

Prudence answered. "Someone broke into the HQ on the first floor. Dismantled the security protocols. Turned off the cameras."

"Wouldn't someone need inside information to pull that off?"

"We suspect Fuentes paid someone on our security team."

Sweeney had an answer for everything. But Kakazu still wasn't sure he bought it.

He paced around the immense office, taking time to admire the fixtures, the architecture, the art. He knew Sweeney had resisted selling art to pay off his debts, but the courts would soon take that out of his hands...

He stopped.

Sweeney was an egomaniac. He loved his art.

But he was savvy enough to know he would soon lose it.

Or more accurately, he would soon lose the art anyone knew about. Everything on display.

The safest way to make sure no one stole your prize possessions was to make sure no one knew about them.

He completed a full tour of the office, carefully measuring it with his eyes. Because this was a crime scene, he had reviewed the floor plans on file before he arrived—and something wasn't adding up.

"Anything I can help you with?" Sweeney asked.

"Maybe." Kakazu took another slow spin. "Is there...more to this office than meets the eye?"

"Isn't it enough?"

"This office should be even bigger than it is." He stepped behind the desk, nudging Sweeney out of the way.

Sweeney never moved far from his desk. Was there a reason for that?

Kakazu examined the wall carefully. Then he knocked on it, hard.

The sound was more of a hollow echo than a solid thud.

Kakazu turned. "Mr. Sweeney—"

"It's Dr. Sweeney," Prudence corrected.

"Dr. Sweeney, then. Is—"

"And he has an urgent appointment. I'll show you the way out."

Kakazu ignored her. "Is there another room attached to this one? Maybe a...secret room?"

Watching Sweeney's expression was like watching a Shakespearean actor at work. Something was going on in there. A flickering behind the eyes. Sweeney was weighing his options...

And finally smiled. "You are an astute observer, detective. There is indeed another room. I didn't show it to you because it has no relevance to this matter. Fuentes was never in there. But just so you know I'm not hiding anything, let me show it to you."

He pressed the edge of the frame holding the spotlighted painting behind his desk. "It's a fingerprint ID scanner. Only opens for my right index finger. No one can get in but me."

Kakazu heard a click followed by a popping sound. The wall behind Sweeney moved slightly.

Sweeney gave the panel a push. A passageway appeared.

Prudence did not look happy. Kakazu was glad she wasn't armed.

Sweeney passed into the room beyond. Kakazu followed him, crouching to pass through the hatch. Sergeant Pemberton followed a few steps behind.

The room beyond was simpler than the one outside and had no furniture except a single recliner that appeared to be on some sort of turntable, like a huge Lazy Susan.

He soon realized why. The walls were lined with paintings. Sweeney could sit in that chair and view one after another without getting up.

"This is where I keep my favorite treasures," Sweeney explained. "Call me selfish, but I think some art should be kept from the masses. A little privacy makes it more special."

Maybe, but he suspected the main motivation was to keep it out of the hands of tax auditors.

"Museums have their place," Sweeney continued. "I thought I might found one someday. But the true connoisseur craves solitude. Privacy. As the great poetess said, 'How public—like a Frog.'"

Sweeney had an aversion to publicity? Then why did he constantly stage high-profile charitable spectacles with himself at center stage? "Is that a Picasso?" Kakazu pivoted. "And a Vermeer?"

"You have a fine eye. Most people would've gone first to the van Gogh. But Vermeer had more talent in a single finger than that Post-Impressionist hack did in his entire body. If the man hadn't killed himself, no one would remember his name."

Doubtful, but Kakazu wasn't here to argue art history. He noticed a refrigerator in the corner, plus what appeared to be a large stainless-steel freezer.

Sweeney opened the fridge door. Only soft drinks. Lots of Fresca. No alcohol. "I'm a simple man."

Right. Kakazu looked at the freezer. The door on the front appeared to lift upward, not horizontally.

Sweeney answered the unasked question. "It's for ice cream. I'm a bit of an expert. I know, another indulgence, but if you can't enjoy life, what's the point?"

"I saw you as more of a soufflé man."

"May I tell you a secret, detective? I worked in a drugstore, when I was a poor youth strapped for cash. Scooped ice cream day and night. This indulgence is a bit of nostalgia on my part. A reminder of my humble roots."

"Is it stocked?"

"Indeed. Come around at dinnertime and I'll offer you the best ice cream you've ever tasted."

"That does sound good…"

"Then it's a date. Prudence, please make an appointment. Have Maurice prepare the duck á l'orange."

Kakazu squinted. Why not offer him ice cream now? He'd been the epitome of hospitality before.

He grabbed the handle on the freezer door and lifted it upward.

Then screamed. He would later claim it was more of a shout, but at the time, the last thing on his mind was pitch modulation.

A human body tumbled out of the freezer. In pieces.

CHAPTER FOUR

DAN SPRINKLED THE SLICED SCALLION INTO FIVE BOWLS, ADDED A dash of red chili flakes, then added a special dressing.

"This is my homemade sweet and spicy soy sauce," he explained. "You're going to love it."

Maria and Dinah sat at the kitchen bar watching. "I don't want to be a wet blanket," Dinah said, "but I don't normally go in for soy sauce."

Dan was undaunted. "You're going to love mine."

"I don't like salty stuff."

Maria nodded. "Smart girl. Salt is bad for you. Causes hypertension. And water retention."

Dan tried not to look perturbed. "Excessive amounts of salt have been linked with hypertension. But it doesn't matter, because my sauce is more sweet than salty." He held out a spoon. "Taste."

Dinah reluctantly did as instructed. "Oh. My. God."

Maria arched an eyebrow. "Meaning...?"

"Meaning I think it's the best thing I've ever put between my lips in my entire life."

Maria smiled. "Ok, Dan, give it to me."

"I can't resist an invitation like that." He leaned forward and planted a kiss on her lips—which lasted longer than he had anticipated.

Dinah looked away. "Ick. Take the orgy somewhere else, you two."

Dan grinned. "Fact of life. Culinary skills are inherently sensual. Cooking is an erotic art."

Maria scoffed. "You probably slipped an aphrodisiac into the sauce."

"A good sauce is an aphrodisiac," he countered.

"Ok," Dinah said, "let's get back to the soy sauce. If that's really what it is. Since it isn't salty."

"It's not what you call it. It's what you do with it." Dan finished dressing the Buddha Bowls and passed them around.

Dinah took hers eagerly. "The master chef strikes again."

He laughed. "Everyone should have a sister." He paused. "And I'm very glad that I do. Lunch is served."

DAN PASSED JIMMY AND GARRETT A BOWL WHEN THEY WANDERED downstairs, Jimmy in his traditional cardigan—despite the heat outside—and Garrett in a Rays ball cap, which he might not have removed since they made it to the World Series. Their law office, a converted Snell Isle mansion, not only provided his team with a kitchen and dining room but private offices upstairs. The kitchen was Dan's favorite part, though. He lived on a sailboat, *The Defender*, docked not far away. He loved his boat, but there was no place to cook. The office allowed him to maintain his gourmet skills.

Dan waited for the response. "What do you think?"

Jimmy wolfed down his bowl in about three bites. "There's enough for seconds, right?"

"Right."

"But don't eat so much you get sleepy," Garrett warned. "Mr. K wants to chat with us."

"New big case?"

"I don't know what's on his mind."

"That's fine, as long as it's not too urgent," Jimmy said. "We have a Gloomhaven game to continue."

"When exactly does this game end?" Dinah asked.

Never, Maria mouthed. "You're still on my bad list, Dinah. You stole my spells."

"I'm a thief. I'm supposed to steal stuff. It's on my player card."

"Female players have to stick together in this rough and sexist pre-Renaissance fantasy world dominated by barbaric male chauvinists."

"Sounds a lot like the real world."

"Pretty much."

"Do we need to play today?" Dan asked. "I think Dinah was hoping for some more kitesurfing lessons."

Maria grinned. "You're only doing it for her, right?"

"The weather's going to be perfect. I thought we might stop by to see Mandy on the way. I think I've almost got her convinced that it wouldn't be the end of the world if she and her puppy moved into an apartment."

"Can she afford it?" Jimmy asked.

"She can if Dan pays her rent," Dinah replied.

"Short term," Dan explained. "The city is trying to create more indigent housing. But their budget has been impacted by the COVID economic meltdown. Demand far exceeds supply."

Maria nodded. "Translation: Dan will be paying her rent."

He took a seat on the sofa beside her. "If it hadn't been for Mandy, I might never have found my sister. I think I owe her a lot more than rent."

"Speaking of our latest teammate," Jimmy said, "how are you liking the legal assistant class, Dinah?"

"I think it's super-cool. Law is my new jam. I can see why you guys are so into it. You can actually help people. And pay the bills."

"Sadly," Garrett said, "some members of our profession forget the part about helping people. We've been fortunate. Mr. K has made it possible to practice our profession in a meaningful way without worrying about financial concerns."

Mr. K paid them a generous salary that bore no relationship to the number of hours they worked. All he asked was that when he brought them a case, they worked it to the best of their ability. His cases were always people who needed lawyers in the worst possible way. He called them the Last Chance Lawyers, because more often than not, their clients had no alternatives.

"I see you as the Black Canary type," Jimmy told Dinah. "Sidestepping the law to mete out your own brand of justice on the mean streets of the city. You know, Black Canary's real name is Dinah."

She was obviously puzzled. "Is this another comic book reference?"

Jimmy nodded. "DC Comics made me the person I am today."

Maria sniffed. "Marvel is cooler."

"Marvel is for children. DC is for adults."

"Is that why every female character is drawn with a D-cup?"

He appeared unperturbed. "The glorification of the human figure has been a constant throughout the history of art."

"Uh huh. Especially when the primary audience is young males suffering from arrested development."

Dan thought it was time to intervene. "Getting back to the topic sentence, Jimmy, why does Dinah remind you of Black Canary?"

"Because she's heroic. She fights for the little guy. Just like you."

Garrett cut in. "Mr. K is ready. I'll put him on the television."

Everyone took a seat in the living room while Garrett transferred the Zoom call to the TV—though Dan never understood why he bothered, since there was no image, only sound. Mr. K preferred to keep his identity private.

"Hello, Last Chance Lawyers!" The friendly voice crackled out of the set. "How's my team today?"

"Basking in the rapture of a fabulous lunch," Jimmy said.

"Something Dan whipped up?"

"Yup. Buddha bowls. It was a religious experience."

"That's good. You may need a little nirvana." He paused. "Because I think the assignment I'm about to give you will shake you to the core."

CHAPTER FIVE

THE ROOM FELL SILENT. IF MR. K MEANT THAT LEAD-IN TO command attention—it worked.

"Perhaps…you could give us a few details?" Dan suggested.

"I'm guessing you've heard about the man who plummeted to his death from Conrad Sweeney's penthouse?"

"It would be hard to miss that one. Even if I wasn't already… focused on the man."

"Focused?" Maria asked. "Try obsessed."

"He's holding back information about my father."

"Maybe."

"Definitely." Dan's father was incarcerated for murder when he was young. He'd recently learned much more about the events leading to that arrest. His father shot a fellow police officer to protect his wife—Dan's mother—and his sister. But he was convinced Sweeney was there and involved in some way. He was also convinced Sweeney built his financial empire by aiding, abetting, and laundering money for a Central American cartel.

"I've talked to former friends in the prosecutor's office,"

Garrett said. "They say they've found no grounds to charge Sweeney."

"That's true," K said. "Sweeney seems to have cleaned everything up and advanced explanations that, however dubious, can't be disproven. He says Fabian Fuentes broke into his penthouse office and attacked him. Says he almost went out the window himself but, at the last moment, he managed to grab a gun and shoot Fuentes, who then tumbled through the damaged window."

Jimmy narrowed his eyes. "Sounds like a scene from a Die Hard movie."

"But so far, all the available evidence supports his claim that he acted in self-defense. He hasn't been charged."

Dan exhaled, chuckling a bit. "For a moment, I was afraid you were going to ask us to represent him. Thought maybe you'd completely lost your marbles. But that can't happen if Sweeney hasn't been charged. Right?"

The line went silent for several moments before K spoke again. "That's just it, Dan. I am asking you to represent Sweeney."

"But—you said—"

"About two hours ago, Conrad Sweeney was charged and booked on a count of first-degree murder. But it wasn't for killing Fuentes."

"Then—who?" Maria asked.

"The identity of the victim is currently unknown. But the dismembered corpse—or parts of it—tumbled out of Sweeney's freezer. In a secret room only Sweeney can access. While Jake Kakazu watched."

Dan's lips parted. "Wow. And you want us to represent him?"

K didn't miss a beat. "He's going to need the best defense lawyer possible. And that's you, Dan."

"But...how can I say this...? I hate him."

"I am aware of that."

"I don't want to be melodramatic, but...he's like my arch-nemesis."

"Aware of that, too. But a lawyer has to be professional. You don't have the luxury of only representing people you like. You have to represent the people who need you."

"K," Dan said, "...this is asking too much."

"You don't think I pay you enough money?"

"I don't think there is enough money in the world to ask me to do this."

Garrett cut in, obviously attempting to alleviate the tension. "How is this a Last Chance Lawyer case? Sweeney can afford to get any lawyer he wants."

"I don't think he can," K replied.

"He's filthy rich."

"Not sure about that, either. He appears to be suffering severe monetary setbacks. The courts are threatening to seize all his assets to pay his debts."

"There are tons of lawyers in this town," Maria said. "He's a prominent citizen. A prestige client. He'll be able to find someone."

"Not so far," K informed her. "He made his traditional one phone call to the lawyers he has on retainer. They turned him down cold." And how did K know that? "Apparently Sweeney already owes them more than a million bucks and can't pay it. Since that porn operation was discovered in the basements of what the locals call Sweeney Shelters, he's become a pariah."

Garrett nodded. "The bigger they are, the harder they fall."

"And it couldn't happen to a more deserving person," Dan added.

"Come on, Dan, open your heart," Mr. K said. "This is a man in need. I know you're used to representing indigent clients and homeless people, but your mission statement is to help those in need."

"No. My mission statement is to help those who deserve help."

"That's not what you told us. Back when Maria first approached you about joining this firm. You said you had a passion for justice. Your father was railroaded by the government and you wanted to make sure that didn't happen to anyone else."

"My father was a hero. A public servant."

"And Sweeney is less than perfect. I'll grant you that. But this is a frame. Everything about it seems wrong."

"Jake Kakazu wouldn't charge Sweeney without a reason."

"Oh, he had a reason. A corpse tumbled out of the freezer in a room that only Sweeney could get into."

"I don't want to get involved."

"C'mon, Dan. Sweeney knew the cops were coming. He's too smart to stash a corpse where it would inevitably be found and blamed on him."

"Maybe he didn't think the cops would discover his private room."

"If he were stupid, he might think that. But he's not stupid."

"He is a crook."

"But a smart one. His MO throughout his entire career has been to use operatives to commit illegal acts so they can't be traced back to him."

"I don't care if he committed the murder or not. If he goes behind bars, the world will be a better place."

"If he goes behind bars," K replied, "he's a dead man."

"Then let him *die*," Dan said, teeth clenched.

The room fell silent for a long time.

Eventually, Dan broke the quiet. "I've been a good soldier for you, K. I've done everything you've asked me to do, even when I didn't want to. But the line must be drawn somewhere. I'm drawing it here."

"I anticipated that you might feel this way, Dan. I wish I could be there in person to persuade you."

"Then why aren't you?"

"Someone else would like to talk to you about this."

"There is no one on earth who—"

"My emissary is at your front door as we speak."

Dan's head drooped. The last thing he needed was some flunky twisting his arm. "Not interested."

Maria squeezed his leg. "If they're already at the door...what can it hurt?"

Dan grudgingly pushed himself off the sofa. "This is not going to change my mind." He walked across the living room and flung open the front door.

Prudence Hancock stood on the other side. "Hello, handsome."

CHAPTER SIX

Dan held up his hands, palms out. "Please don't start."

Prudence walked past him, not waiting for an invitation. "Fine. No banter, no flirting."

"This is not the time for it."

"True. But I thought it turned you on."

Dan eye-checked Maria, who did not appear happy. "Look, Prudence, let me save you some time. Nothing you say is going to alter my opinion in the slightest. I will not be part of your boss's coverup, scheme, murder, manipulation, or whatever this is. That man has been a bloody thorn in my side for years. He's lied, cheated. Told lies about me and my family. Bribed witnesses, threatened my friends, and orchestrated one of the largest criminal conspiracies in the history of the State of Florida."

Prudence pivoted and, to his surprise, he saw her eyes widen, her lips tremble. "He's dying."

It took Dan a moment to find his tongue. "You mean…dying inside? Doesn't want to go directly to jail?"

"I mean dying. Pancreatic cancer. He doesn't have much time left. He was trying to build a legacy. A huge estate to leave to the city and its charities. A business that would continue employing people for decades. The artwork sufficient to create the greatest museum in the Southeast. That was his dream. And now it's shattered, falling apart before his eyes." She paused, wiping her eyes. "Dr. Sweeney is accustomed to the finest lifestyle. Which he earned. And now, the only thing in his future is prison. And the grave. Because he's been framed by a criminal mob that wants him out of their way."

Dan shook his head, as if somehow that might prevent her words from getting inside his brain. "Your boss has been involved in crooked enterprises for decades."

"Perhaps," she said quietly.

"He has hired thugs to hurt, maim, and kill. He's obstructed justice. He maligned my father in public."

"I know."

"And now, I'm supposed to be sympathetic because—"

"He's dying."

Dan threw himself on the sofa wordlessly.

"No one will take his case," Prudence added. "Unless something changes, he's going to show up at his arraignment with a public defender."

Dan had a high opinion of most public defenders, who worked a huge caseload and didn't get paid nearly what they deserved. But the humiliation of standing up in court and admitting he'd been appointed an attorney might be the comeuppance Sweeney deserved.

"You know how it is," Prudence continued. "Once the feds sniff vulnerability, they attack like scavengers. We've had investigators swarming all over his office. I can't stand to go in there anymore."

"Do you seriously expect us to feel sorry for him?" Maria asked. "After all he's done?"

"No, I suppose not." Prudence drew in her breath. "'The quality of mercy is not strained. It droppeth as the gentle rain from heaven upon the place beneath. It is twice blessed: It blesseth him that gives…and him that takes.'"

Dan didn't expect Prudence to be a Shakespearean scholar—or to make a valid point.

His father always told Dan to keep the faith. Meaning stick to your principles. Do the right thing. Go the extra mile. And he had another favorite saying: When you forgive someone, you do a favor for two people.

"Do you know how many enemies Dr. Sweeney has behind bars?" Prudence asked. "If he's in there long, he'll be butchered."

"Regardless of who represents him," Dan said, "his chances of getting bail are slim to none."

"Even if you can't get him out, you could get him moved somewhere safer. That's probably best. I'm not sure he's safe on the outside. I'm not sure I am. I've spotted people watching me. I had one of those doorbell cameras installed at my house."

"Look, I'm not taking your boss's case. But even if I wanted to, he wouldn't agree to it. He hates me, as he has mentioned more than once."

"Yes," Prudence agreed, "but it's hate based upon admiration."

"Hard pass. Sweeney would never go along with it."

"To the contrary. I spoke to him about it. This was his idea."

That took him by surprise. He thought Mr. K contacted her. "Sweeney—wants this?"

"Why else would I be here?" Prudence took a few steps forward, forcing him to make eye contact. "Do you think I wanted to descend into this lion's den? Do you think begging is something I enjoy? But you're the best. And he knows it. Has nothing to do with his personal feelings. You're the best there is."

Jimmy broke the silence. "Hey team—wakeup call. I can't believe we're even considering this. The thought of it makes me want to lose my lunch. And I loved my lunch."

Garrett raised a hand. "Let's hear her out. Then we can discuss it in private."

"Ok," Dan said, "you've explained everything—except, what's in it for me? What's in it for my firm? Why would we want to do this? Your boss is a disgusting excuse for a human being, and the fact that he may have an illness does not make him any less disgusting. You admit he has no money to pay us. And the damage to the firm's reputation would be incalculable."

"Is that what it all comes down to?" Prudence asked. "Your reputation?"

"I've spent years building that rep. Even people who don't like me know what I represent."

"Come on. You've represented all kinds of criminal scum. But you did it because you believed they were innocent."

"That's exactly right. And—" He stopped short, frozen.

He grasped her point.

Prudence stepped even closer, her eyes still wide. "Listen to me carefully. Dr. Sweeney did not commit this murder. I know that for a fact. I am intimately involved in his day-to-day activities. It is simply not possible."

Dan raised an eyebrow. "How intimately?"

"Don't be smarmy. We've never been anything but professional colleagues. But that doesn't mean I don't care about him." Dan realized he had never seen her like this. She almost resembled...a human being. "I've been with him for years. I am not exaggerating when I say I know about everything he does. And some of it isn't pretty. But this is a fact—he did not commit this murder. He is innocent."

Dan turned away. "I'm not convinced."

Prudence grabbed his arms and forced him to face her. "At least give me this. You go meet with him. You're a lawyer, you can get in. Talk to him for ten minutes. And if you're not convinced of his innocence after ten minutes, don't take the case. But if you have doubts...." She folded her arms across her ample chest. "You've been saying for years that you want to prevent innocent people from being railroaded. Let's see you put your money where your mouth is." She cast her eyes around the room. "You say you're the Last Chance Lawyers. Prove it!"

Dan's head shook. "I don't know…"

For the first time since Prudence arrived, Dinah spoke, quietly but distinctly. "That is what you told me, Dan. You said we worked for people who need us, whether they're pretty or poor or even pleasant. You said we performed a necessary function. You said that without defense attorneys willing to take unpopular cases, the system falls apart."

The only sound was the crackle of static from Mr. K's Zoom call, which reminded Dan that he was listening, along with everyone else.

"Fine. I'll meet with Sweeney. But if I'm not convinced he's innocent—I'm out of there."

Prudence exhaled heavily. She looked as if a huge weight had been lifted from her shoulders. "I very much appreciate this."

Dan raised a finger. "I'm not promising anything."

"I understand. But I am…relieved to see that there are still some people with principles in this country." She glanced at her watch. "Visiting hours end at five. What are you waiting for?" She waved her hands, as if urging him toward the door. "Saddle up. The Last Chance Lawyers ride again."

CHAPTER SEVEN

ALEJANDRO HERNANDEZ DESPISED THE UNITED STATES, ITS people, its government, and everything about it. His business required him to come here from time to time, but he obtained no pleasure from the visit. In his homeland, El Salvador, people still had some perspective. They knew what was important. Family. Loyalty. Honor. But in America there was no honor, little loyalty, and the very notion of family had been eroded by easy divorce, loose morals, and the insipid need to accept every possible variation of love and coupling.

He reached for his water with a wrinkled hand. He was appalled by what he saw around him at this bar, Beachcombers, where he had gathered with his two top lieutenants in this region. Women sitting with women. Holding hands. Kissing. Single women sitting at the bar in pants, dishonoring their families. Men with hair like girls and no idea how to drink like a man. It baffled him. How a country with values like this had ever become so rich was beyond his imagining. He knew the American empire was in decline. And he was glad.

He would have preferred a different locale, but public meetings were less likely to be bugged or surveilled. His late lieutenant, Fabian Fuentes, held meetings here. For want of a better idea, he continued the tradition.

"Report," he said to Jose, the younger man sitting opposite him. Jose had worked for Fuentes before he died. "Will the police charge Sweeney for murdering our brother?"

"No way," Jose said. He was dressed like an American, T-shirt and jeans, and appeared to have acquired some of their ways of speaking. Jose had been in Florida too long. "The cops say Sweeney acted in self-defense."

Hernandez smirked. "He probably did. How did that bloated whale ever get the drop on Fabian?"

"I don't believe he did," the other accomplice said. Santiago had come to the States recently, to replace an associate named Roberto who had been murdered. "Fabian was quick and strong. No fat man in a three-piece suit could best him."

"And yet, he did," Hernandez said.

"He must've had help."

"However it happened, Fabian is dead. And killing my top lieutenant was an act of war. Which must be answered."

"Sweeney is behind bars and will remain there for some time," Jose said. "Though he claims he was framed."

Hernandez' smile spread from one side of his face to the other. "That is what people would expect him to say, isn't it?"

"Of course."

"Have the police identified the victim?"

"No. But they will."

"Let them. That will only make the case against Sweeney stronger. What about the woman?"

"Dead by now. A million miles from here."

Hernandez gestured toward the waitress, a tiny blonde wisp who did not appear old enough to enter, much less to serve. The American preference for women too insubstantial to be of use mystified him. Did her father know she worked here? Did he know what riffraff propositioned her every day? "I'd like a Pilsener."

The waitress tilted her head. "I'm not sure we have that."

"Then you will get some."

"I'm not allowed to leave—"

"Do not give me excuses."

"But—" She forced a smile. "Isn't there something else I could do for you?"

"I am not interested in the dubious pleasures of your immature body. Bring me my drink. Now."

She scurried away, scared and perplexed. He predicted ten minutes at best before she returned with his beer.

He had always treated women respectfully—but firmly. They liked that. They wanted a strong man to take control. They felt safe knowing someone more capable was in command. That was a lesson he had learned from his grandfather, the man who started this organization.

He would not be the one who let his grandfather's legacy slip through his fingers. He had to get the family business back on track. But that meant he must eliminate the factors that had damaged the business so severely.

"Watch Sweeney whenever possible."

"I will."

"And then we must focus on the lawyer. Pike. What are we doing to eliminate that blot?"

"He has proved...resilient," Jose explained. "We have struck against him on several occasions. And we have hurt him. But he keeps rising from the dead."

"Put a stake in his heart. End it."

"It is not so simple. He has many friends. And he knows the law."

"That means nothing. Put a gun to his temple and fire. That is the law."

"It is not so simple..."

"Of course it is simple. Killing is always simple."

"Let me be direct, sir," Santiago said. "If we eliminate Pike, one of his partners will take his place."

"Then kill them all!" Hernandez' hands shook. "Kill every last one of them."

"That would attract more attention than you want."

"Fine. What do you suggest?"

Jose glanced at his colleague before answering. "In the past, Pike has not been intimidated by threats to himself. But that is not the only way to control someone."

"Stop dancing and spit it out."

"Pike has several partners who I believe he cares about deeply. And a sister."

"What do you suggest?"

"Santiago and I will monitor the situation. Perhaps, with Sweeney out of the picture, Pike will move on to another crusade."

"And if he doesn't? If he continues to endanger my grandfather's business?"

"Then we act. So quickly and decisively that Pike is powerless to oppose us. I see a new era ahead for our organization, sir. A better future. With renewed profits for all." He paused, taking a long drink of his whiskey. "And all our enemies in the grave."

CHAPTER EIGHT

Maria kept Dinah company while Dan spoke to the elderly gentleman in charge of jailhouse visitation. They'd arrived late and would normally have to wait until tomorrow to speak to Sweeney. They couldn't play the "emergency attorney conference" card since Sweeney hadn't hired them yet. But Dan had known this old coot for a long time and seemed to have an affinity for extracting favors in an old-boy-network way she would never understand.

She noticed Dinah surveying her surroundings with a nervous expression. Despite the lateness of the hour, there were still many people running about, some loudly expressing their displeasure with law enforcement. A parade of arrestees streamed past them on the way to the holding cells. The room was painted a dirty green and was in serious need of a good scrubbing.

Maria thought maybe a few words might help settle Dinah's nerves. "First time?"

Dinah glanced back at her. "As a visitor."

Right. "I have to assume this is better."

"Still creeps me out." Dinah shivered a bit. "Do you think they make it unpleasant on purpose?"

"I do think the experience is designed to make people never want to come back again. A milder form of Scared Straight, I suppose."

"That's no excuse for treating people like dirt. I've seen what happens in here. People become hardened because it's the only way to survive. They come out bitterer and angrier than they were when they went in."

"Everything about the system exacerbates the problem," Maria agreed. "More than half of the people thrown behind bars suffer from addictions and committed their crimes under the influence. Will they be helped by being thrown into a hellhole? It would be smarter—and cheaper—to get them help. For that matter, more than forty percent of the people in American prisons suffer from mental illness. But do we get them treatment? Of course not."

"Because that would be smarter and cheaper."

"Exactly. Most get little to no treatment in prison, but they are subjected to degradation, rape, and perpetual crime school." Maria wondered if she should change the subject. This might be stirring unpleasant memories. "How are you adjusting, Dinah? You've undergone some major lifestyle changes since Dan found you."

"That's putting it mildly. I have a place to live. A room with an actual window. I not only get regular meals, they're meals with names I can't pronounce prepared by a gourmet chef. Who happens to be my brother."

Maria grinned. "O brave new world that has such people in't."

Dinah gave her a look. "Am I going to have to start reading Shakespeare to keep up with you people?"

"Definitely not. I hope you're not getting overwhelmed. I

know Dan comes on strong, but...it's just because he cares about you."

"And that's a pleasant change all by itself. Someone who cares about me. Speaking of Dan—how are you two getting along?"

Maria stiffened slightly. "This might be...an awkward topic to discuss with my boyfriend's sister."

"I'm his older sister, remember. I'm allowed to pry into his business."

"I think it's going well. He's actually acknowledged to the world that we're an item. My associates have accepted it and Jimmy has stopped making that gagging gesture every time we're together."

Dinah laughed. "But...?"

"Is there a 'but?'"

"I had the definite sense that you were coming to a 'but.' C'mon, girlfriend. Spill."

Maria tossed her head to one side. "I can't stop feeling that he's...holding back."

"What do you mean?"

"I think his relationship with Camila seriously scarred him."

"Understandable, given what you've told me."

"I know. And I can be patient. But I feel like he's not...all in. You know?"

"Not really."

"To be perfectly blunt—he hasn't asked me back to his boat."

Dinah waved a hand in the air. "You haven't missed anything. It's so tiny you can barely—" She stopped short. "Oh. You mean—"

"Yeah. That's what I mean."

"Seriously? I mean, I've seen you two together. He's very affectionate."

"I know, right? But...no boat."

"Forget the boat. You two should get an apartment. Or a house. You can afford it."

"Dan is a million miles from getting a house. I don't think he's ready to commit."

Dinah gave Maria's hand a squeeze. "I'm sure it's just a temporary thing. He's been busy."

"And he's about to get much busier, unless I miss my guess."

"He'll come around. I'm sure of it. Wait and see."

"I hope you're right. I can be patient." Her cheek twitched slightly. "But not infinitely patient."

DAN STARED THROUGH THE PLEXIGLAS SCREEN AT THE MAN WHO had caused him so much pain and misery. The man who, truth be told, he had come not only to despise but to fear.

Sweeney did not look so fearsome today. His face was drawn and ashen. His normally shaved head had stubble on top, hair that perversely made him look older, not younger. He had not been behind bars that long, but it was already taking its toll.

Sweeney had trouble positioning his considerable girth on the small stool on his side of the screen, but he eventually settled in. They stared at one another for a long moment.

Sweeney spoke first. "Seems that no matter how much we hate one another, we just can't quit one another."

Dan pursed his lips. "You knew you hadn't seen the last of me."

"True."

"I said that, the last day we were in court." He referred to the civil suit that had been the latest incarnation of the grudge match between them. "I told you I was going to finish what my father started."

"Meaning?"

"Cleaning up the scum that infects this town. The cartel. And everyone who helps them."

Sweeney frowned. "The cartel is fading fast. I've been told Fuentes was their last lieutenant of any competence."

"Is that why you took him out?"

Sweeney smiled thinly. "I acted to defend myself."

"Sure. And the guy in the freezer? Was he cartel, too?"

"I hope you will believe me when I say that I have no idea whatsoever who that man in the freezer was. I don't believe the police have been able to identify him yet. I saw him for the first time when he tumbled out the door."

"Of your private freezer. That no one can access but you. Who has a freezer in their office?"

Sweeney shrugged. "I'm addicted to ice cream."

He wanted to believe that. It would almost humanize the man. If such a thing were possible. "Prudence came by. Begged me to visit you."

"Begged?" Sweeney looked at him skeptically. "That doesn't seem like her style. Persuaded, perhaps. She can be extremely persuasive."

"I'm immune to her charms."

"And yet, here you are." He chuckled. "I've known Prudence for a long time. I recognized her talent early on. I think she's grateful."

"Why else would she be willing to do all the crap she's done for you?" This prolonged exposure to Sweeney made his stomach churn. He wanted to get to the point. "She says you want me to represent you on this murder charge."

"True."

"But you hate me."

"Irrelevant. You're the best."

"There are many fine attorneys in this town."

"You're the best." The corner of his lips turned up. "Ironically, that's why I've tried so hard to eliminate you."

He supposed he should be flattered. In a perverse sort of way. "Can you afford me?"

"I thought the Last Chance Lawyers didn't bill their clients."

True. And Mr. K had already authorized them to take the case, though he couldn't understand why. "Most of our clients aren't able to pay major legal fees."

"My assets have been seized or are in the process of being sold. I'm effectively penniless."

He wouldn't believe anything Sweeney said, but Jimmy had phoned his contacts at the court clerk's office and confirmed most of that. "I wouldn't be able to get you out on bail. I doubt the judge would even let me ask, given the publicity you've had of late. The city would draw-and-quarter anyone who put you back on the streets."

"I can live with that. Believe it or not—I've been in worse environments. All I want is for you to make sure I'm not convicted of a crime I didn't commit. That's supposed to be your forte."

"If you didn't murder this guy, who did?"

"I don't know. Sadly, my arrest has impacted my ability to investigate."

"The cartel?"

"Very possibly."

"Do you have any other enemies?"

Dan was startled to see Sweeney laugh out loud. "Seriously? Yes, one or two."

"Like?"

"The entire Coleman family bears a grudge, though if anyone should be seeking revenge it should be me."

"And?"

"The Democratic Party still blames me for what happened to your former flame. ICE has been investigating me for years. Local gangsters. The IRS."

"I don't think the IRS murders people and stuffs them into freezers."

"You might be surprised what the IRS will do. Absolutely ruthless."

"Anyone else?"

"Many. I'll ask Prudence to draw up a list. If you're taking the case."

Dan stared through the screen at the man. This evil bastard? His client? He couldn't bear the thought. And yet...

"How do I know you didn't commit the crime?"

"I just told you I didn't."

"Something more reliable."

"Do you think I'm an idiot? Would I leave a corpse where it was certain to be connected to me?"

"Maybe it was an emergency. Maybe you were pressed for time."

"That's not how I roll. I had ample knowledge the police were coming. Plenty of time to move the body parts. But I didn't. Because I didn't know they were there."

"When did you last open the freezer?"

"Two nights before."

"And no corpse?"

"Only large quantities of Rocky Road. Shipped in from Vermont."

"And you don't know how the body got there? Or came to be chopped into pieces?"

"I know it couldn't have been done in my office. The police found no blood, viscera, nothing. They wiped the floor and walls with luminol. Nothing. The victim was murdered and butchered elsewhere."

"Who had access to your private office? Other than you?"

"No one. The fingerprint lock requires my index finger. Which I am not in the habit of loaning out."

"Any sign of forced entry?"

"None."

"So basically, the crime was impossible. And yet, it happened."

"It's a classic locked-room mystery. You consider yourself quite the detective, don't you? Surely you can't resist the challenge. A puzzle of this magnitude only presents itself once in a lifetime."

Now Sweeney was playing to his vanity...but he had to admit the puzzle was intriguing.

And worse—he had to admit that what Sweeney said made sense.

Was it possible that, vile though he was, Sweeney was being framed? That this really was a case for the Last Chance Lawyers?

It was easy to pontificate about justice when your client was sympathetic. But what about when he wasn't? Like Dinah said, if no one is willing to take the hard cases, the justice system doesn't work.

"Prudence says you're...ill."

"I don't want to talk about that. It has nothing to do with this."

"If I were to take this case...you can't keep secrets from me. If I don't know everything, I can't do my job."

"I won't withhold any information that relates to this case."

"That's not good enough. You're not the best judge of what might be relevant. I expect total transparency."

"You can't expect me to start revealing everything I've done for the last thirty years."

Dan leaned in closer. "Here's what I expect. I'm convinced that you're the man who was in the passenger seat of the police car driven by Jack Fisher the night he was killed. And my father was arrested. I'm convinced that you were there for a reason. That you hold the final piece of the puzzle that explains what happened that night."

"You already know what happened. Your father executed a man who threatened his wife and step-daughter."

"If you want me to take this case, you're going to tell me what I don't know."

Sweeney looked at him for a long time, drooping eyes, sour expression. "Very well then. But you don't get your answers for merely taking the case. You have to win."

Dan couldn't help but smile a bit. "Challenge accepted."

CHAPTER NINE

DAN KNEW THIS MIGHT BE A HARD SELL BACK AT THE OFFICE, BUT he did not anticipate a reaction like this.

"You said *yes?*" Jimmy screamed. "You're joking. You're representing Conrad Sweeney? *I'm* representing Conrad Sweeney?"

"Well, the firm is, technically," Dan replied. "You knew I was going to speak with him. Why is this so surprising?"

"Oh, I don't know. Because he's a crime lord, cartel conspirator, liar, manipulator, racist, homophobe, and probably a murderer. Because about ten seconds ago he was suing us and threatening to drive us out of existence."

"To be fair, we were suing each other."

Jimmy stood, waving his arms around as he paced the living room. He looked as if he might pop a button on his cardigan. "This is inconceivable!"

"You were here when Prudence came. You knew we were discussing it."

"I assumed your common sense, not to mention your Sweeney hatred, would overcome Prudence's pathetic appeals."

"It has nothing to do with Prudence. I don't think Sweeney committed this crime."

"Who cares?"

"You don't want him to do time for a crime he didn't commit. Do you?"

"Actually, I'm perfectly okay with that. It would be suitable penance for the ten thousand crimes he's committed and gotten away with."

"That's not how the justice system works."

"Tell it to Shawna." Dan knew who he meant. Jimmy was close to the current county clerk, someone who had finally admitted Sweeney blackmailed her into doing his bidding. "He ruined her life."

"He saved her nephew."

"And extracted his pound of flesh."

Dan leaned over the back of an easy chair. "I'm not saying Sweeney is a model citizen. We both know he isn't. But he didn't commit this murder. And Mr. K wants us to take this case. I don't know why. But there must be a reason."

Maria, watching from the kitchen, jumped in. "And you want us to take this case, too, don't you?"

"We've always said we take the hard cases. This is where we prove it." He decided not to mention the part about extracting more information pertaining to his father. He didn't think that would play well at the moment.

Jimmy turned toward Garrett, who was perched at the kitchen bar behind his laptop. "Garrett, please help me out here."

"Actually, I'm okay with this," Garrett said, to everyone's surprise. Usually, Garrett was the most conservative and the first to criticize anything Dan did. "I think it shows that we stand by our principles. As a prosecutor, I had to press charges against people I thought were basically good citizens but who made mistakes. I didn't enjoy it, but that was my role in the system. Similarly, defense lawyers have to take cases for people they don't like. Because everyone is entitled to a defense. A fair trial."

"Exactly," Dan said.

"But you can't go halfway," Garrett cautioned. "If Sweeney is your client, you have to go all in. You can't appear on his behalf while secretly plotting his destruction."

"I understand. I am all in. And Sweeney is too. Says he won't keep secrets from us."

"There is no way this is good for us," Jimmy insisted. "The optics are horrible. We're aligning ourselves with someone who's constantly been maligned by the press."

"Which could in fact create a new niche. Bring us future clients we wouldn't otherwise get."

"So we're doing this for our financial benefit?" Jimmy snapped back. "Like total sell-outs? We're supposed to be above this sort of thing. Mr. K pays our salaries so we don't have to troll in the gutters for work."

"Jimmy, I didn't say—"

"This is just mindless chatter," Jimmy said, much too loudly. "Pontification. Making excuses. I don't know why you want to do this, Dan, but no justification is good enough."

There was no point in replying. Nothing he said would make Jimmy feel any better. "Maria, what do you think?"

"I'm not going to lie to you. I don't like it. In fact, I hate it." She drew in her breath. "But I trust your judgment. And I trust Mr. K. If this is what you think we should do, I've got your back."

Jimmy glared at her.

Dinah scurried in from the kitchen holding a tray of coffee cups. "Anyone need a lift?"

"I don't think we need any more buzz in this room." Dan smiled. "And you're the legal assistant, not the barista."

"I don't like sitting still when there's…conflict. Better to have something to do."

He understood. She had only been with them a short while. She didn't want to be sucked into the maelstrom.

"I'm sorry you feel this way, Jimmy," Dan said. "I mean that sincerely. But I've already told Sweeney we'll take his case and I've entered our appearance."

"Without discussing it with us first."

He drew in his breath. "Garrett, can you start on the research?"

"Of course. What do you need?"

"Anything useful about Sweeney."

"I thought he said he wouldn't keep any secrets."

Dan craned his neck. "And yet…"

"Gotcha."

"Anything about his finances, businesses. And anything about the cartel. Jake tells me Alejandro Hernandez is in town."

Garrett whistled. "The Big Boss. Wow. Why?"

"I'd like to know that myself. See what you can learn. Maria, trial strategy is going to be of critical importance. You see the problem?"

"How do you sell a jury on the innocence of the most notorious person in the city? Yes, a definite problem. I'll get to work on it."

"Dinah, since you've been studying motions practice, maybe you can help Jimmy—"

Jimmy cut him off mid-sentence. "She's not going to help Jimmy do anything."

"I didn't think you mind a helper when—"

"Jimmy isn't doing anything. I refuse to work on this case."

"Jimmy…"

"I won't lift a finger for that disgusting, evil man. In fact—" He marched toward the staircase. "I don't know if I can continue to be a member of this firm. This is not what I signed up for." He marched upward. "You people are not who I thought you were."

He disappeared from sight.

Dan sighed. "He'll get over it."

Garrett shook his head. "I'm not so sure. He and Shawna are close. And Sweeney destroyed her life."

"He'll come around." I hope. "In the meantime, Dinah…this just became a great hands-on learning experience for you."

"Dinah, I've drafted lots of motions," Maria said. "I know the drill. When you have questions, just ask."

"Thank you." Dinah seemed restless. He understood. She liked being part of a family. And hated seeing the family torn apart. "I'm sure I'll have lots."

"Got your back, girlfriend."

"This is going to be difficult," Dan said. "This may be our greatest challenge. The defining case of our careers. But I think we're doing the right thing."

"And if you're wrong?" Maria asked.

He paused. "Let's just get to work…"

CHAPTER TEN

TULIP HAD NO IDEA HOW LONG SHE'D BEEN WALKING, BUT IT seemed like an eternity.

The heat was relentless. Her entire body was slick with sweat. The torn remains of her clothing offered precious little protection against this harsh, killing environment. Every step was an ordeal. Every breath was an effort. The sun baked her brain, made thinking a misery and consciousness a mirage.

How much longer could she survive?

She remembered waking to find a man preparing to kill her. That memory was indelibly etched into her consciousness. After she killed him, she began her search for the car. She found it, though it took hours. The keyless lock worked and let her inside.

But the car wouldn't start. The engine wouldn't turn over, no matter how many times she tried. Was it the heat? Had he left the car running, thinking he'd be back soon? Did sand get into the engine? She didn't know enough about cars to guess.

She sat in the driver's seat, silently begging, trying to will the car into action. She pounded her head against the steering wheel. Tears streamed from her eyes. She was surprised she contained enough moisture to make tears. They came unbidden, and it was a long time before they stopped.

All right. She tried to pull herself together. Plan B. There must be something of use in here, and indeed, she found three bottles of Aquafina in the back seat. That wouldn't last long, but it was better than nothing. In the trunk, she found a packet of cheese crackers and a half-empty bag of almonds. Her would-be killer's idea of a healthy meal? Probably something grabbed in haste at a gas station. Whatever. She was glad to find it.

She hoped the car would have a first aid kit. Or maybe a map. But she never found anything else of use. And the car didn't seem to be on a road or near one, at least not that she could see. Had the man driven off the road to avoid witnesses? The wind had covered the car's tracks. She couldn't tell where or what direction it came from. At best, she could make a vague guess based on the car's position.

She spent the first night in the car to protect herself from the cold, but ultimately, she knew if she stayed there she'd die of thirst or starvation. She left the car behind and started walking with no clear path and she'd been walking ever since. Judging from the position of the sun, she could estimate which direction was south. The man had said they were north of Vegas. Assuming he wasn't lying, if she just kept moving in a southerly direction...

The complete absence of landmarks made accurate navigation impossible. No roads. No signs. No distinctive markers. Just desert.

She couldn't be that far from civilization, could she? He mentioned a private airport. Surely that was near Vegas. And then he drove her off to escape prying eyes. He didn't have to travel hours to do that.

She hoped.

She just needed to find someone. Something. Anything. A

gas station. A store. Weren't there some military bases in this area? Surely, eventually, someone would see her.

The night proved even more unbearable than the day. Given how hellishly hot she'd been, she could never have imagined the night could be so cold. But it was. She shivered and quaked and could not control her body for hours. Baking in the sun was bad but freezing in the cold was worse. She thought she was suffering from exposure, and she wasn't sure that ended just because, at long last, the sun rose. She had never felt such excruciating misery in her entire life.

She had once been so proud of her skin. She had gorgeous, lustrous opaline skin. Men talked about how smooth and clear her skin was. Baby soft, without blemish. But she knew she would never hear that again. Even if she managed to survive this, her skin would never recover. She could feel sores on her face. It was hot and painful to the touch. Regardless of what the future held, she was ruined.

Her feet were worse. Her shoes provided negligible protection from the burning sands. Her feet blistered. She felt weak and wobbly, knees shaking with each step.

She couldn't keep this up forever. That much was certain.

She heard something—a loud noise—in the distance. Her head jerked up. It sounded like...

She wasn't sure.

In truth, she wasn't even sure she heard it. Maybe she just wanted to hear it. Maybe it was an audio mirage.

She strained her wet and blurry eyes, scanning the horizon. Was anything there?

Please, she murmured beneath her breath. Please let something be there. She wiped salty water from her eyes, trying to see more clearly.

Nothing appeared.

She collapsed in a heap, tumbling to the sand.

She lay there for several minutes, until the sand burned her arms and legs.

She tried to push herself to her feet, but she had nothing left.

Except she still had that man's gun. As hot as it was, she'd kept it. And she knew it had at least one more bullet...

No. She clenched her teeth and pushed herself up once more.

That was what they wanted. They thought she was weak. They thought she could be eliminated. But she was stronger than that. She was a woman, a tough woman, and she wasn't going to let this cabal of men eliminate her. She was going to fight those pigs to her dying breath. She would find a way out of this hellhole.

She wiped the sand from her eyes, took a deep breath of the humid air, and started walking again.

CHAPTER ELEVEN

Dan entered the courtroom as quickly as possible. He did not want to attract attention. He spotted a few reporters in the hallway and one shouted a question, but he ignored it. Right now, he didn't care to be interviewed.

Sweeney was already in the courtroom, flanked by two marshals. Since there was no jury today, they left him in jail-house coveralls. His wrists were handcuffed and attached to a belly chain in front. His ankle irons ensured that he couldn't go very far very fast.

Prudence sat in the courtroom just behind the rail, as close to her boss as she could get without being arrested.

Dan approached the table and signaled the marshals that they could leave the accused in his recognizance. Not that they would leave the room. But they would maintain a discreet distance. Sweeney wasn't likely to make a break for it.

"How's jail treating you?" Dan said, taking the chair beside his client. The awkwardness was intense, even palpable.

"The usual. Scorn, insults, and the occasional attempt on my life."

"Can't you do something about that, Pike?" Prudence leaned across the railing. "You are his lawyer."

"I can try to get him out on bail. But I won't succeed."

"He's willing to wear an electronic bracelet."

"I'll make the offer. But..."

"At least get him moved to solitary. Someplace safe."

"That's a decision for the jailhouse authorities. Judges don't normally interfere. I could file some kind of habeas corpus petition. But it wouldn't work. I'd probably have more luck getting this case tried quickly than getting a habeas corpus motion heard in federal court."

Her lips thinned. "Why do I feel you aren't giving this case your all?"

"Because you're used to getting your way. Immediately." He gave his client some side-eye. "You think bluster and bullying can get you anything you want. But it doesn't always work that way. Especially in the courts."

He glanced over his shoulder and saw the prosecutor enter the courtroom.

Jazlyn Prentice. Tall, well-dressed, two earrings in the left ear. Lapel pin with the scales of justice. Jazlyn had been his friend for years. He helped her adopt Esperanza, her ten-year-old daughter. They first met when she was an associate DA, and now she ran the whole office.

Which made it surprising that she was here in person. Surely this preliminary stuff was too trivial for someone of her stature.

"Jazlyn, what—"

She pointedly turned her back to him and walked the other direction as if she hadn't heard.

That was disturbing.

"Feeling snubbed?" Sweeney asked.

Dan bit down on his lower lip. Thank you, Sweeney, for reminding me why I despise you. "She's busy."

"She's giving you the cold shoulder."

"The prosecutor and the defense attorney don't normally socialize much."

"But you and Ms. Prentice do. You went to her daughter's birthday party. I believe you two even dated a little, right?"

Dan slowly turned his head. He knew the man had investigated him, but this was just showing off.

"Get used to it," Sweeney said calmly. "I'm currently out of favor, and that means anyone associated with me will be treated with scorn. You'll survive."

Dan kept his thoughts to himself. *But I don't want to survive this. I want everyone to love me...*

The bailiff called the court to order and Judge Smulders entered the courtroom. When Dan first heard Smulders had been assigned this case, he couldn't believe it. Smulders had handled the Ossie Coleman case, and his combination of immaturity and ineptitude almost derailed the defense. People didn't believe it when Dan told them about the judge's indecisive actions. They naively believed that no one that green would be assigned a capital murder trial. But in this jurisdiction, cases were randomly assigned by the clerk's computer. The idea that a judge had to be "death qualified" or have some elevated degree of experience was a myth.

Smulders took his seat at the bench. Late thirties. Tousled blond hair. Gnawed fingernails. But at least he had his robe on straight.

Smulders called the case. "I will ask my clerk—"

"Waive the reading," Dan said. Always rude to interrupt, but no one wanted to hear that rigmarole.

"Very well," the judge said. "How does your client plead?"

"Absolutely not guilty on all charges," Sweeney said, rising. "And grossly offended that the state would proceed with no evidence whatsoever tying me to this crime."

"I will enter a plea of not guilty," the judge said.

Jazlyn spoke. "Your honor, I can assure the court that we have—"

Smulders cut her off. "No need, counsel. In the seemingly unlikely event that you lack evidence tying the defendant to the crime, he won't be bound over and you certainly won't prevail."

Cool and in control. The little boy had grown up since Dan saw this judge last.

Smulders straightened some papers. "Are there any other matters we can take up while we're gathered together, counsel?"

Dan braced himself. "Your honor, I'd like to ask the court to set bail."

The judge gave him a long look. "Seriously?"

"There is precedent for permitting bail in a capital case."

"Not much."

"But—some."

"Your honor," Jazlyn said, "the defendant has been charged with murder in the first degree. We have already begun convening a grand jury and expect to ask for the death penalty. Plus the defendant is the subject of several state and federal investigations—"

"Not relevant," Dan intoned.

"But true," Jazlyn continued. "Parts of a dismembered corpse were found in the defendant's private mancave, and if the court puts him back on the street, the public outcry will be deafening."

"Should the court's rulings be based upon public outcry?" Judge Smulders asked.

"Well, no..."

"Then would you care to make a legal argument?"

Jazlyn cleared her throat, her face slightly flushed. "Although the defendant's financial empire may be crumbling, we believe he still has access to funds, so he's a flight risk. He's believed to be involved with a Central American cartel, so the chance for more violence is very real."

"Everything she says is supposition based upon rumor," Dan

replied. "Where are the facts? Does she have evidence about the defendant's financial situation? Can she prove a connection to a criminal organization? She's basically asking you to keep my client in jail based upon gossip."

Smulders nodded. "The man does have a point."

"Then let me make a point, too," Jazlyn snapped. "This city will be much safer if the defendant remains behind bars. And we're more likely to have a fair trial, too."

Judge Smulders pushed back in his chair. "The traditional judicial policy in this jurisdiction is not to allow bail in first-degree murder cases, so I'm going to follow that precedent. Is there anything else?"

Dan cleared his throat. "We want to move this case along without undue delay, so I'd like to see what the prosecution has at the earliest opportunity. Exculpatory evidence. Everything."

"We have procedures in place governing this," Jazlyn replied. "As my extremely experienced opponent knows full well. He will see the evidence at the appropriate time."

"And there you have it," the judge said. "Anything else?"

"My client requests the earliest possible trial setting."

"My docket is relatively clear," Smulders said. "That might be earlier than you realize. Are you sure that's what you want? These are serious charges."

Dan drew in his breath. "It's what my client wants. And given the court's denial of bail...who can blame him?"

"Objections from the state?"

"None," Jazlyn said. "The evidence is clear-cut. We could be ready tomorrow."

"Very well. I'll ask my clerk to set this down for the earliest possible trial date. But let me warn you that when that date arrives, counsel, I won't be interested in excuses for why you're not ready. You asked for an early setting. You live with it."

"Understood, your honor."

"Will there be anything else?"

Dan had a hunch he should keep his mouth shut, but Defense 101 said you never missed an opportunity to bend the judge's ear and teach him about your case, even if it was premature. Might make the argument more readily understood when the proper time came. "Your honor, we will move to exclude the fruits of the illegal search made by a police officer in a room in my client's office."

"That would be the aforementioned mancave," Jazlyn explained.

"It was a private room," Dan added. "They did not have a warrant to search."

"Your client invited them in. He opened the door with a fingerprint ID."

"But he did not grant them permission to search the premises."

"Did he think they were wearing blindfolds? He knew both Detective Kakazu and Sergeant Pemberton were experienced officers."

"He did not invite them or grant permission to open the freezer. And that's where the evidence was found."

"Dismembered pieces of evidence," Jazlyn muttered.

"Since they had no right to search the freezer and were never invited to do so, I move to exclude all evidence found within. And without that, the prosecution has no case."

"I disagree," Jazlyn said. "The idea that we should exclude evidence that literally fell into a police officer's lap is beyond ridiculous. While we're at it, why don't we ignore the fact that another body flew out the defendant's window shortly before?"

"That is not relevant to this case," Dan insisted.

"Unless you think common sense is relevant."

"You haven't even charged my client for that incident."

"Doesn't mean we won't."

"He didn't commit either crime."

"Then he's the Typhoid Mary of Murder."

The judge banged his gavel. "Get a grip on yourselves, counsel." They both fell silent.

Smulders pointed the gavel at Dan. "This is not the time to raise a suppression motion, as you know. First, you exchange evidence. Then, if you still think you have a motion, bring it up at the pretrial. But let me caution you. If you're bringing a motion just because you think you have to bring a motion, don't bother. I have no patience for frivolous motions practice."

Dan sensed the judge was telling him to shut up and he probably should. But he wasn't quite done. "Your honor, every day my client is behind bars, not only is his life a misery, but he is literally in danger. He—"

Judge Smulders looked at him sternly. "Counsel...did you hear what I said?"

"Yes, your honor, but—"

"There is no but. I told you to bring it up at the pretrial. Which, given the early trial date you've requested, will not be that long from now. Is there anything else?"

No one dared speak.

"Very good. We are adjourned." Smulders banged his gavel again and made a hasty exit.

Dan turned to Sweeney. "Sorry I couldn't get bail."

Sweeney shook his head. "You had no chance. At least you showed a little fire."

"I could only—"

"Next time, show more."

Dan bit his tongue. Out the corner of his eye, he saw Jazlyn head out of the courtroom.

"Jazlyn! Wait."

Jazlyn slowed, but she did not look happy about it.

He caught up to her. "Can we talk for a moment?"

Jazlyn drew in her breath. "We're on opposite sides of a case. We really shouldn't."

"That has never stopped you before."

"I don't just work in the office anymore. I'm the district attorney. Many people will be watching us. I have to set an example."

"Of being rude to opposing counsel?"

"It's possible to be distant without being rude."

"But—why?"

Jazlyn shifted her weight from one foot to the other. "Was there something you wanted to discuss?"

"Yeah. Why you're being this way."

"Are you kidding?" Her voice boomed, but she reeled it back in. "Dan, you're representing the most vile human being who ever walked the face of the earth."

"Everyone is entitled to a defense."

"Spare me the First-Year Criminal Law lecture."

"It's true."

"Yes, he needed a lawyer. It didn't have to be you."

"But he asked me. And Mr. K accepted the case, and—"

"These are just excuses. I thought you were on a crusade for justice."

"More now than ever before. It's one thing to talk about principles, but much harder to put them into practice."

"I'm sorry, I don't see it that way. I see it as you selling out. And I have to tell you—so does everyone else in the courthouse."

"That's not fair."

"Welcome to real life. It's rarely fair." She poked a finger in his chest. "Here's the reality that your holier-than-thou attitude seems to overlook. Finally, after years of effort, we have a chance to put this disgusting slimeball behind bars. And who stands in our way? You. The person who knows better than anyone how vile he is."

She took a few steps back, then stopped. "I used to admire

you, Dan. Even when we were on opposite sides of the court-room. What happened to you?"

She marched out of the courtroom. Dan stood motionless for several seconds, trying to pretend her words didn't hurt.

But they did.

CHAPTER TWELVE

SOMETIMES DAN FELT LIKE HE SPENT MOST OF HIS LIFE STARING at people through Plexiglas screens. The security at Lake City, a private Florida prison, was higher than at the local jailhouse, but the procedure was essentially the same. He waited more than twenty minutes for the guards to bring him to the inmate he wanted to see. He'd been worried the prisoner in question might refuse to see him, but apparently he was coming. From an isolation cell, which increased the waiting time. Usually, those went to inmates who had mental health issues or needed special protection—meaning cops and pedophiles. This guy was neither, but he was insanely rich. Maybe he could buy some privacy, though he still would be forced to mingle during the day, when he ate, or when he was forced to soak up a little sunshine.

Dan was astounded by how much noisier this place was than the jailhouse, even though the latter had more traffic, more inmates flowing in and out. He heard constant screaming and pounding. He supposed that was to be expected at a joint full of people who didn't want to be there. Or said they didn't deserve to be there which, as Dan knew, occasionally was true.

He also noticed how hot it was in here, which made everything else worse. Beads of sweat rolled down the sides of his face, and all he was doing was sitting. The prison interior was primarily cinderblock walls and cheap linoleum floors. The sweat also contributed to the horrific smell, though he suspected all those unlidded toilets played a role as well. Basically, every cell had an open sewer. Not good for olfactory pleasure or sanitation. On a previous visit, he'd needed to use one of the prison bathrooms. They didn't escort him into a cell, but the bathroom he used was horrifying. He held his breath as long as possible, and for days felt as if he needed to scour his skin with a Brillo pad.

Another five minutes passed before he heard the metallic squeal of an interior door. A moment later, the man in question emerged, flanked by guards on both sides.

Phil Coleman. The youngest member of the billionaire Coleman family, at least prior to Dan's successful representation of the lost heir, Ossie. Phil had squandered a huge portion of the family fortune on an ill-advised venture into bio-quantum computing—in partnership with Conrad Sweeney. Coleman's financial desperation led to the crime that put him behind bars.

Coleman didn't look good, not that anyone did after a lengthy stay in lockup. Light-skinned African-American. Hollow eyes. Gaunt face. Fresh tattoo on the left wrist. He still sported a buzzcut, but most of his muscles had softened. Maybe he didn't spend enough time in the gym or didn't get the opportunity. Or maybe he just didn't care anymore.

"Thanks for seeing me." Dan spoke into the antiquated telephone receiver that permitted communication between the people on either side of the screen.

Coleman looked steadily at him. His expression didn't suggest anger so much as an absence of interest. "My social calendar isn't that busy."

"How's prison treating you?"

"I'm a good-looking rich boy behind bars for the first time in his life and unlikely to get out anytime in the next two decades. How do you think I am?"

"I'm...sorry."

"You should be. You put me here."

"If it hadn't been me it would have been someone else. Eventually."

"Maybe. Maybe not. The only reason I'm surviving is because I got the protection of the cellblock boss."

"I'm glad you've made friends."

"I'm not his friend. I'm his wife."

Dan couldn't think of a thing to say.

"That, plus my last name, conveys a certain status. Whether that's a good thing, I don't know. Without it, I'd probably be dead already. And that might be better."

"Can't you complain to a CO?"

"More violence in here comes from the guards than inmates. I have to keep everyone happy. One way or the other."

He knew he shouldn't ask, but he did. "What's the other?"

"Money, of course."

"How do you pay for protection in here? In cigarettes?"

"You're behind the times, Pike. Almost every inmate has a Venmo account. Hell, some are trading Bitcoin. I have a friend on the outside who transfers money as I direct. And I do a lot of directing."

"But don't you need a phone—"

"It's not that hard to get a cellphone. All the block kings have them. Against the rules, but..." He shrugged. "So is most of what goes down in here."

Dan squared his shoulders. Probably best if they moved on. "You may find this hard to believe, but I'm representing Conrad Sweeney on a murder charge."

"I know all about it. Everyone here does. You're the talk of the town. Daniel Pike representing the Satan of St. Pete."

"He's innocent."

"Sorry, no one here believes Sweeney is innocent."

"I didn't say he was a saint. I said he didn't commit this murder." Tempting though it was, he didn't want to become confrontational. "Look, may I ask you some questions about Sweeney?"

"He's your client. Can't you ask him yourself?"

"I thought I might get more insight from a third party."

"You mean more *honesty*."

"I know you worked with Sweeney on that computer deal that went belly-up. He blames that for his current financial problems."

Coleman blew air through his teeth. "What a crock. He was in bad shape before he came to me. That's why he came to me. Why he allowed himself to be hustled. He had major cash-flow problems."

"That suggests...some line of income dried up."

"The cartel. Money laundering for the El Salvadorean big boys. Sweeney greased the wheels on this side for their smuggling operations and also funneled their cash through various SweeTech subsidiaries. That was the primary source of his wealth for years. Till it dried up. And he blames you for that."

Dan tried to think. High finance was not his best subject, mostly because it bored him to tears. He had an investment advisor who managed his money. Cost him a percentage, but it was worth it not to have to waste his brain cells on spreadsheets. "If Sweeney wasn't making as much income, the normal response would be to reduce expenses."

Coleman chuckled. "Conrad Sweeney is not a normal person. I think he tried to slow some of his business operations. Many were just shell companies and money pits that existed purely for the purpose of laundering cash. But there was one expenditure he couldn't curtail."

"And that was…?"

"Fine art. Paintings."

"I've heard about Sweeney's collection. Supposed to be impressive."

"It's one of the two or three best private collections in the world. Maybe the best. Certainly he thinks so."

"If his money dried up, he needed to stop buying. Maybe even sell a piece or two. Artwork has the advantage of being relatively easy to liquidate."

Coleman smiled. "Have you ever seen Sweeney when he talks about his collection? Or gazes at it?"

"No."

"He gets the same glassy-eyed look that other people get when they need a cocaine fix. He's completely addicted."

"To art?"

"To buying high-priced items normal people can't afford. He's like a junkie, but the hole in his arm is a lot more expensive than most. He couldn't stop buying. And he couldn't sell, either."

"He'll have no choice now. I hear the feds have seized control of his assets. And—"

Dan heard a knock on the other side of the screen. A moment later, a uniformed guard appeared. Holding a cup and saucer.

He set it down beside Coleman. "Teatime."

Was that bone china? It looked like it.

Coleman took the cup and sipped. "I've told you a thousand times I like my tea hot. Piping hot."

"My apologies. I went to your cell first. I didn't know you had a visitor."

"See that it doesn't happen again." Coleman finished the tea, then took a bite out of the cookie—crumpet?—on the saucer. "One of the few vestiges of civilization I've been able to maintain in here."

"You know," Dan said, "I was almost feeling sorry for you. But that's fading."

"Because I can afford to make a few special arrangements? I'm still in prison."

"Does your...husband get teatime, too?"

"He's more of a coffee man. But believe me, if I couldn't afford to treat him right, he'd get tired of me fast. Money doth have its privileges."

So it would seem. Coleman finished his cuppa and the guard carried it away.

"Where did Sweeney find this art?" Dan asked. "I assume they don't sell it on eBay."

"He has a dealer he works with. People said he was just as sleazy as Sweeney, which probably explains why they worked together so well. Word on the street was that some of the art had dubious provenance."

"Meaning they were forgeries?"

"Meaning they were stolen. Museum robberies. Cat burglaries. Some experts say almost as much fine art in the million-plus category is transferred in secret as is sold by conventional means."

"Do you get a discount if you buy hot paintings?"

"Just the opposite. Makes them more valuable."

"Something about this doesn't seem right. Sweeney has always been the exemplar of unemotional rationalism. Ruthlessly doing what needs to be done. Not indulging in bad habits that might impact the bottom line."

Coleman shrugged. "Even Blofeld had a cat."

Dan almost laughed. "Why are you helping me?"

"Just to be clear, I hate you like no one I've ever hated in my entire life. With one exception. Sweeney. And yes, I know you say you're representing him. But I can't help but think this is just a ploy. You're using this to collect information on him."

"That isn't true."

"Which is, of course, exactly what you would say if it were true. But I think you're going to bring the big man down eventually. Nothing could make me happier. And if you damage the cartel, that's ok, too."

Dan pondered another minute. "Did you ever have any involvement with the cartel?"

"Only once. I met the big man himself. Alejandro Hernandez. The Prince of Darkness. The guy is eighty or something, but he could still stop your heart with a cold stare. Scared the hell out of me."

"Why did you meet him?"

"Sweeney asked me to. Said he wanted his partners to know each other. I suspect it was more a matter of informing the cartel that he was developing another stream of income."

"Any takeaways from the meet?"

"Those people have no morals. No principles. It's all business to them. Anything is justified so long as it moves the needle." He paused. "You know they're gunning for you, right?"

Dan felt a cold hand clutch at his heart. "I've had a few indications."

"Don't kid yourself. They want you dead. Frankly, I'm surprised you've lasted this long."

"I'm more resilient than some people give me credit for."

"But no one can survive forever with a cartel bullseye on their back. You need to be careful. Like you've never been careful before."

Message understood. He started to leave, then snapped his fingers. "I forgot to ask. What's the name of the art dealer? The one who's been brokering for Sweeney. And where do I find him?"

"Shouldn't be hard. He has an office in Miami, but he has clients all over the Southeast. Probably all over the country."

"And his name?"

"Christopher Andrus."

CHAPTER THIRTEEN

"CHRISTOPHER ANDRUS?" JAKE KAKAZU SAID. "ARE YOU SURE?"

"Absolutely."

"Who is he? Sex trafficker? Pornographer? Hit man?"

"Worse. Art dealer."

Jake peered at the forensic scientist, Teresa Crosswaite. She was a master of many fields, but at the moment, her expertise in dactylograms rose to the forefront. She'd been with SPPD for almost six months now and Kakazu had repeatedly been impressed by her competence and resourcefulness. Her youth and—dare he admit it?—attractiveness caused some of the old boys to dismiss her, but time and again she was the one who came up with the goods they needed to clinch a case.

Sergeant Pemberton stood at Jake's side. "The art world must be a lot rougher than I imagined."

"You have no idea," Teresa said. "I've done a little research. These people are completely cutthroat. They'd sell your grandmother just to get their hands on a limited-edition Giclee."

Jake decided to nod and act as if he knew what she was talking about. "How did you land the ID?"

"It wasn't easy. Facial recognition got us nothing. Though to be fair to the AI, the head had been damaged during the decapitation. Maybe before. Looked like something out of a Stephen King movie."

"But you had the hands."

"Right. We had a relatively complete set of prints. But they didn't trigger any matches, not locally, not at VICAP."

"Has the FBI helped?"

"Big time. I know some of our officers don't like it when the feds descend and take over a case, but I've found them to be extremely helpful. Not rude, not sexist, and not arrogant. They want the cartel taken down as much as we do."

"And they could ID the prints?"

"No, they came up empty, too. But one of their techies, off the record, showed me how to access some other online databases. That aren't normally part of a law enforcement sweep."

"Okay, stop building the suspense. Where did you find his prints? A laptop? Phone? Small-town speed trap? Bar Association?"

She shook her head. "Disney World."

Jake blinked. "I know they've had to heighten security, but I wasn't aware that the Mouse took prints."

Crosswaite laughed. "I can see you haven't been to Disney World in a while."

"Or ever."

Crosswaite and Pemberton peered at him in disbelief. "Tell me you're joking."

"I'm an adult. I don't have children."

"You've never been to Disney World? It's only two hours away. Where do you go on vacation?"

"I'm very fond of Tuscany..."

Crosswaite showed no disrespect to her senior officer, but he got the impression it was a lot of work. "Andrus apparently loved Disney World. He was an Annual Passholder. Which meant he had one of those cool plastic watchbands that get you through the gate. But Disney wants to make sure people don't transfer their watches to others. So when you show up, you not only get your watch scanned—"

"They check your prints."

"Bingo. Right forefinger. They had Andrus on record. And it's an almost perfect match."

"Disney let you access their records?"

"Not in a million years."

Jake's eyes narrowed. "Tell me you didn't do something you shouldn't have."

She coughed into her hand. "Or...maybe it's best you don't know..."

"How are we going to establish Andrus' identity at trial?"

"The feds have sent me all kinds of information on the guy. Photos, employment records, address. I'm sure you'll be able to find his prints in his apartment."

"And how do I explain why I went there in the first place?"

Crosswaite and Pemberton spoke in unison. "Anonymous tip."

"I'll go out there this afternoon," Sergeant Pemberton added. "See what I can find."

"Take the dusters. Above all else, we need prints."

"Right."

Jake sat beside the slender forensic scientist. "Can you copy me on what the FBI sent you about Andrus?"

"Sure. Apparently he's been an art dealer for decades. He's developed quite a reputation."

"As a...reliable professional?"

"As a sleazeball who sells stolen art. Stuff too hot for Christie's and Sotheby's. Paintings most museums wouldn't touch."

"But Sweeney did."

"Repeatedly."

Jake nodded. "I believe it. Near as I could tell, the whole

point of that hidden room was so he could sit around alone and pleasure himself with his secret art stash."

"Eew." Crosswaite pursed her lips. "That's an image I won't be able to get out of my head. Thanks."

"But we still don't have a motive."

"Perhaps they had a falling out. Perhaps Sweeney couldn't pay his bill. The papers say he's in serious financial trouble. And I doubt being in jail is helping his portfolio."

"True. But I'd like something more concrete. Even if a deal went bad—why murder Andrus? And for that matter, why do it in such a grisly way?"

"Maybe Sweeney gets off on violence." Her face contorted. "There's another nasty mental image. Do you really think Sweeney could do something like that?"

"Could? Yes. Would? I don't know. His MO has always been to act through hunchmen."

"Might be harder if he's got money problems."

"He'd find a way. But we're still dodging the big question. One we'll have to answer during the trial."

"And that is?"

"Why would he stuff the body into that freezer?"

"Maybe it was a way of...admiring his handiwork. Like the paintings."

"Hard to imagine."

"Maybe he thought it would be easier to transport once it was frozen."

"Then where's the rest of the body?"

"Maybe he's a cannibal and—"

"Okay, stop." Jake thrust his hands into his pockets. "Let's hope the apartment search produces some answers. In the meantime—good work. If I can thank you in some way—"

"Surf and turf at Chez Guitano."

Today was just filled with surprises. "Probably not a good idea..."

"C'mon, Kakazu. Go big or go home."

He took a moment and peered into her lovely blue eyes.

"Well, copper? Waiting for an answer here."

Jake drew in his breath. "Do you think they have those battered hush puppies? I love those."

CHAPTER FOURTEEN

DAN WANDERED AROUND THE CEMETERY FOR MORE THAN TEN minutes before he finally spotted the funeral. The day was overcast, which explained why a tent had been erected over the gravesite. A group of maybe twenty people sat in folding chairs.

He heard noises, shouting. Angry shouting. Several people rose from their chairs, pointing, yelling. What in the world?

He quickened his pace. Apparently this was not your run-of-the-mill funeral.

The ceremony was for a man named Christopher Andrus, the art dealer Phil Coleman said was Sweeney's partner who had been identified as the victim found in Sweeney's freezer. Sweeney acknowledged that he had done business with the man on numerous occasions, though he adamantly maintained that he had not killed him.

Dan assumed this was not an open-casket funeral, since most of the body parts had not been located and the parts in the freezer were in hideous shape.

Some sort of scuffle was taking place at the front of the tent just behind the coffin resting on a raised mechanical platform that would later lower it into a grave. One of the people struggling up front was the man he came to meet.

The other appeared to be a preacher.

"You are desecrating a holy ceremony," the preacher said

"You mean I'm making it honest." The other man, who Dan recognized as Bernard Jamison, held his ground. Goatee. Oxford button-down shirt but no tie. Blue stud earring on the left. "Kit never wanted a religious service."

"His widow does," the preacher muttered.

"Is this her funeral? No. It's Kit's, and he gave me specific instructions on how he wanted it to go down. None of this religious huggermugger. No more lies. No more deception."

Dan assumed the woman in black sobbing on the front row was Andrus' widow. The crowd reactions ranged from perplexed to disturbed. "Please leave," the widow cried. "I want Kit's soul to go to heaven."

"He didn't believe in heaven," Jamison said. "And from what he told me, neither do you."

"It isn't true. Please. You're turning this into a...a farce."

"The farce was your marriage."

Audible gasps emerged from the crowd. Two people rose and walked away in disgust, muttering as they went.

The preacher tried unsuccessfully to dislodge Jamison. "You have no authority here."

"No, that's you. I have written instructions from Kit and the right to take the corpse out of here right now if you don't let me speak. I showed you the disclosure documents. Now stand down."

The preacher grudgingly retreated, though he clearly wasn't happy about it.

"As for Kit's marriage," Jamison continued, "let's take a moment to acknowledge what I think most of you already know. Kit was gay. Mary here is bi and theirs was a marriage of convenience necessitated by the outmoded mores of an earlier era. Two beards living a lie to appease the majority."

The widow's cries heightened. She folded forward, hands covering her face. A woman sitting beside her reached an arm across to comfort her.

"And while we're at it, Mary, why don't we be honest about the woman you brought to this event? Willa isn't your cousin. She's your lover. Your true spouse. And she has been for more than two decades."

The announcement that Kit was gay had barely raised an eyebrow, but this revelation popped eyes all across the tent.

"Don't bother protesting, Willa. I won't try to throw you out. Kit didn't mind the fact that you were sleeping with his wife. But he did mind you sneaking around his office photocopying his financial documents. Did you really think he couldn't tell? He wasn't an imbecile."

"He was an imbecile," the woman apparently named Willa said. "He had the best woman in the world. And he didn't appreciate her."

"That's where you're wrong. He wasn't sexually attracted to Mary, but he held her in high esteem. What he didn't appreciate was you two putting tenterhooks into his estate while he was still alive. Were you planning a divorce? Building your stash of evidence so you could rob him? I suppose it doesn't matter. He's gone now."

Dan stared at the audience, which seemed simultaneously appalled and mesmerized. This was certainly not the funeral they expected. But it was weirdly spellbinding. As if Andrus were telling tales and spreading gossip from the other side of the grave.

"It's not like being gay is unusual in the art world," Jamison continued. "Maybe if we all started being more honest, the need for this kind of deception would disappear."

Dan noticed that some of the tumult quieted.

"Kit was taken from us much too soon. We still don't know what happened. But we know this. He was a bright spot, a flash of color in a world that too often seems gray and colorless. He lived in the world of art, but the truth is, Kit was a work of art himself. He found joy in his work and he spread that joy everywhere he went."

Dan wasn't sure this qualified as a eulogy, but if so, it was one of the most interesting he'd ever heard. Though the remaining crowd seemed to have settled in for the ride, the preacher stomped off in a huff.

"Kit Andrus was a great human being," Jamison continued. "A jubilant, gay, atheist soul who loved art and knew how lucky he was to find a way to live in the world he loved so well. He told me he wanted to be an artist himself, but found he lacked some of the essential ingredients. Like talent." Jamison laughed. "So he became a dealer and surrounded himself with the finest work in private hands. His life was a triumph over adversity and discrimination. Don't be sad, my friends. Celebrate. That's what Kit wanted, not all this morose handwringing and blathering about a non-existent afterlife. Take the love Kit held in his heart and spread it throughout the world. That's how you honor him best."

AFTER THE FUNERAL ENDED AND THE OTHER ATTENDEES LEFT, Dan introduced himself. They strolled through the spacious cemetery, past rolling hills and well-kept gardens. Dan suspected a corpse needed some serious wherewithal to get into this cemetery. Before he left the office, Garrett told him the place was so popular "people were dying to get in."

Dan stared at the business card in his hand. "You're a coffin confessor?"

"That's what I call it," Jamison replied. "You got a better name? I'm open to suggestions."

"You mean you've done this before?"

"I do it several times a year. Kit knew that."

"Kit" was apparently what friends called Christopher Andrus. "And he…asked you to create a scene at his funeral?"

"He didn't specify 'a scene.' But he knew what he wanted and authorized me to make it happen."

"His widow seemed pretty upset."

"And that's a shame. But it was inevitable. I warned both her and the preacher that I was coming. Showed them the authorization documents Kit signed empowering me. Maybe they didn't think I was serious."

"But you were."

"Are you kidding? I gave Kit my solemn promise. Plus, he paid me 10K."

"You got ten thousand bucks to disrupt a funeral?"

"To make it honest. We need more honesty in the world, don't you think?"

"Yes, but—"

"We live in a world of fake social media posts and troll-farm dark-web conspiracy theories. Some people can't separate truth from fiction anymore. They want to believe what pleases them, even if there is no evidence whatsoever in support. A person's legacy, an entire life, can be rewritten by a few fake tweets. It was worth it to Kit to see that people told the truth about him after he was dead."

"Did Andrus suspect his end was approaching? Is that why he made plans for the funeral?"

"I got no hint of that. He was an advance planner, maybe even a little OCD. I do several of these a year which he knew, since we were friends. I was instructed to blend in, sit with the family and friends quietly. But if anyone started any religious nonsense, I was authorized to stand up and speak out."

"I think that's the part where I came in."

"It got dodgy for a while. But Reverend Wolverton backed off pretty quickly. He'd seen the documents. He knew I wasn't talking through my hat."

"Still didn't seem to like it much."

"I'm sure it's hard for an old school guy like him. He's used to being the big deal at the party. A funeral is supposed to be a somber bon voyage."

"That scene with the widow and her partner was ugly. More like an assassination than a bon voyage."

"They deceived Kit while living off his support. Hard to be more backstabbing than that. Kit wanted them called out at the funeral. It's going to get worse for them later. Kit only left his wife a tiny support package. Just enough to make sure she had nothing to complain about in court. The vast majority of the estate is going to a nonprofit organization."

Dan followed the path around a hill and found a large pond with a fountain. Geese floated on the edge. "Were you really prepared to take the casket?"

"Absolutely. I had written authorization from the deceased himself. It's an insurance policy. A way to make sure no officious so-and-so tries to prevent me from completing my appointed task."

This whole coffin-confessor business was too bizarre. Grief was hard enough for most people. A funeral was meant to provide solace and a sense of resolution. A tumultuous ceremony like this one was more likely to have the opposite effect.

But he hadn't come here to judge the funeral or its participants. "Can we talk about Andrus? Did you know much about his business?"

"Just enough to be envious. He was an art dealer."

"Like Al Capone was a used furniture dealer?"

The man laughed. "In a way. He might've been covering other activities. He usually had several irons in the fire. But he also trafficked a lot of art. I've dabbled a bit in art myself, but not on his level. He always seemed to have a line on the most valuable pieces. Today, fine art is so expensive it's almost impossible to sell without a middleman. Maybe several middlemen. But galleries and auction houses take a steep percentage. Kit managed to avoid those by finding people with the cash to shell out major bucks."

"Like Conrad Sweeney?"

"Kit knew what Sweeney liked and usually managed to find it. Sweeney had always dreamed of owning a Vermeer. Today, that would seem virtually impossible. All known Vermeers are believed to be in museums. And yet, Kit managed to sell one to Sweeney not long ago."

"Where did he find it?"

Jamison smiled. "If I knew that, I'd pick one up myself."

"When did you first meet Andrus?"

"While I was still in the Army. I was a medic, believe it or not. Saw some action in Iraq. Was stationed in Paris for a while and started going to museums to pass the time. That's when I fell in love with fine art. Kit was at the Musée d'Orsay one day and we bumped heads. Been friends ever since."

"You must've been aware that...some of his deals with Sweeney, and perhaps others, were thought to be...on the criminal side. Stolen work. Paintings with dubious provenance."

"I've heard those rumors, sure. But I don't know that they're true. Here's the reality. Anytime someone is as successful as Kit, there's going to be some trash-talking. People get jealous. Insecure. It's hard to admit someone else is better at the job than you are. Easier to call them crooked."

"Do you know whether Andrus sold stolen paintings?"

"I have no information about that whatsoever."

"Did Sweeney have any reason to kill Andrus?"

"Far as I could tell, Kit was doing exactly what Sweeney wanted him to do. And doing it well."

"When was the last time you saw Andrus?"

"Two days before his body—or part of it—was found in that freezer. I bumped into him down at the Crislip Arcade. I was doing a little shopping for my mother and I ran into Kit...and a woman he called his intern."

"What was her name?"

"I'm sorry. I don't remember."

"Did you believe the intern story?"

"Sure. Why not? Kit was gay, and even if they were having a fling, he had no reason to hide it. His wife had been in a relationship with someone else for years."

"Did he tell you anything?"

Jamison thought for a moment. "He said he was meeting someone for dinner. A guy named Ray Carvel."

"Another art dealer?"

"Far from it. Architect. Reasonably successful once, but I hear he's fallen on hard times."

"I need to talk to him. Can you give me his contact info?"

"Carvel is currently...unavailable."

"A recluse architect?"

"An on-the-lam architect. I don't know all the details, but he's been involved in some dubious ventures."

"Like what?"

"I don't know. Something bad enough to have the feds after him. And maybe the cartel as well. Look, I've told you everything I know. But consider the facts. Carvel met with Kit. And forty-eight hours later, Kit was dead."

CHAPTER FIFTEEN

GARRETT HAD BEEN STARING AT HIS COMPUTER SCREEN SO LONG his eyes started to water. Which was usually the sign that it was time to take a break.

He looked away from the monitor, rubbing his eyes. He was glad he invested in this high-tech high-resolution curved screen. Letting the images wrap around him created an immersive environment that helped him get his work done. At the moment he was watching grainy footage from a security surveillance camera, but his computer and software's enhancement capabilities elevated it significantly. Which was useful when searching for minute details, minor incongruities the police might have missed.

He'd been holed up in his office since the team took this case. He'd been reviewing footage from the SweeTech security cameras since five in the morning. And he had about reached his limit.

What had he learned? Bottom line: nothing useful.

He'd scoured every online source he knew, trying to find something to help Dan win this case. Before that, he explored Sweeney's financial situation, which proved to be truly horrific, worse than anyone imagined. Sweeney owed creditors more than four-hundred-million bucks. Given the kind of people he'd been doing business with, they were unlikely to consider filing bankruptcy a suitable excuse for not paying his debts.

Garrett had also investigated the cartel that had been using St. Petersburg as a crime nexus and debarkation point. In no small part due to the efforts of Dan and Jake Kakazu, the human trafficking ring it ran for more than two decades was in tatters. Organ smuggling was similarly disrupted because they couldn't get the goods into the states and sadly, because they were getting so much competition from dark web sellers. The cartel was no longer cutting edge. They were Sears in an Amazon world.

But today he concentrated on the hundreds of hours of surveillance camera footage from SweeTech, which only reinforced the case against Sweeney. Footage showed Christopher Andrus entering the building on the day in question and riding the elevator to the penthouse floor—with Sweeney.

And never leaving.

He detected no signs of tampering. The camera angles and shadows were correct. This footage definitely came from those security cameras. Besides, the only person in a position to tamper with anything was Sweeney, and he wouldn't fake footage certain to lead to his arrest.

He heard a rustling in the hallway outside his office, the familiar swishing of a cardigan sweater.

"Jimmy?"

The swishing stopped. He knew his partner was there, though he didn't know if Jimmy would answer. He wasn't even sure why Jimmy still came into the office, since he adamantly refused to work on the Sweeney case.

"Are you out there?"

"Yes."

A less than enthusiastic response. "Can I get you to look at something? I could really use a second set of eyes."

"Does it involve the Sweeney case?" Jimmy wrapped himself around the open door. "Because if it does, forget it."

Garrett drew in his breath. "It...does."

"Ask Dinah. I'm not interested."

"But I value your input. We all do."

"If that were true, you wouldn't have taken this case."

"Jimmy." He started to argue, then stopped himself. There was no point. "You've always been my ace consultant. There's no substitute for the insight you have. No one knows this city the way you do."

"Please stop. Just leave me alone."

"I don't know why you're being so difficult about—"

"You don't? You really don't?" A deep furrow crossed Jimmy's forehead. "Then let me explain it to you. Conrad Sweeney is a racist. He's homophobic. He blackmailed one of my favorite people in the world. He wants an America where everyone looks like him, rich and white and selfish. He spews hate about everything that is important to me."

"If we don't help him, he'll die in prison."

"I'm okay with that." Jimmy strode into the office. "What the hell happened to you, Garrett? You're a former prosecutor. You used to know the difference between right and wrong."

"Now wait a minute—"

"Now you're helping a man with no moral compass, which seriously suggests that you have no moral compass."

"Jimmy, you're still a member of this firm—"

"And that's the next thing that needs to change around here."

Garrett bit down on his lower lip. Nothing would be served by them both becoming angry. "Jimmy, you and I have been here the longest. I would be...deeply saddened if you left."

"Me too. But I don't have any faith in this place anymore. I came here to be on the right side of the law, not to aid racist felons. This whole mess is turning me upside-down. Hank says I'm becoming irritable. I mean, more so than usual. I haven't slept in days."

"I hope you'll reconsider," Garrett said.

A new voice emerged from the hall. "Me too."

They both turned. Dinah stood in the doorway. She had a tall stack of papers in her arms. Garrett knew she was trying to draft the motions and briefs that Jimmy refused to do. She wasn't qualified to handle that kind of work yet, but he supposed there was no better way to learn than being plunged into the fire feet first. Maria would review everything before it was filed.

"Please don't leave, Jimmy," she said. "It wouldn't be the same around here."

Jimmy shuffled his feet. "Your brother will take care of you."

"He'll teach me how to do the work. But you're the one who makes it fun."

Jimmy's chin lifted a bit. "I am?"

"Come on, you can't talk about cases all day long. You're the one who brings in Gloomhaven—"

"You are an excellent thief."

"—and Black Canary and comics and...and...cardigans." She clasped her hands together. "We need you, Jimmy."

"I appreciate your kindness." The coldness returned to Jimmy's demeanor. "But this is where I draw the line. I will not defend Conrad Sweeney. And I don't want to be associated with anyone who would."

He rapidly exited the office, not glancing at either of them.

Garrett looked at Dinah and saw her eyes well up. "I think he means it," she said, choking.

"Yes," Garrett replied. "I'm very much afraid that he does."

CHAPTER SIXTEEN

ALEJANDRO HERNANDEZ TURNED THE KEY IN THE IGNITION AND started the yacht. He had originally planned the day as a marlin-fishing expedition, but eventually settled on a simple pleasure cruise. He knew that with all the turmoil in his brain, he wouldn't have the patience for fishing. And that was not the primary point of this excursion anyway.

He needed to have a delicate conversation in a location where he could not be overheard. The feds could not know in advance that he would rent this yacht. They had no reason to bug it, and even if they did, the roar of the engine would make it unintelligible.

And, he admitted to himself, there was another reason for the offshore meeting. Anyone who knew anything about organized crime, or for that matter, anyone who knew nothing about organized crime but had watched *The Sopranos*, knew that anytime the boss gathered people together on a boat, there was a strong chance someone was about to be rubbed out.

Never hurt to let the minions fret. Usually improved productivity.

Once he thought they were sufficiently far from shore, he

slowed the engine and gathered his associates, Jose and Santiago.

"Report," he said, in his usual crisp manner. "Tell me about the money."

"That is…difficult," Santiago replied. "Complex. We are still working to forge new connections. The heat is on and no one wants to do business with us."

Hernandez pounded his fists against the dash. His frustration was not just for show. "Forget Sweeney! Forget Andrus! Find someone else. They are not the only crooked businessmen in America. Far from it!" Bad enough to have so many problems maintaining the business. Worse that they had no effective means of masking their diminishing profits. He knew all too well that the once invincible Al Capone had eventually been laid low by charges of tax evasion.

"Tell me about the placing." "Placing" was cartel jargon for getting money into the legitimate financial system.

"I have been to Miami. I think casinos are the best way to go."

"You live in the past. The federales are onto that."

"But the feds watch for big spenders. Large suspicious amounts of cash. The law requires casinos to report such things."

"But we must move large sums of cash. What do you recommend? Smurfing?" Meaning, breaking the total into smaller, less conspicuous amounts below any reporting threshold.

"We are recruiting men as we speak."

"The more hands involved, the greater the chance someone will talk."

"We will make sure they understand the consequences of any betrayal."

"See that you do." As Hernandez knew, fear worked wonders. But if the FBI threatened someone with imprisonment, or worse, threatened a family member with imprisonment, loyalty to the cartel might seem less of a priority. "You said 'men.' But you should target middle-aged women. They can be bought in Miami for ridiculously small sums. And they attract less attention. Today, it is suspicious to see a casino that is *not* filled with middle-aged women."

"Understood."

"We will still need more fronts. Even if you can't find something with the scope of SweeTech. You can smurf this as well. There are many smaller businesses with legitimate reasons to take in cash. Laundromats. Check-cashing services. Travel agencies. Small groceries. Pawn shops."

"We are assembling a portfolio. But we are also pursuing other possibilities. Like…the stock market."

"Explain."

"Many different accounts under different names with different brokerages. Relatively small amounts of startup cash in each. Brokerage firms don't talk to each other, so no one understands how much money is involved in the entire operation. We buy lots of stock, letting capital gains accumulate, only selling when we need cash."

For the first time, Hernandez' eyes lit. "I like this. Clever. Innovative. But you must obscure the trail. If you sell, wire the cash to an offshore account. Not the usual island paradises. Luxembourg. North Dakota." This was what they called "layering," moving the money around to disguise its origin. "Can we use the investment without selling?"

Santiago nodded. "We take out a loan, using the account as collateral. Paper the transaction. If the FBI gets curious about the money, we explain that it's a loan. And we have documents to prove it." He winked. "Though sadly, the loan may never be repaid." That was the final stage of any money-laundering operation. "Integrating"—commingling it with other spendable income.

"Excellent. Jose, tell me what is happening with our former associate, Mr. Sweeney. Is he enjoying his time in jail?"

"He is surviving. But now he is being represented by an attorney of your acquaintance. Daniel Pike."

The cry of the seagulls was not nearly so loud as the cry inside Fernandez' head. "How can that be? I thought they hated one another."

"I believe that is true. But still, Pike has agreed to serve as his lawyer."

"So the heroic Pike turns out to be a prostitute selling himself to the highest bidder."

Jose shrugged. "He appears to be doing it because…he believes Sweeney is innocent."

"Conrad Sweeney is the least innocent man who ever walked the face of the earth."

Jose held up his hands. "I know. But there are many who suspect he is not guilty of murdering the art dealer." He paused. "You can…see why this might be so."

Fernandez nodded. "And the woman. Has she been eliminated?"

Jose and Santiago exchanged a concerned glance.

"That is a problem," Santiago said. "No one seems to know. But so long as she is off the radar, she poses no threat to us."

"Until she suddenly reappears. If you are not capable of handling this, I—"

"It will be done."

Hernandez gripped the steering wheel of the yacht so tightly his knuckles turned white. "And take care of the lawyer. You said his attachments create a vulnerability."

Jose spoke. "He is a member of a team. A firm. He has friends. Family. A sister."

Hernandez revved the engine, executed a ninety-degree turn, and steered the yacht back toward shore. "Do it."

CHAPTER SEVENTEEN

DAN APPROACHED THE TENEMENT WITH THE UTMOST CAUTION. He had not expected a rooming house in this neighborhood to be nice, but he hadn't expected it to be this horrific either. Dilapidated, dirty, disintegrating. Missing bricks, graffiti on the side, a dangling fire escape clanging in the alley. No one would live here—in fact, no one would pass a minute here—if they had any other choices. But in this neighborhood, they probably didn't. Most of the residents were transient, poor, living on the edge. Not the cutting edge. The slicing and dicing edge.

Wasn't Ray Carvel supposed to be an architect? And yet, he chose this meeting place? Why?

He couldn't put his finger on the danger, but he felt it, just the same. It had been hard to persuade Jamison to arrange this meeting, so he readily agreed to any conditions. But coming here was tempting fate. He knew he had a target on his back. He could disappear from a place like this and no one would ever know.

He especially regretted bringing Maria. "Who set up this meeting? Count Dracula?"

"Not exactly," Dan replied. "But Jamison does have a fondness for coffins." He walked down the sidewalk, then stopped before the front door. "I think it would be best if you waited in the car."

"In this neighborhood? Forget it."

"Ok, go for a drive. Get a pizza. Pick me up in an hour."

"Not happening."

"I'd feel better if—"

"You might need someone to pull your butt out of the fire."

"I am perfectly capable of pulling my own...you know."

"You stumble into trouble like a blind man, then act surprised when something bad happens."

"I assure you I'm not stupid and I can take—"

All at once, she leaned in and clasped his hand. "I was the one who found you outside your boat after three thugs almost killed you. I'm not letting that happen again." She leaned forward and kissed him lightly on the lips. "Please don't argue with me."

It wouldn't do any good. "I should've researched the location before we came."

"But you didn't. And you know why? Because you're used to Jimmy handling that sort of thing."

He sighed heavily. "It's true. Jimmy knows this city like the back of his hand. He would've warned us."

"Or dressed you in a suit of armor."

"Or sent some of his street friends to keep an eye on us."

"Or notified his husband to keep an eye out for you at the ER."

He gave her a look. "Now you're getting morbid."

"Sorry." She paused. "Maybe you should take me back to your boat later and...scold me."

His head twitched. "Okay, now I'm getting mixed messages."

She smiled. "Are you really?"

"Let's focus on the task at hand."

"Sure. Exactly what I was hoping for."

He knocked, but no one responded.

Maria pursed her lips. "Apparently Lurch is off duty tonight."

"But we're expected." He turned the doorknob slightly.

Unlocked.

The door creaked when he pushed it open. That seemed appropriate. He stepped inside, Maria huddled close behind.

"No receptionist?" she said.

"You were expecting Della Street?"

"More like Rod Serling."

"Our guy is in 2D. Let's just go there." He pointed toward a rickety staircase that looked like it dated back to prehistory and might give at any moment.

Get a grip, he told himself. The tenants must walk these steps every day. You'll survive.

He started upward, one careful step after another. Maria followed close behind. They ascended slowly, the wood creaking beneath each footfall.

At the top of the steps, he spotted the door marked 2D. "We've arrived."

He raised his fist to knock, but before he made contact, the door opened. "Get in," a shadowy figure hissed.

Dan hesitated a moment, wishing again that he'd left Maria behind, then stepped inside.

The apartment was as bleak as could be. The only illumination was an unshaded light bulb that dangled from the ceiling. The ratty bed looked like it might be infested. The easy chair was so worn Goodwill would turn it down.

The man standing before him was short, thin, and bespectacled. Bald at the top, with Dagwood tufts on both sides. Shoulder stoop. Hole in his left sneaker.

The small man gestured. "Come into my parlor."

Said the spider to the fly. Dan gestured toward the grungy chair. "Maria?"

"No way in hell."

"Then I guess we'll stand." He glanced at his host. "Thank you for meeting with us. I'm sure you had other things you'd rather do than welcome strangers into your...home."

"Home?" The man made a snorting sound. "I don't live here. I rented this dive to meet you. Rented for an hour, so maybe you should start talking."

"You're Ray Carvel?"

"That's what people around here call me."

Oooh-kay. "I was told you knew the late Christopher Andrus."

"Sure, I knew Kit." His hands twitched. "What about it?"

"May I ask how you knew him?"

"I did some brokering, of a sort. Not just artwork."

"Then what?"

"Whatever I could lay my hands on."

"Were you a broker," Maria asked, "or a fence?"

He smiled thinly. "You think you're pretty smart, don't you, lady?"

"Well, now that you mention it, yes. And you don't look like you've been brokering deals for the Dali Museum."

"Right about that." Carvel moved toward the window, avoiding eye contact. "I haven't had the luxury of restricting myself to fancy deals. I took whatever came my way."

"But you knew Andrus," Dan said. "Jamison told me you had dinner with him shortly before he died."

"We had a mutual business associate."

"Sweeney?"

He shook his head. "The cartel."

Dan and Maria exchanged a look. "What did you do for the cartel? Jamison told me you were an architect."

"Once upon a time. Back in Seattle, where I used to live. Lost my license."

He decided not to ask. "I'm sorry."

"Which is what led me to this sorry state of affairs. Scraping the barrel to stay alive."

"So you got involved with the cartel. Doing...something."

"Haven't you figured it out yet? They needed someone to launder their cash."

Dan nodded slowly. "Because Sweeney couldn't—or wouldn't—do it anymore."

"I couldn't handle all the cash they brought in but I could do a lot. I got friends with nail salons and car washes and stuff. Cash businesses. The cartel boys were happy for a while. Till the old man turned on me."

"You mean Alejandro Hernandez?"

"That's the bastard. About a year ago, he found out I was an architect. Wanted me to design a hacienda for him, a huge sprawling mansion back in El Salvador. I'd have to leave the country. He didn't even plan to pay me. Said I'd been paid handsomely enough already."

"So you...?"

"Told him to go screw himself. Not exactly in those words."

"That required courage," Maria said.

Or extreme stupidity, Dan thought. "I'm guessing Hernandez is not accustomed to being told no."

"Pulled a gun and tried to plug me right there on the spot. I managed to knock it out of his hands and ran. His bodyguards chased after me, but I lost them." He paused. "I've had a lot of practice disappearing."

"And that explains why you're here. Hiding. Jamison said the feds are looking for you."

"I'm not worried about them. But the cartel—that's different. They'll plug me the second they see me. No questions. No remorse. They're coldblooded killers."

This part, at least, Dan knew to be true.

"How do you disappear?" Maria asked. "In this day and age. When everything is stored on computers and credit cards and cell phones and you can't walk down the street without leaving a record six different ways."

"It ain't easy, that's for damn sure." He sat on the edge of the bed. "Fortunately, I knew some people. Good forger. Good computer geek. They helped."

"You created a false identity."

"Actually, I created a false corporate identity."

Maria tilted her head. "You're a corporation now?"

"If you're going to survive in today's world, you have to be able to transact business. You need credit cards. You can't do everything in cash. And once your bankroll runs out, you can't even get cash without a bank account. So I created an LLC."

"A limited liability corporation?"

"My people said that was the way to go. Way further under the radar. The feds look for fake IDs, identities that don't seem to have a past. But people create new companies all the time."

"I suppose that's true."

"We created the corporation in Wyoming. I didn't have to reveal any personal info. They don't require corporations to identify their owner. Then we opened a bank account in the corporate name, stashed some cash, and got a credit card. I could hole up for a long time."

"The cartel isn't stupid," Dan warned. "They'll figure it out."

"I use burner phones and change numbers constantly. Only a few people, like Jamison, know how to contact me. I don't use my phone for directions. All the geolocation functions are shut off. I don't go anyplace I used to go in the past. I use a fake name when I'm forced to interact with someone."

"Your name isn't really Ray Carvel?"

"See? I knew you could keep up."

"Do you go on the internet?"

"No choice there. But I use a VPN to shield my location. I drive the world's most boring car, nothing that would attract attention. The LLC's company car. My name is not on the title. I even bought a decoy house."

"That seems extreme."

"To register the car, I needed a street address, so the corporation bought a tiny home. Complete piece of crap."

"You have to go out sometimes. Groceries, gas. What if someone recognizes you?"

"I wear a disguise. Nothing fancy. Just a big floppy fishing cap and sunglasses. I work remotely from home. I encrypt all my data. I've hired private investigators to try to find me. They couldn't. I think I'm safe."

Dan shook his head. "I don't want to throw cold water on your enthusiasm. But the cartel is extremely resourceful. And persistent."

"And yet, here I am. Alive."

"For now." He drew the conversation back to the Sweeney case. "The prosecutors are claiming there was a meeting between Sweeney and Andrus. Shortly before he was killed."

"Right. At Beachcombers. I was there."

"What can you tell me about it?"

"Not much. I kept my distance. I was suspicious that the cartel might be watching. Kit asked me to come, though I still don't know why—and it's too late to ask. I think he didn't trust Sweeney, which is understandable. He wanted friendly faces around just in case Sweeney had something planned."

"The cops say there was some kind of fight."

"I never saw any fighting. They talked for about twenty minutes. Had a drink. Then everyone left."

"What was the point of the meeting?"

"I assume Sweeney needed to sell some of that artwork fast, on the QT. Andrus would be able to handle that without attracting any press."

"Do you think Sweeney killed him?"

"Why would he? He needed Andrus. I'm telling you, there

was no fight, no threat, no disagreement. The three of them just had a pleasant drink together."

Dan felt a tingling inside his skull. "The three of them?" He pondered. "Was Prudence Hancock there?"

"She was at Beachcombers, watching from a distance like me. I meant the three people at the table. Sweeney, Andrus, and the woman."

Dan leaned forward. Jamison had also mentioned a woman. "Who was she?"

"Don't know her name. She's the one you want to track down. Except good luck with that. From what I hear, she's gone completely off the grid."

Dan glanced at Maria. This was going to be the difficult part, but he had to ask. "I was hoping you would testify."

The little man's eyes bugged. "Have you listened to a single thing I've been saying? The cartel wants to kill me. No way in hell I'm testifying."

"I could subpoena you."

"How? You don't know where I live. You don't even know my name."

The man had a point. "I have a terrific researcher on my team. If anyone can find you, he can."

"He can't. And don't try."

"If you won't help, why did you agree to talk to us?"

"Excuse me, but I already helped you. Do you think I like my current situation? I hope to God you can shut down this cartel. Then maybe I can poke my head out of the shell someday. I'm desperate to get back to Seattle. I got family there. But I'm not going to commit suicide."

"We can offer you the best protection—"

"Do you not understand how dangerous this is? Be smart. Don't stick your hand in the fire. Leave it alone."

"I have a client on trial for murder."

"Who the hell cares? It's Conrad Sweeney. Let him fry."

"I can't do that."

"Then you're even stupider than I thought." The little man rose off the bed and scurried toward the door. "I'm getting out of here. Before you get us all killed."

Dan grabbed his arm. "Please wait."

"Let go of me."

"I—need you—"

The man tried to shrug his hand off, but he wasn't strong enough. So he punched Dan in the side.

"Ow!" Dan pushed him against the wall. "Son of a bitch."

The man started to leave again, but Dan grabbed him by the collar.

"*Let go of me.*"

Maria tugged on Dan's sleeve. "Let him go."

"We need him."

"What are you going to do? Hold him against his will until trial? Throw him in the basement and lock him up? And what would his testimony sound like then?"

She was right, of course. He let go and watched as he disappeared down the hallway.

"Right back where we started," Dan said. "No witness. No case."

"Not true," Maria said, wrapping her arms around him. "That loser would be a horrible witness anyway. We need someone better."

"Any suggestions?"

She hugged him tightly. "*Cherchez la femme*, Dan. Find the woman."

CHAPTER EIGHTEEN

DAN ENTERED THE COURTROOM WITH MORE THAN THE USUAL amount of trepidation. He still didn't have any useful information to build a defense, so he was reduced to poking holes in the prosecution case which, judging from the evidence shared so far, was getting stronger every day. They still didn't have enough to charge Sweeney with the Fuentes murder, but he suspected they weren't too worried about that, since they were certain they would get a conviction for the murder—and dismemberment—of Andrus. That should be enough to assure Sweeney either got the death penalty or spent the rest of his life in prison.

Jazlyn was still cold-shouldering him. Maria declined to come because she couldn't bear to sit at the same table with Sweeney. And his client—well, the less said the better. He could rationalize taking this case, but a tiny voice at the center of his soul still didn't believe he was doing this. Once again, he was putting himself in the line of fire—and for what exactly?

He took a deep breath and made his way through the courtroom.

He spotted Jake Kakazu sitting behind the prosecution table

beside another man he didn't know. They were both dressed in street clothes, but he suspected Jake's friend was a police officer.

They greeted one another cordially. "This is Sergeant Mark Pemberton," Jake explained. "He's been working with me for some time now."

Pemberton shook Dan's hand. Baby-faced. Skinny. Missed a belt loop.

"Good to meet you, Mr. Pike. I've heard a lot about you."

"At the police station? I don't wanna know."

"Everyone is highly respectful of your legal ability," Pemberton said.

Dan tilted his head. "But...?"

Pemberton just smiled.

Didn't matter. Dan knew the end of the sentence. We respect your talent, but wish you weren't always aiding the forces of darkness.

Jake pulled him aside. "Dan, I understand why you're doing this. But I wanted you to know...we didn't do anything wrong. I didn't break the rules."

"My argument is that you exceeded the scope of your invitation."

"No one was more surprised than me when I opened that freezer unit. I expected ice cream. Not body parts."

"That part I absolutely believe."

Jazlyn saw them talking. "Dan, you're not trying to taint my witness are you?"

"Jake is not taintable."

"Too bad we can't say the same about you."

Ouch. "Jazlyn, I'm just doing my job."

"For a man I not too long ago heard you refer to as an acid-spitting toad."

Damn her and her steel-trap memory. "Everyone is entitled to a defense. Some say that representing unpopular defendants is a lawyer's highest and best calling."

"I would agree with that. But I still draw the line here. You know better than anyone how many lives Sweeney has ruined. He's a sham and a liar and a bully and—"

Dan raised a hand. "This is probably not a conversation we should be having in the courtroom. How's Esperanza?"

Jazlyn's adopted daughter. "Very well. Thanks for asking."

"Still setting the curve in the fourth grade?"

"She's as smart as they come."

"Still into Hello Kitty?"

"Oh, Dan, come on. She's ten. She's moved on."

For some reason, that saddened him. "No more big-eyed cat toys?"

"No. Now she collects Gudetama. Another import character. Which, as near as I can tell, is an animated egg."

"And people say my hobbies are weird."

Typically, defendants did not appear at motion hearings, since only legal issues were resolved—but Sweeney had insisted and the judge permitted it. To be fair, the issue of what permission Sweeney gave, and whether Kakazu exceeded it, was central to this motion. No facts were in dispute, but it was still possible something might arise which required Jake or Sweeney to be called to the witness stand.

Sweeney had changed into one of his trademark white suits. He was shaved and groomed, but Dan could see he'd lost some of his usual color. His eyes looked tired.

Prudence sat in the first row beyond the rail, making some kind of signals with her hands. Technically, no one was supposed to communicate with Sweeney but his lawyer and the judge.

Dan sat in the chair beside his client but found it hard to make eye contact. "How's prison life?"

"I'm still alive. How about you? I hear you've been haunting funerals."

Dan's brow furrowed. How the hell did he know about that?

Sweeney's apparent knowledge about his every move was even spookier than Mr. K's.

"I did get some information about a meeting you allegedly had with the victim shortly before he died. Funny you didn't mention that."

Sweeney turned his head slowly. "If you'll recall, when last we spoke, we had no idea who the victim was."

"Certainly I didn't."

Sweeney drew in his breath. "I had no reason to mention that banal and unproductive meeting with Andrus."

"The prosecution will ram that meeting down your throat. They say there was some big fight. Shouting. Threats. Or to put it differently—motive."

"Poppycock."

"We need someone to take the stand and say that. I hear there was someone else sitting with you."

Sweeney allowed himself a small smile. "You've been talking to Carvel. Why?"

"Because I'm doing my job."

"You'll never get him to testify."

"How do you know?"

"Because he's a coward. Always has been."

"He says the cartel wants to kill him."

"Join the club." Sweeney let out a sad chuckle. "If you'll recall, that old bastard Hernandez sent Fuentes to my office to kill me. And almost succeeded. But I didn't go into hiding."

No, Dan thought, you went into the slammer. "I did my best to shame Carvel into testifying, but it didn't work. But he saisd-Andrus brought a woman."

"Tulip Krakowski. She worked with Andrus. Probably the smartest card in that dirty deck."

She couldn't be too smart, if she hung with this pack. "Is she an art dealer, too?"

"I think she was his intern or something like that. Probably banging her on the side."

"Andrus was married."

"You are so naïve."

"And gay."

That slowed Sweeney slightly. "You need to find her."

"I'll do my best. Can you tell me what the point of the meeting was?"

"It's irrelevant. There was no fight. No threats. We were business partners. I had no reason to kill Andrus. In fact, killing him was distinctly against my best interests. I would never do that."

"Are you saying you would never kill someone? Or that you wouldn't do it if it were against your interests?"

Sweeney looked him square in the eyes. "I'm telling you that if I did it, the cops would never have found the body. Or any part of it. Especially not in my freezer."

CHAPTER NINETEEN

JUDGE SMULDERS ENTERED THE COURTROOM. HE APPEARED CALM and reasonably chipper. He chanted through the preliminaries, then took up the matter at hand.

"Mr. Pike, this is your motion?"

Dan rose. "Yes, your honor."

"Very well. Let's—" Smulders stopped short. "Counsel...are you getting enough sleep?"

That was unexpected. "I'm...uh...fine."

"You look tired."

He cleared his throat. "The boat rocked a lot last night. High winds..."

"I'm sure it's stressful, handling a high-profile, high-stakes case like this. Do you meditate?"

"Uh...no. One of my partners—"

"You might consider it. It isn't hard. You can download apps that lead you through the process. It's done wonders for me. Believe it or not, I used to be somewhat nervous and insecure."

Do tell.

"But meditation and mindfulness training helped me pull myself together. And gratitude thinking will increase your positivity, which in turn increases your productivity." He paused. "Maybe you should take some time off. Get away for a while. Learn a foreign language."

Dan drew in his breath. He wasn't accustomed to having a judge as his spiritual counselor. "I'll give that some thought, your honor. After this case."

"I hope you will." Smulders glanced down at his papers. "I thought we agreed to table the suppression motion until the pretrial."

"I thought this might be close enough, your honor. The pretrial is just around the corner."

"On the expedited schedule you requested."

"That's correct. So far as I know, discovery is complete."

The judge shifted his gaze to the other side of the court-room. "Is that correct, Madame Prosecutor?"

"It is." Jazlyn stood. "Though we continue to investigate."

"As do I," Dan echoed. "And I assume that if the prosecution finds anything of interest, they will share it."

"Indeed," Jazlyn said. "May I assume that you will do the same?"

"We have no obligation to produce anything and you know it."

Jazlyn pursed her lips. "But I always hold out hope for a fair and balanced proceeding." She turned to the judge. "I know Mr. Pike talks a lot about justice. I wondered if he might be willing to actually put that principle into practice."

The judge intervened before Dan had a chance to make a snappy comeback. "Let's talk about the motion. Perhaps if we get this out of the way now, it will help you streamline your cases and improve the quality of your pretrial submissions. I don't want any endless exhibit lists, counsel. That tells me you haven't done the prep work. Ditto for every-name-in-your-contacts-file witness lists. If you send me that—I might send it back."

Dan raised an eyebrow. Smulders was running a tight ship and letting them know he wouldn't tolerate any half-assed lawyering.

"Please tell me about your motion, Mr. Pike. You want to suppress all evidence pertaining to the dismembered corpse?"

"Partial corpse, your honor. Found in my client's freezer. Which the police had no right to search."

"The defendant was the one who invited them in," Jazlyn said. "The facts are not in dispute. Lieutenant Kakazu and Sergeant Pemberton requested a meeting, which the defendant granted. Kakazu discovered the secret room behind the main office, and the defendant invited them to look around. Access could only be granted by a keypad that responded to the defendant's right index finger. Once inside, the defendant told them to make themselves at home."

"That's hardly the same as permitting them to conduct a search," Dan said. "They needed a warrant if they wanted to do that."

"The defendant watched the two police officers at all times," Jazlyn explained. "He told Kakazu why he had a large freezer in his little mancave."

"But he did not invite him to open the door and take a look inside."

"Was the defendant surprised when he did? He certainly did not forbid the police from looking. He expressed no objection whatsoever."

"Which is still not the same as granting permission. This was an unauthorized search."

"It was done in plain sight and without objection from the owner of the premises. Frankly, your honor, Detective Kakazu had no way of knowing he was about to discover a corpse. But he had to act appropriately when the corpse fell into his lap."

The judge nodded. "Sounds like we might have a technical,

teeny-weeny Fourth Amendment violation. But not much of one."

"I disagree," Dan said. "If Detective Kakazu had not improperly opened that freezer door, we wouldn't be here today."

"I don't know that that's true," Jazlyn said. "The police were already investigating the defendant in connection with another—"

"Which is not relevant, since you haven't brought charges for that crime," Dan said. "Let's not muddy the waters."

Jazlyn's voice rose. "Let's be realistic for one moment. This defendant is surrounded by murder. When you have corpses falling all around you, it's going to attract interest. It was just a matter of time before the police learned about this second murder."

"You might never have learned about it," Dan said. "You still haven't found the rest of the body."

"Which suggests that it...probably is not in a state to be found."

"Your honor," Dan said, "the bottom line here is that the police had no probable cause with respect to the freezer. My client did not waive his rights. This is cut-and-dried fundamental constitutional law."

"I can't agree with you there," Judge Smulders said. "I might feel differently if your client had posed an objection. But he didn't. Are you familiar with *State v. Bingley*?"

Dan stopped. "Uh, do I know..."

"It's a case. Precedent."

"I know, but—"

The judge cut him off. "The facts are similar to those in the present case. The defendant admitted the police to his home but did not specifically give them permission to search the safe in his library. He didn't waive any rights, but he didn't assert them either. He allowed the police free rein to poke around and only posed an objection after the police found the counterfeit bills in the safe. The court ruled that Bingley had implicitly waived his rights by asserting no objection to what the police did in his presence and with his knowledge."

"But your honor," Dan said, trying not to sputter, "that was not a murder case. When the stakes are life-and-death, a higher standard should be applied."

"No," Smulders said firmly, "the law is the law. Regardless of the charge. If your client had stopped Kakazu or asked him to leave, the officer would have complied. But he said nothing. He cannot complain now about the inevitable consequences."

"But your honor—"

Smulders raised his hand. "I've ruled, counsel. Will there be anything else?"

No one spoke.

"Very well." The judge banged his gavel again, then left the courtroom.

Dan slumped into his chair. "That was a complete disaster."

"True," Sweeney said, his eyes dark. "You were."

"I'm sure you're disappointed."

"I'm disappointed in you."

"Now wait just a minute."

Sweeney shifted around to face him. "Let's be candid for a moment. You don't like me. Fine. I can live with that. I'm not that crazy about you myself. But you took this case. You made a professional obligation."

"I am a professional."

"A professional leaves no stone unturned. A professional takes every legitimate step to benefit his client. Did you research this motion? The judge came up with the controlling precedent, not you. You didn't seem to know what he was talking about."

"I didn't mention that case because it didn't help us. And our usual brief writer—" He stopped short. Sweeney didn't need to hear about Jimmy. "Frankly, there were no cases that helped us but I still made the motion, because even though the odds were against us, I had to try. Because I'm a professional."

"Only losers make excuses."

"Suppressing evidence is always an uphill—"

"You've done it a million times. I know that for a fact. You said you'd go all in on this case. But you haven't. You're keeping your cards close to your vest. Playing both ends against the middle, leaving yourself room to bail if the proper justification presents itself."

"That is simply—"

"Don't BS me. You think you're the only one who knows how to make observations? I can read you like a book. You're keeping your distance. Taking the case, but trying to remain above the fray. And that is not how you win cases."

The marshals moved forward, ready to return Sweeney to his cell.

Sweeney drove a finger into Dan's chest. "Commit to the case, Pike. Or get the hell out of the way."

CHAPTER TWENTY

TULIP'S EYES FILLED WITH SWEAT. SHE FELT AS IF WITH EACH STEP, she staggered a little more. She had lost all track of how long she had been walking, stumbling, trying to find some trace of civilization—without success. The water ran out a long time ago. The food ran out after that. She didn't know where she was and she didn't know where she was going. She hadn't seen a soul since she confronted the man who dragged her out to this wasteland—the man she had to kill.

It was self-defense, she kept telling herself. She had to kill him before he killed her.

But in killing him, she may have killed herself. He could've have shown her the way out of here.

She remembered a story she'd learned in Sunday School all those years ago, about people who wandered in the desert for decades. Forty years. She wouldn't last that long. She wasn't sure she'd last another forty minutes. And she wasn't expecting any manna from heaven, either.

She'd had fantasies, delusions about miracle rescues. The helicopter that spots her from above. A tourist shuttle full of drunken gamblers. A family in an RV that stumbles across her during a potty break. "Hey, Dad, there's a lady lying in the sand…"

But none of that happened and, at this point, she'd given up all hope that it would. The chances that she would survive this ordeal seemed slim to none. At times she wondered if she even wanted to survive. She knew her skin was ruined. There wasn't enough moisturizer in the world to heal the damage. Her stomach hurt. All the time. Sure, she had eaten too little for too long, but there was more to it than that. Maybe something happened during the fight. That bastard had kicked her several times in the gut.

Her throat was parched. Baked, might be the more accurate word. It hurt. Fortunately, she didn't have to speak. There was no one to speak to except herself, and she didn't do that aloud. It might be comforting to hear a voice, even if it was only her own. But she would have to live without that comfort. Like so many others.

How had she gotten herself into this mess? What choice led her to this disaster? She had openly rejected anything resembling a conventional life. She didn't want to be a drone. She didn't want to work nine-to-five, to spend her days in some cubicle hating every moment.

She also rejected the other alternative. Finding a husband. She had nothing against women who married and actually admired women who were good homemakers, good mothers. But she knew that wasn't for her. She didn't want to be limited. This world was full of possibilities and, one way or another, she had been determined to find them. She had one life. She wanted to make the most of it.

That had certainly turned out well, hadn't it?

When Kit invited her to the meeting, she obediently complied. Conrad Sweeney was a big attraction. For years he had been the Big Kahuna in St. Petersburg. The most famous citizen. The most respected philanthropist. Now people were saying he was involved with human trafficking. And porn. She knew she should be repelled, but in a perverse way, it made meeting him more exciting. Beat working in a cubicle.

She thought that was why Kit invited her. He cared about her. He wanted her to succeed.

Now she wasn't sure she could make it to the next day.

She wiped the sweat from her eyes again. It stung and it made it harder to see, which was difficult enough already. She could barely trust her vision. The monotony of the landscape, the relentless sun, the shimmering heat waves rising from the sand, all conspired to make sight the least trustworthy of her senses.

Was that a road ahead? She strained, trying to bring it into focus.

Was that shimmering surface paved? Had she finally found some sort of...path? To people and civilization and water? Food? A chance to survive?

She put all her strength into her legs, quickening her pace, trying to move faster. She had to know. Was it real or just another mirage? Was she seeing what was there or what she wanted to be there?

She put a foot down and the sand shifted beneath her feet. She tumbled hard. Her head slammed against the sand and all at once the world was spinning, even more than it had before.

Sand burned against her cheek, but she couldn't seem to move, not even to alleviate the pain. She writhed but that seemed the most she could manage. Squirming. Helplessly.

Had she finally reached the end of the struggle?

She felt her consciousness fading. She tried to fight it—but how? The light was dimming, and at first, she welcomed it. The dying of the light. Peace at long last.

No, she told herself. You are not a quitter. You are a survivor. You are a woman. You have refused to let men control you.

Refused to let others determine how you should live your life. She would not...would not...

But the darkness was overpowering. Hard as she tried, she wasn't able to beat it back. Her eyelids were closing, even as she tried to force them open.

Maybe she had fought long enough. Maybe she should let the warm nothingness wrap around her like a soothing blanket. Maybe it was time to let her eyes close once and for all...

"Hey Dad, there's a lady lying in the sand..."

CHAPTER TWENTY-ONE

DAN UNTETHERED HIMSELF FROM HIS KITESURFING GEAR AND splashed his way back to the shore. He almost felt guilty about taking personal time so close to the start of the trial. But he also knew this time wasn't entirely for himself. When he was in the water, he found a serenity never equaled anywhere else. The water let him clear his head. Sometimes he got his best ideas and devised his snazziest trial tactics while skittering across the surf.

But it hadn't worked today. No fault of the environment. The sun was bright and the wind was absolutely perfect. But he couldn't pretend he'd had any brilliant insights.

Maybe he was tiring of this routine. Maybe it was time to take a sabbatical.

Or maybe he didn't get brilliant insights because there weren't any brilliant insights to be had.

He splashed saltwater on his face, trying to snap out of it. Why did life always have to be so complicated?

As he approached the beach, he noticed a slender woman holding a cell phone. She seemed to be waiting for him.

She was talking aloud, and not to him. No one else was nearby.

She was talking to the phone. In an extremely animated manner.

Wait a minute. Was she live-streaming?

"Here he comes, cyberbuds. The Corporal of the Courtroom. The Florida Felon's Friend. The man some call the trickiest defense lawyer since Clarence Darrow." She paused. "And judging by my view of the man in a swimsuit, he's pretty damn cut, too."

Dan hesitated, wondering if he should walk away. He wasn't prepared to meet anyone, much less appear in someone's vlog.

She strode right up to him, holding the phone at arms' length so it covered the both of them.

"Daniel Pike," she said with enthusiasm. "We meet at last."

Black hair, buzz cut on the left, flipped from the part to shoulder-length on the right. Mid-thirties. Black skinny jeans, gray T-shirt, black leather jacket. "You're going to get your shoes wet."

"No problem. I believe in sensible shoes." She turned toward her phone. "As all women should."

"If you'll excuse me—"

She took a step forward, blocking his path. "Whoa there, Big Boy, I have thirty thousand followers who want to meet you."

"You'll need to find another form of entertainment. And grow up."

"Hey, don't @ me."

"I have work to do."

"Does that work involve kitesurfing?"

"In a way…"

"I got some great footage. You look good out there." She gave the phone some side-eye. "And I'm not just talking about your surfing style, either."

He didn't like being video-ambushed. And he especially

didn't like being the target of her smarmy asides. "I don't have time for social media influencers."

"Hey, I'm a lawyer. I've come all the way from Seattle to talk to you."

"That may have been a mistake."

She did not move. She didn't lower the phone, either. "It's very important."

"It can't be too important, since you're broadcasting the conversation live."

"My followers demand that I keep them up-to-date on the latest and greatest, right?" She winked into the phone. "Hashtag Kenzi. Hashtag Splitsville."

He tilted his head. Something rang a bell. "Your name is Kenzi?"

"As if you didn't know. Kenzi Rivera, at your service."

"And just what services do you provide?"

"That depends on you." She winked, then immediately looked at the phone. "What do you think, KenziClan? Are you shipping us yet?"

He did not have the time or patience for this. "Sorry to disappoint your legion of fans. But I really can't—"

"Even if I have information about Freddie Lombardi?"

Dan pulled a face. "Never heard of him."

"I think you know him by his most recent alias. Ray Carvel?"

He stopped in his tracks. "What about him?"

"I hear you're looking for him."

"Already met him."

"I mean, looking for an address. To serve a subpoena."

"If I force him to testify, I probably won't like what he says."

"That all depends on how you handle it. Sometimes a little quid pro quo is more effective than threats and legal maneuvering."

Seemed dubious, but he supposed he had an obligation to his client to pursue every possible lead. "Spill. What do you know?"

"A lot more than you."

He took a step forward and got right in her face—even though he knew it put him squarely in the camera frame. "Stop messing around. If you actually know something, I want to hear about it. Right now."

Kenzi offered a mock shiver. "KenziClan, am I the only one who had a little moment there when he started getting tough with me? I can just imagine what he's like behind closed doors."

"I am not remotely interested—"

"What do you think, KenziClan? Should I pursue? Vote now."

"What is this KenziClan?"

"That's what my fans call themselves."

"I wasn't aware lawyers had fans. At least not the good ones."

"Ooh. Burn." She dropped her voice. "Could you speak a little louder? And look into the phone when you deliver your zingers."

"I'm not putting on a show."

"You do in the courtroom. This is just a different courtroom. Of popular opinion. Loosen up." She dropped her voice again. "Don't be a spoilsport. You're trending. You were barely on the radar, but in the last two minutes you've hit the Twitter Trending Top Ten."

"I don't care about that."

"You should. Opinions are formed online these days. This is how you reach jurors before they become jurors. Also how you find future clients. It's branding."

"There's more to practicing law than branding. You should spend more time with your clients and less time with your social media manager."

Kenzi laughed out loud. "What an arrogant so-and-so. FYI, Boomer, my clients love me. And my social media manager is my teenage daughter."

She had a teenage daughter? She must take care of herself

and visit the gym regularly. And take care of her complexion. And…

He realized he had been staring and looked away.

"I'll tell you what I know about Lombardi, my friend. But I expect something from you in return."

"What? Skinny Girl popcorn?"

She glanced again at the phone, tapping it several times. "Fifty-seven percent of those watching this livestream event want us to go out to dinner."

"They're going to be disappointed. I'm seeing someone."

"Oh, boo hiss." She made a sad face for the camera. "Pity. Your approval ratings will go into freefall now."

"Your fans would rather I cheated on my girlfriend?"

"No. They'd rather you sent a text dumping her, then went out to dinner with me."

"That is not going to happen."

"Fine. Then my backup request is that you come to Seattle and testify for me."

He didn't like being confused, especially when he knew his state of bafflement was being broadcast live into cyberspace. "Do you have a criminal case against Carvel too?"

"Perish the thought. I don't do criminal. Way too grimy for me. I handle divorces."

"Of course. Nothing grimy ever happens in family court."

"Not to me. I only represent women. Wronged women. Women who need help to make sure they aren't railroaded by the system."

That sounded somewhat familiar. "Is Lombardi getting divorced?"

She touched her nose with her free hand. "Ding ding ding. Now you're onboard. She's dumping that deadbeat daddy. She wanted an architect, not a mobster."

"I don't see how I can help you."

"If you talked to him, you can testify about what he said. His business dealings and assets."

That wasn't preposterous. What Carvel hinted about his criminal activities could be useful to his wife in a divorce case.

"Look," Kenzi said, "I'll offer Lombardi a break on the marital property division percentages if he agrees to testify for you in your murder case. I think he'll go for it, if we promise to keep him safe. Once your case is over, you can testify for me. I'll add you to the witness list. If he thinks he's in danger of being arrested for money laundering, he'll agree to anything. Might even lead me to his stashed assets, deliberately or unintentionally."

"You need to look for an LLC registered in Wyoming."

"Brilliant. See? This is working well already. He'll pay through the nose, even though I agreed to a reduction of the division percentages."

"Sounds good in principle. But did you find Carvel? I haven't been able—"

"That's because you don't have a Clan."

"You've lost me."

"Do you know how many photos are uploaded to the internet every day? How many videos? Billions. It's virtually impossible to step outside without ending up in the background of someone else's video."

"You combed through billions of photos?"

"Don't be ridiculous. I bought some high-end facial recognition software. And I posted images to my Clan. Someone spotted him yesterday buying groceries and followed him back to his apartment. I confirmed that it was Lombardi."

"That's actually…impressive."

"Well yes," she said, mock-blushing for the camera. "I am rather impressive. That's my superpower. But the point is, I've found Lombardi."

"And you just said that live on the internet, so he's probably already packing."

"I have detectives watching his place. He's not going anywhere."

"This might actually work. Thank you for your help."

"It's my pleasure. Want Carvel's address?"

He glanced at his dripping swimsuit. "I don't actually have pen and paper on me."

She grinned. "That's okay. If your brain is as tight as your abs, you'll remember."

CHAPTER TWENTY-TWO

Dan gathered the team for a pretrial meeting. As usual, he'd made a little something to gnaw on while they laid their final plans. It seemed to improve the quality of the meetings.

He tried not to be depressed about the fact that the biggest fan of his cooking, Jimmy, would not be partaking. He still refused to have anything to do with this case. He was upstairs in his private office but wouldn't come down. Not even to listen.

Dan hoped Jimmy came around before this nightmare trial began. He'd never seen Jimmy behave like this. He was always amiable. Upbeat. He was the one who reminded them there was nothing wrong with having a little fun now and again.

While Dan stirred vegetables in the sauté pan, he felt two arms reach around his waist.

"Hey, good lookin'. Whatcha got cookin'?"

Maria. "Just a little stir fry. Nothing fancy."

"Good thinking." She nuzzled the crook of his neck. "You don't want to be talking to a bunch of hangry lawyers."

"Amen. I think I need more diced tomato."

"I can help with that." She took two tomatoes from the veggie basket and grabbed a knife.

"Uhh…" He clenched his teeth.

"Stop. I know I'm not much of a cook, but I am capable of slicing a tomato."

"Okay, but…don't use that knife."

"It's a sharp knife. Made for slicing and dicing."

"But it will smoosh the tomato. Use a bread knife." He handed her one. "Works much better. Slices through the tomato clean."

She took the knife. "What a fussbudget. I can't imagine—" She stopped short. "Okay, that does actually work better."

He smiled.

She pointed the knife at him. "If you say, 'I told you so…'"

He returned his attention to his stir fry. "I would never."

The team assembled around the kitchen bar and Dan distributed the plates. "Where's Dinah?"

"She has class," Maria explained. "I didn't think you'd want to wait. I'll fill her in later. I'll give her the pep talk, too."

"What makes you think I'm going to give a pep talk?"

"Maybe 'pep talk' isn't the right phrase. 'Dramatization of the impossible odds against us and the dire consequences if we fail.'"

"I would never do that."

"You do it every time." Maria smiled. "And we love it. Wouldn't be the same without it. So please proceed."

He tried not to show any irritation, but it required effort. "Anyway, without being…dramatic…we are not in good shape. To be blunt, we're not ready to go to trial. We served Carvel and swung a deal, so he's agreed to testify. Says he'll tell the truth about the meeting at Beachcombers. But I fear that's not going to be enough."

"Could we ask the court for a continuance?" Garrett asked.

"I was the one who asked the judge for the earliest possible setting."

"So you have to tuck tail and say you were wrong. It's not the end of the world."

"I don't think that's in our client's best interest. And I'm not sure the judge would agree to it. Smulders seems determined to show his mettle. He's had a personality makeover or something."

"He's matured. Gained confidence."

"I guess. At any rate, we have to move forward."

"Have you hired security? Carvel thinks the cartel is gunning for him. And he's probably right."

"We will take every possible precaution to ensure his safety. The cartel isn't going to whack him while he's on the witness stand."

"Are you sure? There is some precedent here..."

Dan knew what Garrett was talking about. Only a few months before, a courtroom sheriff had been blackmailed into killing a cartel informant while he testified. "We have to call him. He'll back up Sweeney's account of the meeting. Let's just hope for the best."

"You've given Sweeney the speech, right?" Garrett asked. "The one about how if he withholds information from his lawyers, he puts his case in jeopardy."

"Of course. Zero impact. Sweeney is so accustomed to keeping secrets he's barely aware he does it anymore. Just second nature."

"He needs to get over that. If he doesn't want to finish his distinguished career with a lethal injection."

"I know. But here's the thing." Dan wasn't sure he should say this aloud. He hadn't worked it out completely in his head. "Sweeney is not a stupid man. So anytime it appears that he's making a seemingly stupid move, I have to wonder what's really going on." Especially since his family was involved. He had adjusted to knowing that his father committed a murder—to prevent a murder. To protect his wife and stepdaughter. But he was convinced Sweeney was in the deceased's cop car that night. Why?

"I can say this with certainty," Dan continued. "I don't believe Sweeney committed this crime. Killing a man who was helping him. Dismembering his body for no apparent reason. Stashing it in his private freezer and leaving it there when he was expecting the police. Sweeney is not stupid. Hell, no one is that stupid. He's being framed."

"Then we're honor-bound to fight hard to get him off the hook."

"I know. But how? Even if Carvel testifies, it's not enough. The forensic evidence paints a damning portrait. The prosecution has eyewitnesses and motive and…if we don't come up with something more soon…Conrad Sweeney is going down for good."

CHAPTER TWENTY-THREE

CARVEL WALKED FAST AND WHENEVER POSSIBLE, KEPT TO THE shadows.

He never even thought of himself as Lombardi anymore. That name was a part of his past, like the wife and the daughter and the Seattle condo and...all those dreams. These days, all he dreamed about was staying alive.

He didn't like going out. He knew he was being watched. Ever since he'd been outed by his wife's mouthpiece, he felt eyes burning down upon him at all times. It wasn't paranoia. It was reality. If a divorce lawyer could find him, how long until the cartel did?

But he was out of Wheat Thins, out of peanut butter, and worst of all, out of smokes. Despite all he had to handle right now, he still felt compelled to put cancer sticks in his mouth. But these days, inhaling smoke was the only comfort he got. And he couldn't pretend that tobacco might kill him anymore. With so many people gunning for him, something else was bound to get him long before cancer did.

He picked up his supplies at the convenience store near his

flophouse, then turned around and started back, still moving fast.

It wasn't that late but it was dark, and the sidewalk and streets seemed deserted. Which normally he would consider a good thing. But just this once, he might feel safer with more company.

He passed a pawnshop that had once been one of his favorite stops. He liked to browse through other people's trash to find treasures. But not today. Too risky.

His father had never believed he would be successful at anything. More than once his father had told him what a loser he was. Even after he got his B. Arch. Daddy couldn't get past the fact that he had a son, not a clone. If you didn't do what he did, you weren't worth anything. The old man probably gloated when Carvel lost his job with the Seattle firm.

What an ego that man had. Well, Daddy, I'm sure you wouldn't approve of me now, but the truth is, I could've saved the world from the zombie apocalypse and you wouldn't approve of me. I made a life for myself on my own terms.

He crossed to the street where he lived. A chill raced down his back. The sun set early tonight and the ocean breeze was strong. He got a sudden shiver. These days, it seemed like he spent most of the time shivering. Even in his sleep.

He headed toward his apartment building.

Someone was waiting for him.

Tall. Overcoat, which looked ridiculous. This was Florida.

He took a closer look.

The man wasn't wearing it for comfort. He was wearing it to hide what he was packing.

Carvel moved away in the opposite direction. Had the man seen him?

A glance over his shoulder confirmed his fear. The overcoat man was coming after him.

No point in subtlety. He ripped into high speed, running as

fast as he could. He turned left, avoiding the bright lights of the liquor store and the streetlamps. He came to a corner, made a quick judgment about which path looked darker, and took it.

He spotted an alleyway splitting the block. There was no time for careful deliberation. If he could disappear, the man might give up the chase.

He took the alley. He veered hard and ran as fast as he could.

Right into a brick wall.

It was too tall to climb and there was nothing to hold onto anyway. He looked on both sides, hoping for an escape path. Side doors? Windows? Even a Dumpster?

Nothing. He was trapped. He started back the way he came—

The overcoat man appeared, silhouetted by the faint glow from a nearby lamp.

If Carvel had any doubts about what his future held—and he didn't—they would've disappeared when he saw the man's face.

"You don't have to do this." Carvel held his hands up, as if somehow that might stop him. Why hadn't he brought a gun? Or even a crowbar? "I'm not going to squeal. I would never do that."

The man kept coming.

"Are you worried about that subpoena? It's just a piece of paper. They can't make me talk."

The man moved closer.

"Listen to me. Your boss wants me to design his mansion? Fine. I'll do it. Anything he wants."

The man kept walking.

Carvel backed up against the brick wall. There was nowhere he could go. "Take me to Hernandez. Let me explain. I can clear up everything."

The man reached into his coat pocket and slowly withdrew a large object. It wasn't until he raised it over his head that a faint glint of light told Carvel what it was.

A hammer.

DINAH WONDERED WHETHER SHE HAD MADE THE RIGHT CHOICE, walking home from class. Dan warned her not to make the mistake of thinking that because this was a beach town, everyone was a laid-back surfer. They had crime. Too much.

Like she needed the warning. She suspected she knew more about the pennyante crime in this town than he did. She'd lived in and among it for far too long. He might know about the high-profile murders and crooked politicians and white-collar chiselers. But she knew more about the real people. The ones who weren't evil, just trying to survive. Far too often, they were forced to take actions they'd rather avoid.

She knew how to take care of herself. And she wasn't going to do anything stupid. Not now, when she was enjoying life more than she had in years.

Years? Try ever. She enjoyed school. She liked hanging out at the office, being involved in their cases. It was exciting.

What she liked best of all, of course, was the fact that Dan trusted her. And loved her. She could see it in his eyes.

She hadn't done a thing to deserve it. But there it was, just the same.

How could life be better than that?

She couldn't walk all the way back to Snell Isle, but there was a bus she could catch nearby and that would take her most of the way. Dan had offered to buy her a car, but come on. At some point, she was going to start feeling like a complete leech. She'd respectfully declined.

Without telling him that, actually, she didn't know how to drive.

She turned a corner and almost collided with someone.

A man in an overcoat who did not appear to be moving.

Was he waiting for her?

"Sorry," she said, and tried to squeeze past.

He grabbed her arm and held her in place.

"Excuse me." Not the first time a man had grabbed her without consent, but that didn't make her like it any better. She squirmed, trying to break his grasp.

"Let—go of me." She shoved him hard, but he still didn't release her. "Mister, if you don't let go of me right now, I will scream my head off."

"If you like," he said quietly.

"I have a phone in my pocket, and it's on. My friends are listening to this."

"I doubt that." He reached into his coat pocket and slowly withdrew something about a foot long.

A hammer.

And it was covered in blood.

"I hope one of the friends listening is your brother," he said, breathing heavily. "We are sending him a message. And we want to make sure he gets it."

THE COLOR OF JUSTICE IS GRAY

CHAPTER TWENTY-FOUR

DAN PACED BACK AND FORTH IN THE LIVING ROOM OF. THEIR office, trying not to collide with Jake Kakazu, who was basically doing the same thing in the opposite direction. Kakazu yakked into his phone, calling in favors, talking to every available officer. Dan tried to eavesdrop, but following one side of a conversation was difficult. All he could gather was the gist.

No one had a clue what happened to Dinah.

Kakazu thrust his cell phone into his pocket. "Sorry. No one's seen her."

"People don't just vanish. There must be some explanation."

"Is it possible she met a friend? Decided to go out for a drink?"

"All night?"

"You know how it goes. You start having fun, time gets away from you. Maybe she decided to crash somewhere."

"She would've called. Or texted."

"Sometimes people forget when they're tired or tipsy."

"She would've called. Or texted."

"You can't be—"

Maria cut in. She sat on the semicircular sofa, not moving

but looking just as agitated as Dan. "I know Dinah, too. We've spent time together every day since she joined the firm. She's not a little kid. She's a grown adult and knows we care about her. She would not fail to come home without telling someone. If she could."

Kakazu didn't argue.

Neither did Dan. He knew Dinah and Maria had become fast friends. It was probably conceivable that Dinah might run off on a whim and neglect to contact her brother. But her bestie? Never.

"Does she have a cellphone?" Jake asked. "Have you tried tracking her that way?"

"Yes. Garrett has been doing everything he can. Dinah has an iPhone, but as far as we can tell, she never activated Find My Phone or anything like it."

"Describe her route home for me again," Kakazu said. They'd already covered this, but he supposed it was possible the repetition might reveal something fresh.

"She takes the bus. I offered to get her a car, but she declined. I should've insisted."

"You couldn't know this would happen," Maria said.

"I could've. I should've."

"She didn't want to be a burden. You've already done so much for her."

Dan slammed his fist into a sofa pillow. "I was asleep at the gate."

"Dan, stop." Maria wrapped her arms around his shoulders. "This is not your fault."

"Are you sure? I'm not. How can you be sure when we don't even know what happened?"

"I know this is not your fault."

Kakazu glanced at his phone, reading something. "I've contacted her instructor. Class ended at the usual time. No one observed anything unusual about Dinah." He looked up. "And by the way, her teacher says Dinah is the class superstar. Thinks she should go to law school after she finishes her legal assistant training."

Nice to hear. But she couldn't go to law school if…

"I've sent officers to interview all the bus drivers on duty in that area around the time she got out of class. No one saw her."

"Then she never got on a bus," Maria murmured.

"Looks that way to me. I've got detectives scouring the area."

"Have you—" Dan's voice choked. "Have you called the hospitals? Clinics?"

"Of course. No one remotely resembling her description has arrived."

He felt Maria give him a tight squeeze. But he wasn't sure if this was good news or bad. At least if she were in the hospital, they'd know where she was. They'd know someone was looking after her. "Ambulances? Mortuaries?"

"No sign of her."

Dan pulled away from Maria, his fists clenched. "This is Sweeney's work."

Maria clasped his arm. "Dan, try to stay calm and think. Sweeney is behind bars."

"That doesn't mean he's powerless."

"True. But it does mean he has no incentive to screw with you or your family. You're the only hope he has of regaining his freedom."

"I have to agree with her," Kakazu said. "If something has happened—and I emphasize the *if*, because at this point we don't know—I doubt Sweeney was involved. Over three-hundred-thousand females are reported missing each year in this country. Most of those cases are resolved in twenty-four hours and have perfectly innocent explanations."

"But thousands remain unsolved. Every year." Dan squared his shoulders. "You're thinking about the cartel."

"How can I not? We know it has a long history of...you know."

Dan pressed his hands against the wall. He felt as if he were about to explode. "I can't stand...not knowing."

Kakazu's phone buzzed. He pulled it out with lightning speed. "Yes?"

A second later, he spoke to Dan, covering the phone. "They've found her."

Dan whipped around. "Where is she?"

"Kindred Hospital."

"Condition?"

"Not sure yet."

Dan raced to the kitchen counter and grabbed his keys. "On my way."

Maria skittered behind him. "I'm coming with."

"You don't have—"

"I'm coming with." And that was the end of the conversation.

DAN RACED TO THE DESK ON THE FIFTH FLOOR. "I'M HERE TO SEE Dinah Fisher. Where is she?"

The attending nurse swiveled around and glanced at a computer screen. "I'm not sure she's allowed to have visitors yet."

Dan clenched his teeth. *"Where is she?"*

The nurse sighed. "Let me check with the doctor."

A middle-aged woman in scrubs appeared beside them. "I'm Dr. Thompkins. I've been treating Dinah. Are you a relative?"

"Yes. I'm her brother. What happened?"

"I don't know. She was brought in about half an hour ago, unconscious. She had a concussion. She was fully dressed and showed no signs of any kind of assault. Just some bruises and a head contusion."

The color drained from Dan's face.

The doctor continued. "It could've been a lot worse. Fortunately, someone found her and called an ambulance. We ran an MRI and a CT scan. So far as we can tell, there's no cerebral trauma. She's awake and answering questions."

"She's awake? What room?"

Dr. Thompkins hesitated a moment, then relented. "314."

Without another word, Dan raced down the corridor. He tore into the room.

Dinah lay on the hospital bed wearing the traditional gown, no covers.

She smiled as soon as she spotted him. "'Sup, bro?"

He ran to her side and took her hand. "What happened? Tell me who did this."

"Really? Not even a 'How are you' first?"

Maria came in behind him and crossed to the other side of the bed. "He's been worried sick about you, Dinah. But you know how he is. Always on the case."

He drew in his breath. "Ok. How are you, Dinah?"

She shrugged. "My head is throbbing. Tummy hurt, but they gave me something for it. The attending nurse is kinda stern but, on the upside, they gave me some ice cream and it was excellent."

"Okay, is that enough chitchat? What the hell happened?"

Dinah exhaled heavily. "My memory is spotty. They say that's typical after a concussion. But I do remember that I ran into someone. Someone who wouldn't let me pass."

"You should've screamed. Immediately."

"I'm not the screamy sort."

Maria leaned in closer. "There are times when every woman should scream," she said firmly. "Even if you're not the screamy sort."

"I guess. Anyway, he must've hit me or something. Dragged me into the alley."

Kakazu entered the hospital room. "Do you remember what he looked like, Dinah?"

"I really don't. It was dark. I never got a clear look at his face."

"What did he sound like?"

"Very deep voice. Of course, he was trying to be all scary and threatening. And he had an accent."

Dan and Kakazu eyed one another. "What kind of accent?"

"I'm not an expert, but I think it was Spanish."

"Central American?"

"Maybe."

Cartel. Jake was right.

They didn't kill her. Yet. Though they could have and wanted him to know they could have.

The message was clear. Drop the case and get out of our way. Or you sister dies.

And given the brutality they'd displayed in the past, there was no reason to think they would stop with his sister.

"I'm resigning from this case."

Maria stepped toward him. "Dan—"

"No one can fault me for quitting after this."

Maria fell silent. To his surprise, she wasn't going to argue.

But Dinah was. "You can't do that, bro."

"I sure as hell can. All I have to do is file a Withdrawal form. The trial hasn't started. If Sweeney can't find a lawyer, the judge will appoint someone—"

"I guess I should've said that differently. I know you *can* do that. But you shouldn't."

"You don't know…as much about this…"

"Dan, I don't want you to quit."

He felt his eyes itching. "Dinah…someone attacked you."

"So we'll all be more careful from now on. But you're not a quitter, Dan. I know that. And frankly, neither am I."

"These are special circumstances."

"Are they? You told me our mission statement was to prevent people from being railroaded the way your father was. Because any miscarriage of justice proves the system isn't working. Every miscarriage of justice weakens us all." She clasped Dan's hand. "Please, Dan. Don't give in. I don't want to be the reason you betrayed your core principles. You know what your dad said. Keep the faith."

"It's not like we have a sympathetic client. We're talking about Conrad Sweeney."

"And you're his last hope. Even if he doesn't deserve one."

Dan drew in his breath. He wanted to argue, but when he stared into those blue eyes, hearing her say what she said, even after what had happened to her—he couldn't.

He turned. "We have to take this cartel down. Immediately."

Kakazu twisted his neck. "Easy to say…"

"No. This time we have to do it."

"We've been trying for some time."

"I know you have. We both have. We've dented and dinged and interfered with their business. But it has to end. Totally." He turned back toward his sister. "Or no one is safe."

Maria cut in. "Maybe we should let Dinah rest."

"In a minute." He leaned toward his sister. "Anything else you remember? Any distinctive markings? Anything unusual?"

"He was wearing a coat. Like a trench coat or something. Looked awfully hot for this climate. And he was holding a hammer. Threatening me with it."

Dan's mouth went dry. "A—A hammer?"

"Yeah. Mean looking. Ball peen job, I think."

Kakazu spoke softly. "I didn't mention this before because I didn't want to worry you, but…we had a murder last night. That victim was also found in an alley. And it looks like he was beaten to death. Possibly with a hammer." Kakazu turned his head away. "Bloody mess. Brutal. Face is like hamburger meat."

Dan looked him straight in the eye. "Same assailant?"

"Possibly."

"And the victim?"

Jake hesitated. It was clear he did not relish answering.

"Come on. Spill."

Jake pursed his lips. "It's Ray Carvel."

Dan's eyes bugged. "Our star witness? The one I moved mountains to persuade to testify?"

Jake nodded slightly. "I don't think he's going to be available for trial…"

CHAPTER TWENTY-FIVE

NORMALLY DAN ENJOYED BEING IN THE COURTROOM. HE MIGHT not admit it, but he did. Even when he had a tough, impossible case—he liked the challenge. Courtroom battles got his blood flowing. He liked finding a way to solve the indecipherable puzzle.

But not today. He should be in the hospital with his sister, not screwing around at the courthouse trying to....

He could barely say it to himself. Trying to get the most despicable man on earth acquitted so he could run amok once again, creating misery and ugliness everywhere he goes.

He didn't try to speak to Jazlyn. He already had enough pain in his life. He understood her position but...that didn't mean it hurt any less. He hoped their relationship would improve once this damnable case was over.

Maria had arrived earlier. She was already sitting at the defendant's table. Prudence was behind the rail, as usual. As he approached, he noticed Maria seemed to have less trouble being near Sweeney than he did. Her forbearance and tolerance put him to shame.

The courtroom gallery was almost full, though he suspected

that at least half of the people in the throng were reporters. He spotted one face he didn't expect to see: Bernard Jamison. The coffin confessor and friend of Christopher Andrus. What brought him here?

He decided to ask. "Surprised to see you this morning."

"Well, my workload has been light."

"No good funerals?"

"Or art deals. Kit hogged most of that when he was alive, and he seems to still be doing it even though he's dead."

"You're going to need another whale. If you hope to make the kind of deals Andrus made with my client."

"I've been working on it. Hard to find people with that kind of money. But they do exist."

"And…that's why you're here today?"

"Oh. No." He glanced over his shoulder. What was he looking for? "I was just curious. I want to see that justice is done by Kit. I owe him that much."

Dan passed on to the defense table.

"There he is," Sweeney said. "The man of the hour. I was beginning to wonder if you were coming."

Today, since there would be a jury, Sweeney had been allowed to dress and groom. Prudence made all the arrangements. Even picked out the suit from what Dan guessed was an ample clothes closet. He noted that she had not chosen Sweeney's trademark white suit. Too flamboyant for a jury?

Sweeney leaned forward. "Let me say that I am horrified by what happened to your sister. If there's anything I can do, just tell me. I don't know what it would be, but I'm more than ready to help."

"Thank you," Dan said, not really meaning it. "But Dinah is going to be fine."

"Thank goodness. Remember, Prudence is still on the outside. Anything you request, she can make happen."

"And I will," Prudence added.

"My client is lucky to have someone like you he can depend on," Dan told her.

Sweeney spoke before Prudence did. "Don't I know it. I thank my lucky stars for her every day."

"She's been with you for..."

Prudence filled in the blanks. "Almost twenty years."

Sweeney whistled. "Where does the time go? When we first met, she was a college intern. I didn't give her that much to do at first, but it didn't matter. She found things to do. She made herself invaluable."

Dan spotted some action near the door to chambers. The judge was probably preparing to emerge. "I'm sure you're familiar with general courtroom procedure—"

"Maria explained our trial strategy," Sweeney said. "Seems sound to me. In fact, Maria, I want to compliment you. You haven't let the loss of our key witness hold you back."

She shrugged. "It's what I do."

"You know, I could use someone like you in my organization."

Dan didn't have to be a mind reader to detect Prudence's reaction to that suggestion.

"Please don't make this awkward," Maria replied. "I'm very happy where I am."

"I understand," Sweeney said. "But if that ever changes, you come to me. I'll find a place for you in my organization."

"If you still have an organization," Dan couldn't resist saying.

Judge Smulders emerged from chambers and started the proceedings with the brisk and efficient manner that was apparently now his norm. He blew through the preliminaries with impressive alacrity.

"Sounds as if we're ready to begin. All parties prepared to select a jury?"

Jazlyn rose to her feet. "The prosecution is ready, your honor."

"We are as well," Dan replied.

"Good. I'll ask my clerk to call the first slate of venirepersons, and then you can begin questioning. Let's see if we can get this done in less than a week, shall we?"

IN FACT, THEY WERE DONE IN LESS THAN A DAY. THE LEAD attorneys on both sides were extremely experienced, no one was playing games, and the judge kept a tight rein on the questioning. He didn't wait for counsel to object to irrelevant questions. If he thought one of Dan or Jazlyn's questions was a waste of time, he cut it off before the jurors answered.

Dan was not accustomed to seeing a state court judge plunge so aggressively into the jury selection process. He was also surprised to see how much and how often Sweeney butted in. Most defendants kept their mouths shut and let the lawyers do their work. To be sure, Sweeney was not your average client and this was certainly not your average case. But he commented almost as often as Maria did. And most of what he said made sense.

Sweeney took notes from Prudence, quietly passed over the rail. If you judged only by appearances, it looked like she cared more about what happened to Sweeney than Sweeney did.

The most controversial moment came as Jazlyn questioned a middle-aged African-American woman on the front row. Without any discussion, Sweeney leaned forward and whispered, "Get rid of her."

Dan kept his head down and tried not to attract attention. "Why?"

"She doesn't like me. I can tell."

She doesn't like you, Dan wondered—or you don't like her? "I'm not seeing the problem."

"I am. Give her the heave-ho."

"If you could explain—"

"As I understand it, you work for me. You're supposed to implement my wishes."

"Yes, but—"

"Get rid of her."

Fortunately, Maria was listening, because Dan was missing half the questioning. "Is this…a black thing?"

"Of course not. I know there will be minorities on the jury. That's why I didn't wear a white suit."

Dan squinted. *What?*

"But I will do better with real Americans. Successful Americans. People who are living by the fruits of their ingenuity. Not people who go through life asking for handouts and feeling entitled."

Oookay… "We still have three peremptory challenges. But since this woman is black, we'll still have to assert a non-race-based reason. Removing a juror based upon race is forbidden by Supreme Court precedent."

"I'm sure you'll be able to think of something. Get it done."

The rest of the jury selection went smoothly and predictably. By mid-afternoon, they had a jury of twelve, plus six alternates. Dan had no idea whether it was a good jury for his client, but he thought they had eradicated all the obvious bias which, given the high profile of their client, was no small task.

"Very good," Judge Smulders said. "And we still have time left on the clock to knock out those opening arguments. Thirty minutes per side, and I will be keeping time. Madame Prosecutor, would you care to begin?"

CHAPTER TWENTY-SIX

DAN WATCHED AS JAZLYN CONFIDENTLY STRODE TO THE JURY BOX and positioned herself in the center, just beyond the rail dividing the attorneys from the jury. During the questioning, she had been friendly, cordial, and at times, even funny. He assumed she was trying to humanize herself, to fight against the stereotype of female prosecutors as ice queens. But all that was gone now. Her somber expression and no-nonsense language made it clear the fun was over and it was time to get down to business.

"First of all, ladies and gentlemen, I thank you for your service, and I mean that sincerely. This trial will take many days and will require you to confront matters you would probably rather avoid. You will have to make tough decisions and give force to the law, to take the theoretical and make it real. It's a hard job, so I thank you."

Off to a great start, Dan had to admit. Jazlyn was always good, but he hadn't heard this bit before. Lawyers usually started by sucking up to the jury, but this had a note of sincerity that he could see played well with the people in the box.

"As you have likely already gathered from the questions put to you, this case involves the worst of all possible crimes— murder. We will be asking for the death penalty, but as you hear about the crime, the motivations, and...the way the victim was killed, I believe you will understand why that ultimate sanction is necessary. Asking for anything less would do a great injustice to not only the victim but the criminal justice system itself. This case involves a heinous crime of the worst order. Most people would be incapable of exacting such brutality. When we find someone who is, it is vitally important that we take all possible measures to make sure that individual never has a chance to repeat his offense."

He noticed that Jazlyn slowly scanned the jury box as she spoke, not fast enough to make anyone seasick, but enough to make them all feel included, like she was speaking to each member individually.

"Most of you acknowledged during the questioning that you had at least some passing familiarity with the defendant, Conrad Sweeney. He has been a high-profile citizen in St. Petersburg for at least the last two decades. He's a successful businessman—or so it appeared. He's a great philanthropist— though of late, the true nature of those endeavors has been called into question. We will discuss that more during the trial. At this time, I will simply remind you that you said you would be able to set aside any preconceived ideas and make your evaluation based upon the evidence presented at trial. That will become important, because as you will see, nothing about this defendant is what it appeared to be."

At the pretrial, Jazlyn sought permission to show the jury a photo of the murder victim—predictably, one taken from the coroner's office that showed a bloody decapitated head bashed virtually beyond recognition. Dan objected and the judge agreed that it would be more inflammatory than probative.

Jazlyn was still putting a photo on the screen, but it was a standard passport photo, not a decapitated head.

"Christopher Andrus was an art dealer, among other things. His friends called him Kit. Some people called him a hustler, and to be fair, he was involved in many different projects, some of them more than a bit on the shady side. That may be why he worked so long and so well with the defendant, Conrad Sweeney. We know that Andrus brokered the sale of many rare and valuable works of art to the defendant. We are still undergoing the difficult process of cataloguing the pieces found in the defendant's home and office. But the point is, the evidence will show that the defendant and the victim knew each other and worked closely together on many occasions."

She took a deep breath, as if to express regret, before she plunged ahead. "The evidence will also show that there was a major falling out between the parties, which eventually led to Andrus' death. We will have expert testimony explaining that Sweeney was in serious financial trouble. He was in near bankruptcy and, in all likelihood, prison, based upon financial malfeasance and perhaps his links to organized crime."

Dan instinctively started to rise, but Sweeney grabbed his wrist and gave him a tiny shake of the head. Dan did not appreciate a client advising him about whether to object. But at the same time, he understood. Objections during opening were relatively rare and juries didn't like the interruption. An objection to this mention of organized crime might be sustained, but it would underscore the words in the minds of the jurors. Better to wait until closing and then double-down on the fact that the prosecution never substantiated its claims.

Painful to admit it. But Sweeney was right.

"Multiple witnesses will testify that Sweeney was seen meeting with Andrus shortly before his death, and that meeting was hostile and angry. Sweeney threatened him. Security footage shows Sweeney and Andrus both entering Sweeney's penthouse not long after. And Andrus never came out."

Jazlyn clasped her hands and lowered her head, as if she were forced to address an unsavory subject. That was how she won the jury over. By making them so repulsed by the crime that they were ready to convict anyone.

"We will have police testimony describing the victim's remains exactly as they were found. I regret to inform you that the body was dismembered. The head was severed from the torso. The hands were severed from the arms and legs. The head and hands were found in a freezer unit in a secret room only the defendant could enter. The lock to this hidden room required the defendant's fingerprint. No one could get in without his help. And that's where the body was found."

Jazlyn drew in her breath, then continued. "The torso and legs and other body parts have never been found. Neither has the murder weapon. Neither have the tools that must have been used to tear the body apart. But it doesn't matter—because we know what happened. We know Andrus entered the defendant's office and never left. And we know where the body parts were found—in the freezer of the man who had a motive to kill him, who had been seen violently arguing with him only a few hours before."

Jazlyn inched closer and gave them her most earnest expression. "I know you will honor the oath you have sworn and take this responsibility seriously. Your job is not a pleasant one, but it is an important one. You are the people who hold this fragile thing we call law and order together. Crime must be punished—especially crime of this magnitude. Otherwise, our society descends into chaos. We will provide incontrovertible evidence that will allow you to find this vile man guilty beyond a reasonable doubt. We will do our part. We only ask that you do yours. Thank you."

While Jazlyn returned to her seat, Dan heard Sweeney murmur. "Good opening."

"She's a pro," Dan whispered back.

"And smart. I can see why you dated her."

On the other side of Sweeney, Maria's head whipped around. "What?"

Sweeney arched an eyebrow. "Didn't mention that to her?"

Dan felt his steam rising. "We…didn't really date."

"Not what I heard."

"We went out to dinner once." He looked at Maria. "I'm sure I mentioned it."

"No," Maria whispered.

"Well, it was nothing."

Maria turned her head front and center. "We'll talk about this later."

Dan glared at Sweeney. Who just smiled back.

The judge was looking at Dan, obviously expecting him to launch his opening.

Thank you, Sweeney, for giving me another reason to hate you. As if I didn't have enough already.

Dan rose and faced the jury. "Let me welcome all of you who have agreed to perform your civic duty. Like the prosecutor, I thank you. I cannot promise this will be over quickly, but I can promise that I will not waste your time. I will not call witnesses who have little or nothing to contribute, or redundant witnesses. I will not make emotional appeals or try to get you so worked up about the crime that you forget to look at the evidence. Instead, I will ask you to focus on the evidence, such as it is, and make your decision based upon it. Because at the end of the trial, the judge will instruct you that to convict, you must find the defendant guilty beyond a reasonable doubt. That is a super-high standard. A standard which the prosecution cannot meet in this case."

That was all he had to say, in a nutshell, but he knew the jury would be disappointed if he didn't talk more. If he spoke for significantly less time than the prosecution, some jurors might think his defense didn't amount to much.

"You may be surprised to hear me say that I actually agree with some of what the distinguished district attorney has said." Never hurts to be a reasonable person. "My client and Andrus did know each other. They worked together, and my client bought several paintings that Andrus brokered over the years. And they did meet shortly before Andrus disappeared. But that's where the agreement ends, and that alone proves nothing about who committed the murder. Everything else is disputed. You will have to decide what you think happened. And your decision about the facts will inevitably lead to your conclusion about the guilt or innocence of my client."

He paused, giving them a moment to soak that in. "My client and Andrus did meet, but the evidence will show that there was no argument. What would they argue about? As the prosecutor has suggested, my client was in no position to buy expensive paintings. He did not kill Andrus and the idea that this pillar of our society would hack up a body is preposterous. C'mon, people—look at him. Does this look like a guy who would do that? Sure, appearances can be deceiving, but not *that* deceiving. This is an educated, cultured man who built a successful tech business, not a barbarian."

He pivoted slightly. "And that brings up another issue we should address up front. You can already tell from the prosecutor's opening that she intends to trash my client, to accuse him of all kinds of crimes. Basically, she's suggesting that since he's committed other crimes, you should convict him of this crime. That is absolutely wrong. You can only convict him of this crime if it is proven that he committed this crime. You will hear me object any time she tries to sling mud or discuss other possible crimes, and for a good reason. Ask yourself—if they are so sure my client committed other crimes, why haven't they charged him?"

He stepped closer to the defendant's table, forcing them to look at Sweeney. "Here's another thing I want you to remember about my client. He may not be perfect, but he is definitely not stupid. They can accuse him and malign him, but they will not say he's stupid because they know better. Any time they suggest that he did something stupid—like leaving body parts in his ice cream freezer when he knew the cops were coming—you should see a big red flag waving. None of you would do something that stupid. Why would you imagine Conrad Sweeney would?"

He took a moment as if gathering his thoughts, but of course, that was for show. He'd worked out this opening long before, practiced in front of a mirror, performed it for Maria and taken her notes. After all, it was designed to introduce her strategy, her theory of how they might win this case. But jurors liked to think these talks came from the heart more than the head, so he delivered the Oscar-worthy performance that allowed them to believe that.

"I think most of you appreciate straight-shooters, people who say what they mean and mean what they say. Let me bottom-line this for you. This is a frame. My client did not commit this crime. He is not a perfect person, but neither is he a murderer. You want to criticize his business, his art collection, even his personal life, fine. But he is not a murderer. A body was discovered and the police have no clue what happened. They can't even find the rest of the body. They can't find the murder weapon. So they grabbed the obvious suspect—obvious because he was obviously being framed."

Dan knew he was getting dangerously close to argument, which supposedly was not permitted in openings, so he dialed it down. "For some time, law enforcement has been circulating rumors, planting stories, and indirectly accusing my client of many things. But what have they been able to prove? Nothing. Then this opportunity dropped into their hands—literally—and they milked it for all it's worth. But make no mistake, people—my client did not commit this crime, and they cannot prove that he did—because he didn't. I will ask you to perform your civic duty…and find Conrad Sweeney not guilty."

CHAPTER TWENTY-SEVEN

WHEN THE TRIAL RESUMED BRIGHT AND EARLY THE NEXT DAY, Dan found himself struggling to shake off the early-morning cobwebs. He hadn't slept well, Maria seemed angry, and Garrett hadn't found any useful leads. The press badgered him constantly. Somehow his cell phone number leaked and reporters phoned more relentlessly than robocallers. Social media was all over the case, and what he read on his phone during breakfast was particularly vile.

IS PIKE GETTING A PIECE OF THE PORN ACTION? #JUSTICEFORSTPETE

WHAT'S SWEENEY'S FAVORITE FLAVOR OF ICE CREAM? YOU. #sweeneyisguilty

WOULD YOU TESTIFY? LOOK WHAT HAPPENED TO THE LAST GUY THEY put on the stand. #lawandordersp

DAN DROVE TO THE COURTHOUSE AND SAT AT THE DEFENSE TABLE beside Maria.

"Is this seat taken?" he asked, smiling.

"Sure you wouldn't rather sit next to Jazlyn?"

Yup, definitely a chill in the air… "I'm sure."

"You're saving her for dinner?"

"Maria." He tugged at her elbows, trying to get her to face him. "Jazlyn and I only had dinner once. Nothing happened. And that was before you and I were together. In fact, it was before you and I met."

"Then why didn't you tell me about it?"

"I thought I did. I guess it never came up. At any rate, it was no big secret."

"Jazlyn never mentioned it to me either."

"I doubt the DA yaks much about her dinner with the city's best-known criminal defense lawyer."

Maria frowned a few moments, then caught his eye. "And this will never happen again."

"Of course not. Jazlyn and I are just friends. Will you forgive me?"

A small smile emerged. "I'll take it under advisement."

JAZLYN OPENED HER CASE WITH WITNESSES WHO WERE BORING BUT essential. First, the medical examiner, to establish that a death occurred. Then Jake Kakazu, to describe how Andrus' head was found.

Dan had cross-examined Dr. Zanzibar on many previous occasions. He was competent, prepared, and always wore his white coat, even though it seemed unlikely that he'd be performing an autopsy on the witness stand. Maybe it was his security blanket. Or maybe he thought it lent him an air of authority. Which was probably correct.

Jazlyn established that Zanzibar had received the body parts found in Sweeney's office and performed an autopsy—or as much of an autopsy as was possible, since he didn't have a complete corpse. Some of the normal procedures, like the toxicological panel, were either unavailing or impossible given how little of the body he had to scrutinize.

"Could you please describe your conclusion for the jury, doctor?"

"Of course. Cause of death is more difficult to conclude here than in most cases. But there are several conclusions I can reach with certainty. Andrus was struck from behind. I observed a depressed skull fracture that in all likelihood was caused by blunt force trauma."

"Did you observe anything unusual?"

"That depends on what you mean by 'unusual.' What I observed would be unusual for someone walking and talking, but not someone who died as a result of blunt force trauma. His contact lenses had fused to the corneas of his eyes. I observed lots of petechiae—that's the red splattered result of burst blood vessels."

"What could cause that?"

"Strangulation could, but given the skull fracture, it's more likely that his brain started swelling after the injury. Skulls are closed containers. The brain can swell but the skull can't. Kind of like inflating a balloon inside a lockbox. It can't push through the skull, so instead, it swells into the brain stem, which would cause the burst blood vessels. And of course, it's possible the victim was hit in other places. The same weapon that caused the skull injury might've damaged the brachial plexus nerves, which would immobilize the victim's arms, making it impossible to fight back."

"Can you tell what weapon was used?"

"Judging from the depression, it appears to be a heavy object, probably swung at high velocity. Several teeth were dislodged. Two right-side molars were cracked at the root. His jaw and orbital bone were fractured on the same side."

"Would he have remained...conscious? After the blow or blows?" Not really relevant—except for generating jury sympathy and repulsion.

"He was probably conscious until he died, and that did not occur instantaneously with the first blow. He would have felt pain, then nausea. Probably cloudy thinking and blurred vision. How functional he remained, I can't say. This is a brain injury, and everyone reacts differently."

"Was the brain injury what killed him?"

"In all likelihood, what killed him was either shock or loss of blood. Exsanguination. But given that I can't examine the rest of the body, it's hard to reach definitive conclusions. It's possible something was happening to the rest of the body that I don't know about. But based upon my professional expertise and more than twenty years as the county medical examiner, I believe it was blunt force trauma to the head, probably repeated, that eventually led to death."

"Dr. Zanzibar, have you seen the photographs taken in the defendant's office, where the victim's head was discovered?"

"I have."

"Did you see anything that could have caused the blunt force trauma you described?"

"Objection," Dan said. At last. A valid opportunity to interrupt the flow. "Calls for speculation."

"Not really," Jazlyn replied. "I'm asking for an expert opinion about what could and could not cause the injury he described."

The judge nodded. "An expert witness can offer reasonable speculations so long as it is relevant and within the realm of his expertise. The witness may answer."

Dr. Zanzibar cleared his throat. "There is a heavy metallic

paperweight on the defendant's desk. Flat on the bottom and rounded at the top. That would be more than sufficient, if it came swiftly enough."

"Thank you. No more questions. Pass the witness."

Dan knew he would gain little from crossing, but he didn't want Sweeney whining that he wasn't committed to the case. "Dr. Zanzibar, you've suggested a paperweight could be the murder weapon. But you can't say for certainty that it *was* the murder weapon, can you?"

"It complies with the profile—"

"Doctor, you're not answering my question. Can you say with certainty that the paperweight was the murder weapon? Or are there other possibilities?"

Zanzibar shrugged. "There are always possibilities."

"And the paperweight is a convenient one, but you have no way of knowing whether it is the actual murder weapon or not, correct?"

"I can say that it absolutely could have been—"

"But you cannot say that it absolutely was. I get the picture. Tell me, doctor—you said you detected an indentation in the skull. Could that have been made by a different weapon?"

"It is…possible…"

"Could it have been made by a hammer?"

That caught the doctor by surprise—and most of the jurors. They'd probably read in the papers or online about the attacks on Carvel and Dinah. Though they were forbidden to read about this case, they weren't in a total news blackout. If he could establish the hammer as a possibility, that suggested Andrus' killer was the person who attacked Dinah—and was still on the loose.

Zanzibar frowned. "That is…possible, I suppose."

"Would the use of a hammer comply with your profile?"

"It might."

"Thank you for your honesty. Have you actually seen or held

the physical object you just proposed as the instrument of death?"

"No. It's not in the police evidence locker."

"Was it tested by the forensic department?"

"I believe so, but—"

"And in fact, they found no traces of blood, hair, skin, or other body matter, correct?"

"Yes."

"And it isn't broken or cracked."

"It's solid steel. I wouldn't expect it to be damaged."

"But you would expect to see residue from a collision with someone's head, if that's what happened. Wouldn't you?"

"Not necessarily. The assailant could have put the paper-weight into something else, like a sock. That would make it easier to swing. Easier to get some serious momentum. Even a rock in a sock is enough to kill a person if it hits the soft part of the skull."

"Did the police find any evidence of a sock at the crime scene?"

"In the office? No. But I assume your client has a few." The doctor smiled. "That sockless Miami Vice look is so passé."

CHAPTER TWENTY-EIGHT

FOR HER NEXT WITNESS, JAZLYN PUT JAKE KAKAZU ON THE STAND. That was expected and inevitable, given that he was the one who found the head in the freezer. Jazlyn established who and what he was, his experience and credentials, and of course, his Oxford education. That didn't bear on the case at hand, but it was bound to impress a few jurors. With impressive speed, Jazlyn arrived at the fateful day Jake and Sergeant Pemberton arrived at Sweeney's office.

"What was the reason for the visit?"

"Shortly before, a dead body was found on the pavement outside Sweeney's building. We believe the man plunged through a floor-to-ceiling window in Sweeney's office. When we contacted the defendant, he acknowledged that it was true—but claimed that the man attacked him and was killed in self-defense. I wanted to see the site where it happened."

"Did you doubt the claim of self-defense?"

"We weren't to that point yet."

"Is the SPPD investigating the defendant?"

"Yes. As has been widely reported, many of the women's shelters the defendant helped create were fronts for—"

"Objection," Dan said. "Relevance."

The judge nodded. "Sustained. Let's stick to the crime that forms the basis of this case."

Given what he had learned during the jury examination, Dan suspected most of the jurors already knew all about the video porn operations Dan uncovered in the basements of the so-called Sweeney Shelters. Helping women above ground, exploiting them below. But he couldn't sit still and let them tarnish his client with every possible irrelevant dirty dealing. That could go on forever.

"Did you learn anything during the visit?"

"About the first murder? No. Everything Sweeney told us checked out. Just to be clear, I'm not saying it was true. But I saw nothing that disproved his story. According to him, he and the victim, a man named Fabian Fuentes, were the only two present, so I had no means to verify his story. I was about to leave when Sweeney offered to let me peruse his office and artwork. And during that tour, I noticed something unusual about the shape of his office."

"Please explain."

"Given Sweeney's claims about the window, I made a point of looking at the blueprints for the building filed at the county clerk's office. I eventually realized that this office was not as large as it should be. Could be hidden storage space, of course, but given the nature of the defendant, I thought it more likely that he had a sanctum sanctorum, a private area within an already private office. Someplace he could be alone." He paused. "Someplace he could put things he didn't want disturbed."

This was complete speculation, but Dan saw no point in objecting. Kakazu was simply laying a predicate for what came next, and they were going to get there one way or the other. He decided to save his objections for when it mattered.

"Did your suspicions prove true?"

"Yes. Sweeney readily admitted there was another room. A

private room only he could enter. The door was hidden and a fingerprint scanner controlled the lock. His right index finger was required to open the door."

"Did he take you into the secret room?"

"He did."

"And just to be clear, did he invite you in?"

"He did."

"Did he put any restrictions on what you could do or examine while you were inside?"

"Not at all."

Jazlyn gave Dan a little side-eye. "What did you find inside the private room?"

"The same, except even more ornate and plush. Had the vibe of a British men's club. A big plus-sized stuffed chair on a rotating platform. Tea service. More artwork, some of it... edgier. Nudes and such."

At least two jurors raised an eyebrow. Dan knew that point hadn't been dropped by accident. Porn would be discussed later.

"Some statues," Kakazu continued. "Big home-theater screen. Built-in speakers. Sweeney seems to favor classical music. And of course, as everyone must know by now, there was a freezer."

"Why did he have a freezer?"

"It was a complete mini-kitchen setup. Fridge, sink, pantry. But the freezer was bigger than the fridge. He told me a story about his nostalgic affection for ice cream. I felt he was inviting me to look inside—"

"Objection," Dan said. The time had come. "The witness' feelings are not relevant."

The judge didn't wait for a response. "Sustained. I'll ask the witness to stick to what he saw and heard."

"Of course." Kakazu continued. "The defendant talked about the contents of the freezer and did not indicate in any way that he objected to me looking inside. So I opened the freezer." He inhaled deeply. "And Christopher Andrus' head rolled out. Right into my arms."

Several of the jurors recoiled in horror, turning their heads.

"Peering inside," Kakazu continued, "I saw the hands. Blood-caked ice."

"What did you do then?"

"I asked the defendant about it. He declined to answer."

"What exactly did he say?"

"He said he was calling his lawyer. I told him he could do that from the station and placed him under arrest. Sergeant Pemberton cuffed him."

"Was there any trouble?"

"Not from him. But we got a lot of blowback from his assistant, Prudence Hancock." He pointed. "She's sitting in the courtroom, just behind the defendant. She yelled and threatened and told us we didn't know what we were doing. Said we were bringing down a hailstorm of trouble so bad we wouldn't know what happened. I came close to arresting her as well, but she finally backed off. Pemberton took the defendant downtown and booked him. I remained at the office to conduct a more thorough search. Obviously, at that point, I had probable cause."

"Did you find anything of note?"

"Several things. I visited the building security office. Turns out they have a twenty-four-hour security team on the ground floor and security cameras posted all around the building."

"Were any of those cameras in Sweeney's office? Or the secret interior office?"

"Unfortunately, no. But there were cameras in the elevator lobby. I made copies of the footage from that camera for the prior week."

"And what did those tapes reveal?"

"They show Sweeney rode the elevator to his office with another man, a man we now know to be Christopher Andrus."

Jake briefly described the process that allowed them to identify his remains. "We know for a fact that Sweeney and the victim went to his office. And we know for a fact that Andrus didn't leave alive."

"Thank you, Officer Kakazu. I pass the witness."

Dan had little to say, since he knew Kakazu wouldn't lie. But there were a few points of clarification worth cementing in the jurors' heads.

"Let's start with the first death. Fabian Fuentes. Has the SPPD charged anyone with that crime?"

"No."

"Would it be fair to say the police do not have sufficient evidence to charge anyone with that crime?"

"If we had the evidence to charge someone, we would. That's our job."

Dan was careful not to ask Kakazu what he thought happened, or what leads they might be pursuing. What mattered was the evidence. "At this point in time, you cannot dispute my client's statement that Fuentes attacked him and that my client acted in self-defense."

"We have not charged him. At this time."

"Let's talk about the next matter. Christopher Andrus. You say my client talked about ice cream. That's hardly the same thing as inviting you to open the freezer, is it?"

Jake hesitated. "It is not exactly the same thing, no."

"And you said my client did not pose any objection to you opening the freezer. But did you tell him you were about to open the freezer?"

"Not in so many words, no."

"So he had no way of knowing. Why would he expect you to

open the freezer? It's common knowledge that police can't search beyond what's in plain sight unless they have a warrant."

Kakazu wasn't taking it lying down. "He could see that I was scrutinizing the premises. I'd been poking around since the moment I entered."

"Did you open the fridge?"

"Well...no. Sweeney—"

"Did you open the pantry?"

"No."

"Why would he expect you to behave differently with respect to the freezer?"

Kakazu's voice took on a slight edge. "Because we were talking about ice cream."

"Is there any reason why my client should not be permitted to have a private room stocked with ice cream?"

"I don't know what you mean."

"It was his building, wasn't it?"

"Yes."

"A busy businessman might understandably want to get away from the madding crowd every now again, don't you think?"

"I wouldn't know."

"A lot of men have so-called mancaves. Even a few on this jury, I believe. You've heard of that, right?"

"Of course."

"And my client had more artwork than he could fit in the exterior office. A busy man might like a private retreat decorated in a pleasing way."

"The fingerprint scanner suggests that what he wanted was a place no one else could enter. A place where he could stash things."

"Like artwork for his private enjoyment."

"Or a body," Jake mumbled.

"Sweeney knew he was under investigation. Wouldn't this be the stupidest possible time to commit a murder?"

"Maybe it couldn't wait."

"Sweeney knew you were coming. Wouldn't it be smarter to get rid of the body parts before you arrived?"

"Criminals don't always do the smart thing. That's why we catch them. Successful men tend to become smug. Over-confident."

"For that matter," Dan continued, "my client didn't have to admit you to the private room. You didn't have a warrant. Doesn't the fact that he took you in there suggest he had no idea there was a partial corpse in the freezer?"

Jake shook his head. "Smug. Superior. Over-confident. Or maybe he didn't have the time or means to get rid of it."

"Have you found the rest of the body?"

"We don't know where it is. Maybe your client could tell me."

"Objection. Move to strike."

Judge Smulders looked down at the witness sternly. "Officer Kakazu. You know better than that. Answer the question."

Kakazu looked repentant. "I'm sorry, your honor. To answer the question, I don't know where the rest of the body is."

"Your version of what happened is missing a lot of key details. And doesn't really make any logical sense."

"I don't agree with—"

"And if someone could get most of the body out of the office without being detected, they could get it in without being detected."

"There is no—"

"Thank you, Officer Kakazu. No more questions."

CHAPTER TWENTY-NINE

DAN KNEW JAZLYN'S FINAL WITNESS FOR THE DAY, THE accountant, played a key role in the prosecution's plan to establish motive—but he wasn't sure that would make the testimony any less boring. Numbers, equations, spreadsheets—it all tended to make jurors' eyes roll up into their heads. He'd never once seen an accountant-witness who wasn't snooze-inducing on the stand.

But then again, this case had been full of surprises from the get-go.

Jazlyn called Hannibal Busey to the stand. Thin, floppy hair, glasses taped at the bridge. What his generation would've called a nerd, but Dan knew nerds were a lot cooler today than they were once upon a time. He also knew the man had been buried in work Dan wouldn't want to do even if it came with a ticket to heaven.

Jazlyn walked Busey through his education and background. Two Masters and a Ph.D. A thriving accounting business. Had consulted with law enforcement on several previous occasions. And most relevant to this gathering—he'd been scrutinizing Sweeney's financial books since the day the cops seized them.

Jazlyn whisked Busey through the fundamentals of Sweeney's business. It was obvious she wanted to get somewhere—before the jury fell asleep.

"What conclusions can you draw from your review of the defendant's books?"

"First of all," Busey said, raising a finger, "I assume that when you mention the defendant, you mean his business, SweeTech. Since he is the sole shareholder, there is little practical difference between the two. And in addition to the financial books, I reviewed his tax returns, although he made it difficult for us to obtain them. We had to go to court."

"Is that unusual?"

Busey smiled. "No one ever refuses to release their tax returns unless they have something to hide."

"What's the portrait you obtained of the defendant's financial situation?"

"Desperate. And getting worse."

Beside him, Dan could sense Sweeney stewing. This must be a blow to his massive ego, hearing people suggest in open court that he was a business failure, just the opposite of what he'd been trying to convince people for years.

"Please explain," Jazlyn said.

"For a long time, SweeTech and its many diverse subsidiaries did quite well. Massive amounts of cash flowing through them. Big dividends for the sole shareholder. He mitigated his income tax in a variety of ways, including charitable donations, all the money he gave to the foundation that created the so-called Sweeney Shelters. But not long ago, he invested in a bioquantum computing venture that turned out to be a complete bust. The man who organized the deal is now behind bars. It's doubtful whether he ever had anything real. But the point is, Sweeney lost close to half a billion bucks."

Jazlyn craned her neck. "Was that enough to make an impact on his bottom line?"

"That would be enough to make an impact on anyone's bottom line. Yes, it hit Sweeney hard. And soon thereafter, much of the cash flow in those subsidiaries dried up. In some cases, it completely evaporated."

Jazlyn nodded. "As if...someone had been siphoning a lot of cash through Sweeney's companies but suffered a severe business interruption. Or took their money elsewhere."

"Exactly."

Jazlyn was getting dangerously close to talking about the cartel. At the pretrial, the judge had forbidden any mention of Central American cartels unless directly relevant to the question of who committed the murder. The potential prejudice outweighed the probative value.

"Were there other problems?"

"Yes. I mentioned the Sweeney Shelters and, as most people know, those have been closed following the discovery of a large-scale video-porn—"

Dan rose. "Your honor—"

Jazlyn cut him off. "We're not going to describe the criminal operation in any detail."

Then why mention it? "I still object."

The judge nodded. "I'm going to allow it, but I'm watching you carefully, Madame Prosecutor. If this veers into irrelevant matters or baseless character assassination, I'll shut you down."

"Understood." Jazlyn returned her attention to the witness. "What do you know about the video-porn operation, sir?"

"Porn is extremely profitable, even in the short-term." Busey paused. "It's exactly the sort of business an unethical person might use to generate large amounts of money—"

"Objection," Dan said. "This is precisely what I predicted. Despite the court's ruling, they went straight to the baseless character assassination. I move for a mistrial."

The judge raised his hands, looking extremely unhappy.

"Your motion will be denied. But your objection will be sustained. Ms. Prentice, you made a promise to the court."

"And I believe I have kept it. No one has said outright that the defendant—"

"Stop playing games. Everyone in this courtroom knows what you were implying. I'm going to instruct the jury to disregard this entire line of questioning." He looked at the jurors directly. "The defendant is on trial today for one crime and one crime only. Murder. Any allegations regarding anything else are irrelevant and should be completely ignored during your deliberations."

He pointed his gavel at Jazlyn. "If this happens again, I'll issue sanctions. Have I made myself clear?"

"You have. I...apologize, your honor."

"Anything more from this witness?"

"Just one thing." Jazlyn turned back to Busey. "You said you've made a thorough review of the defendant's assets. Do you see any hope that he might pull himself out of this financial tailspin?"

"Only one. The defendant owns a huge collection of extremely valuable art. Vermeer. Basquiat. He even owns a van Gogh, as we discovered when we searched his premises. If he sold his art collection, it would go a long way toward healing his financial wounds. It might not pay everything, but at the very least it would buy him time."

"And if he wanted to sell that work, how would he go about it?"

"This collection is far too valuable for the average art gallery. He'd need a broker. Someone experienced at handling highly valuable art."

"Someone like the victim. Christopher Andrus."

"Yes. But we haven't been able to trace the provenance of many of those paintings. To put it more simply—we don't know where Sweeney got them. If he obtained them by...inappropriate means, or illegal means, any relationship with a broker would present a danger. Which might explain—"

"Objection," Dan said. "The witness is speculating. And this is not his area of expertise."

"Goes to motive, your honor," Jazlyn argued. "The existence of someone who knew that the paintings were illegally obtained, and thus unsellable, posed a threat to the defendant's financial recovery. And the fact that they argued—"

"I'm sustaining the objection," Judge Smulders said. "And I will remind you that if you are going to make a lengthy talking objection, you need to approach the bench and do it quietly."

"Yes, your honor. I understand. We will call another witness at a later time who can testify about the angry meeting between the defendant and the victim. No more questions."

Beside him, Dan heard Sweeney grunting. "Damn bean-counter."

He turned. "Not a fan?"

"If his own business was making any money, he wouldn't be working for the government. Loser."

Dan sighed. "But I still need to cross."

"Two words. Cloud computing."

And the most embarrassing thing was that he immediately understood what Sweeney was saying.

Dan rose and stood a few feet from the witness. "You didn't say anything during your testimony about my client's more recent financial ventures."

Busey shrugged. "I wasn't asked."

"Are you familiar with SweeCirrus?'

"The cloud-computing venture? Sure. But it's new and thus far hasn't generated profits."

"A new venture requires startup cash, doesn't it?"

"Or course."

"Where did my client get the startup cash?"

Busey paused for a moment. "I don't know."

"You spent days poring over those records. You've told the jury you're an expert in every aspect of my client's business. But you don't know how he funded this new operation, one that is projected to make more money than all his other ventures combined in two years or less?"

"I can't review the books for businesses that don't exist yet."

"Would you be surprised to learn that my client redirected the cash from failing operations to fund the new one? What you're suggesting is criminal is actually just smart. Abandoning less profitable ventures and initiating new ones."

"I doubt a cloud-computing business would be enough—"

"Are you aware that Amazon makes more money from its cloud-computing operations than it does from retailing? And it's the most profitable retailer in the United States. If Sweeney could capture even ten percent of that business, it would cure his financial problems, wouldn't it?"

"There's still the matter of the failed bio—"

"Is SweeTech the only corporation that ever made a bad investment?"

"Of course not."

"In fact, it's fairly common, isn't it? It's the cost of doing business. You never get anywhere if you don't take risks. But not all risks pay off."

"That is certainly true."

"I will suggest, Dr. Busey, that you ignored the obvious in pursuit of a motive that does not exist. Everything you've discussed can be explained as commonplace corporate reorganization. All these accusations about funneling cash are unfounded and, frankly, unprofessional. Did the district attorney's office encourage you to make these statements?"

"I object," Jazlyn said. "Counsel is suggesting the witness was encouraged to make statements that are not—"

"You wouldn't put him on the stand unless you thought he could help your case. You don't have a real motive so you're trying to invent one with incomprehensible babble about corporate financing. You're just slinging mud."

"Your honor," Jazlyn said, "I renew my objection and call for a bench conference."

Judge Smulders pursed his lips. "No need. I'm ruling now. The objection is overruled. The defense is well within its rights. This is cross-examination."

Jazlyn was seething and Dan could see it, but she sat down. He was always pleased to win an objection—but hoped he hadn't lost a friend in the process.

"Dr. Busey, do you have any proof that any illegal crime organization is or was funneling cash through my client's businesses?"

Busey looked thoroughly chastened. "No."

"Do you have any proof that my client was in any way at any time connected to the illegal video-porn operation?"

"No."

"And in fact, when he found out about it, my client was the first to call for the closure of the shelters and arranged for all the women housed in them to be transferred to other facilities at his own personal expense."

"I didn't mean to give offense—"

"Well, I take offense," Dan said. "I take offense to this entire misleading line of irrelevant testimony. This is beneath the integrity of this court and an offense to all right-thinking people. You may step down, sir. I have no more questions."

He was not surprised that Jazlyn chose not to re-direct.

Sweeney leaned in close. "Looks like you finally found your fire."

Dan said nothing. He was glad he'd been able to bury someone who might have been a damaging witness. But getting praise from Conrad Sweeney still made his skin crawl.

CHAPTER THIRTY

JIMMY WAS NOT SURPRISED WHEN SHAWNA, THE COUNTY CLERK, texted him suggesting a meeting. They'd been friends and worked together for years. Even in recent times, when the heat was on and Shawna was far too involved with Conrad Sweeney, they'd continued to see one another—but usually in secluded, low-profile venues. It was clear that she did not want people to know she was meeting with a member of Dan Pike's law firm.

But this time she suggested meeting at the kids' playground behind the courthouse childcare center. There could not be a more visible location.

Had she finally stopped fearing Sweeney and his minions?

Or had she stopped caring what happened to her?

He found her on the swing set. Since she was swaying on the far right swing, it seemed natural to plop down into the swing beside her.

"What's going down, compadre?"

"Big news shaking, Jimmy."

He straightened his cardigan. "Talking about the trial in Courtroom One?"

"No. Talking about me. I've tendered my resignation."

Jimmy's eyes bulged. "You're quitting? But you've been in the clerk's office—"

"All the more reason. The courthouse needs new blood. And I need a change. I'm going to make a fresh start."

"I haven't heard a thing about this."

"That's the way I wanted it. A formal announcement will be made at the end of the week. At the end of the month, I ride off into the sunset."

"What brought this on? I mean, I knew you were unhappy, but—"

"Unhappy is putting it mildly. I got in way too deep."

"With Sweeney."

The mere mention of his name seemed to give her a shiver. "I thought I was doing the right thing. Helping my nephew the only way I knew how. But the price was too great."

"Because Sweeney kept calling in the marker. Over and over again."

"Every time he needed information. Every time he wanted a room bugged. He had me by the short hairs, so to speak."

Something wasn't clicking. "That's been true for some time. What's changed?"

Shawna cast her eyes downward. He could tell she didn't want to proceed.

"You're Lori Lemaris," he said.

She blinked. "Um...excuse me?"

"Clark Kent's college sweetheart. He loved her dearly—he always falls for girls with double-L initials—but when he discovered Lori was a mermaid from Atlantis, the romance seemed impractical."

Shawna laughed, despite herself. "I would imagine so."

"The point is, Lori wasn't trying to deceive him. She knew Clark was Superman and she loved him. She just couldn't force herself to tell him the truth. Because she knew it would end the romance. But hiding the truth only makes matters worse."

Shawna gave him a wry smile. "Very subtle, Jimmy."

"When you've read as many comics as I have, you can always find an appropriate analogy."

"Here's what I haven't told you yet. I won't even ask you to keep quiet. I trust your discretion."

"Understood."

She took a deep breath. "That other murder? The guy who flew out the window?"

"Fabian Fuentes."

"Right. Everyone assumes Sweeney killed him. But here's the truth. It was defensive, sort of. Fuentes almost killed Sweeney."

"How do you know that?"

Shawna clenched her eyes shut. "Because I was there."

"*What?*"

"Sweeney had gathered all his minions. He was in serious trouble and had assignments for everyone. But Fuentes tried to kill him."

"So Sweeney killed him first."

"Not exactly."

"Someone else killed him?"

"Can we just leave it at that?"

"Shawna, this is important. You need to go to the police."

"If I do, the next person behind bars will be me."

"Was someone else there? Someone free to speak?"

"Marjorie was there. The court reporter who screwed Dan over. And some turncoat cop. I don't know his name." She paused. "Marjorie disappeared right after. She regrets her involvement with Sweeney as much as I do, so please don't chase her down."

Shawna had screwed up royally, but he still didn't want to see her arrested. "I suppose if Fuentes was trying to kill Sweeney, the person who shoved him out the window didn't exactly commit murder."

"Exactly. It was justifiable homicide."

"Why are you telling me this?"

"Because I'm aware that your firm is currently defending Sweeney. Everyone assumes Sweeney killed Fuentes. But he didn't. And if he didn't commit that murder…it's just possible he didn't kill Andrus either."

Jimmy's voice dropped. "Dan should know about this."

"That's why I'm telling you. And…there's more."

Jimmy stiffened. They were getting close to a line he didn't want to cross. She wanted to help with the current case. Which he wanted nothing to do with.

He pushed the ground with his feet, moving the swing. "You should probably talk to Dan."

"I don't know Dan. I know you. I trust you."

"Yeah, but—"

"Something hinky is going on at the DA's office."

A deep furrow crossed his brow. "Jazlyn is doing something crooked? I don't believe it. The main reason she ran for the office was to eliminate the corruption of her predecessor."

"I know," Shawna said. "But still…it is what it is."

He closed his eyes. He wanted nothing to do with this case. Nothing whatsoever. But here it was, thrust in his face, whether he wanted it or not. "Maybe you'd better tell me what you know."

Shawna grabbed the chain on his swing to stop it. She forced him to look at her, eye-to-eye. "One of the people on the prosecution witness list isn't testifying voluntarily."

"They subpoenaed him? They would have to reveal—"

"Originally. They originally subpoenaed him. Filed it in my office, as they should. Signed by a judge. And they brought him in. Had a few conversations."

"Worked him over?"

"The next thing I knew, the subpoena was withdrawn and he was testifying voluntarily."

"They made a deal."

"Certainly looks that way."

"But the original subpoena would still be in the file."

"Not anymore. They got it expunged. Got a judge to sign off on that, too. No trace left behind."

"And no notice to the defense." He pondered. "I don't even know if that violates a rule. But it certainly is...unusual."

"To put it mildly."

"Deceptive, to put it strongly." He paused. "On cross, Dan could ask the witness if he's made a deal. But people in that situation often say no and it's not a complete falsehood. A deal may have been discussed but never finalized. In some instances, formal discussion is not necessary. A guy behind bars expects early release if he testifies. Everyone already knows what the deal will be—after the trial is over."

Shawna nodded. "At any rate, the whole procedure raises a lot of questions. I wanted you to know. I don't want your team to be blindsided."

"And this is where it all gets...complicated." Jimmy pursed his lips. "I should have told you this sooner. I'm not actually working on this case."

"I thought you guys always worked as a team."

"Not this time."

"But you can still tell Dan, right?"

"Shawna...I've sworn I won't have anything to do with this case."

Shawna looked distraught. "Are you resigning from the firm?"

"I'm thinking about it."

"But—why?"

"Shawna—it's Sweeney!" His teeth clenched. "He's a bigot. Racist. Sexist. Homophobe. He worked with sex traffickers and the same organ smugglers who made it so difficult for your nephew to get the kidney he needed. He needs to be put away. And I don't care how it happens."

"Even if it's for a crime he didn't commit?"

"Yes!" Jimmy pushed out of the swing, barely able to contain himself. "He's Satan, for God's sake. He needs to be sent to hell and kept there."

Shawna's head bowed. "I...see."

"You think I'm wrong?"

She licked her lips, obviously thinking before she spoke. "Jimmy...no one has more cause to despise Sweeney than I do. He's ruined my life. I'm hoping to start over now, but even as I do, I know he could come after me. I hope he'll be too busy with his own troubles. But it would be safer for me if he were in prison." She drew in her breath. "But I still don't want him convicted for a crime he didn't commit. I couldn't live with that."

Jimmy grabbed a fistful of dirt, slowly letting it trickle through his fingers. "I...could."

"I don't understand."

"That's exactly right. You don't understand what it's like to live in this country as a Black man. A gay Black man. As if it weren't bad enough having to look over your shoulder, constantly worrying about cops or white supremacists or gay-bashing religious zealots, you've also got big business bigots like Sweeney doing the same things but more subtly. This man represents everything that needs to be changed in this nation."

Shawna rose from the swing. "I don't disagree with a thing you've said. But you're not addressing the problem the right way."

"Are you going to give me a lecture on appropriate social activism?"

"No. I'm going to ask you to look deep inside your own heart. Dan needs this information. And you need this team."

"I got along just fine before Mr. K drafted me into this weirdness."

"You've told me many times this is the best job you've ever had."

"Doesn't mean I'm dependent upon it."

"Maybe not financially. But your teammates are your best friends."

"Dan betrayed that friendship."

"Dan? Your Aquaman?"

"Everything has changed. And there's no going back."

"There's always a road back, Jimmy. If you want it. You just have to decide what's most important."

"You're not hearing me."

"I am. But I may know you better than you know yourself. You love this job and you love your team. Don't let one ugly trial spoil that. I don't know if taking this case was right or wrong, but I know Dan thinks it's the right thing to do or he wouldn't be doing it. Sometimes we have to support the ones we love. Even when we think they're making a big mistake." She paused. "As we all do."

Jimmy crossed his arms. "I will not walk this back. Conrad Sweeney is reprehensible and I will not participate in his exoneration. Nor will I assist or associate with those who do. Call me old-fashioned if you like, but there is a difference between good and evil in this world. And Sweeney is the most evil person in this world."

"You may be right." She reached out and touched him on the side of his face. "But Dan is one of the best."

CHAPTER THIRTY-ONE

DAN RETURNED TO THE COURTROOM THE NEXT DAY FEELING upbeat. They'd weathered the initial volley of prosecution witnesses. Jazlyn's first-day slate didn't help Sweeney, but they didn't nail him to the lethal-injection gurney, either. If she wanted to win a case for first-degree murder, she would have to present more damning evidence than this.

Unfortunately, Dan knew Jazlyn wouldn't have brought the charges if she didn't think she could win. And she was usually a good judge of cases.

He spotted a familiar face in the gallery. Took him a minute to recall who it was. Colin Baxter. He was a hacker Garrett had used in a previous case. Baxter created what he called a "fingerprint glove," something that allowed him to break into an iPhone.

He extended a hand. "Daniel Pike."

Baxter nodded. "I know who you are." Young. Hair down to his shoulders. Pale skin. Needed to get out more. "You're famous around here."

"What brings you to the courtroom?"

Baxter shrugged. "It's Wednesday. There's no new Star Trek till tomorrow."

"Got any business here?"

"Am I being cross-examined?"

Dan smiled. "Not yet."

"Truth is, I need to refill the coffers and I hoped there might be a lawyer here who needs a hacker."

"I see. Good luck with that."

He spotted Maria coming through the back doors. He knew she'd stopped at the hospital earlier. "How's Dinah?"

"Strong. They're going to let her go home today."

"Emotionally?"

"If she's shaken, she's hiding it well. No whining. Kinda reminds me of someone else I know. Someone closely related to her."

Good to hear. But not for one moment did he forget that the attack on Dinah was also an attack on him. A warning shot. Every day he moved forward with this trial, he was potentially putting himself and others in danger.

Mr. K had hired security to watch the team, but even the Secret Service couldn't stop a determined wild man with a gun. Dinah had begged him not to quit, but he couldn't stand the thought of harm coming to someone. He would be glad when this case was over.

"C'mon, slugger," Maria said, offering him a smile. "It's going to be okay. Let's just win this case. Then we can all go on a long vacation."

"Kitesurfing?"

"Sure. Or possibly even...you know. Something fun."

Jazlyn called Deanna Folsom, a forensic scientist Dan had cross-examined on two previous occasions. She had worked for an online genealogy site that collected DNA samples from people wanting to know more about their heritage. He knew she'd been petitioning for a fulltime position with the SPPD. Maybe she hoped this testimony would get her the good conduct medal she needed to get the job.

Dan hated DNA evidence. There had been so much blather about it on television, mostly inaccurate, that people had come to believe it was incontrovertible, when nothing could be further from the truth. Sure, when you had verified samples and they were handled by trained experts, there was a fair chance of finding meaningful matches—but there was also a lot of guesswork and interpretation involved. As he had proven on more than one occasion, DNA at best indicated likelihoods. Furthermore, it was easily manipulated, doctored, or planted.

Nonetheless, Jazlyn was leading the forensic show with it. Because she knew it would have a major impact on the jury.

Jazlyn established Folsom's credentials and that she had testified in court on numerous previous occasions. "What is your occupation?"

Folsom sat up straight. Older woman. Mandala pendant. Black sweater. "I'm between jobs. The online genealogy sites have come under fire recently because they've shared information with law enforcement agencies, something most people submitting DNA samples never anticipated. During the cutbacks, I lost my position. I was planning to get out of the DNA field and return to my first expertise, skin and scalp analysis, and thought I had a position lined up in Tampa, but it fell through. Nonetheless, I keep up with the latest developments and maintain my expertise in DNA forensics."

"Can you explain briefly what DNA evidence is?"

"Sure. When we talk about DNA, we're talking about genes. Every person has a unique DNA profile—except identical twins. Even a small sample of genetic material—skin, saliva, blood—is sufficient to make an analysis. It's like fingerprints, only better."

And of course fingerprints also were not nearly as reliable as most people believed, Dan mused. As he had proven on previous occasions.

"Have you had a chance to review the relevant files?"

"I have. Especially a skin fragment that was found on the head in the freezer. The head belonging to Christopher Andrus."

"I don't see any reason to prolong this. What were the conclusions of your analysis?"

"The skin fleck came from the defendant. Conrad Sweeney."

"Is there any question in your mind?"

"It's a ninety-four-percent match to samples taken from the defendant after he was arrested. In my field, that's more than enough to be considered proof positive."

"I think we've got the picture. I'll pass the witness."

Dan rose. "No questions."

The judge did a doubletake, as did the jury. "You have...no questions?"

"Not at this time." He was taking a gamble. But Folsom would be unlikely to give up much. He was planning to call his own DNA expert during the defense case, and he would get further with that witness than he could with this woman.

The risk, of course, was that this evidence would sit with the jury unrefuted too long. If they got an idea fixed in their heads, he might not be able to dislodge it.

"Very well," the judge said. "Ms. Prentice, please call your next witness."

CHAPTER THIRTY-TWO

DR. MARK COLUMBO, A BITE-MARK EXPERT, LUMBERED TO THE stand. He was a heavy-set man. White shirt. Long red tie. Hush puppies. Back pants pocket untucked.

As he explained, Columbo had been trained as a forensic scientist, worked in several jurisdictions, and operated out of Orlando. He had an impressive array of degrees, commendations, and awards.

"Could you please describe your areas of expertise?" Jazlyn asked.

"Of course." Columbo turned slightly so he spoke to the jury, without making so much eye contact that he made anyone uncomfortable. He was a pro. "I'm trained in dentistry and in forensic science, so I can use my knowledge of both to provide insight into evidence. In this case, a bite mark."

Dan rose to his feet. "I object, your honor. We addressed this at the pretrial. This evidence is unreliable and doesn't meet the current scientific standards for admissible forensic evidence. The court will recall that I—"

Judge Smulders shut him down with the wave of a hand. "I

recall what you said perfectly well. I also recall that I denied your motion to suppress."

"Your honor, courts all around the nation are—"

"Stop. I will not permit talking objections. I want the jury to make its decisions based upon the evidence and nothing else. Mr. Pike, you will be permitted to cross-examine and to raise any issues you wish at that time. You may call an expert of your own during the defense case. But this witness may testify. So please sit down."

Dan did as he was told. It was too early for outright contempt.

Jazlyn continued. "Did you examine the bite mark in the present case?"

"Yes. There was a pronounced bite mark on the victim's right hand. One of the two…dismembered hands found in the freezer. I was able to detect and analyze a clear bite mark."

"I'm sure many people are wondering why anyone would bite the victim's hands."

"I wasn't there so I can't say with certainty, but in all likelihood, it was a defensive move. Someone attacked the victim, perhaps with a paperweight in a sock, and the victim raised his hands to block it. The attacker grabbed the hand and bit it, perhaps in anger or in an effort to subdue the victim."

Smart witness. He was saying what they wanted him to say but acknowledging that complete certainty was impossible—rather than letting Dan make that point on cross-examination.

"Did you conduct an analysis of the bite mark?"

"I did. As I'm sure you know, everyone has a unique dental pattern. The arrangement and size of everyone's teeth differ. That's why dental records are used to identify bodies. That pattern changes little over the course of someone's life, once they reach adulthood."

"Is it possible to determine who bit the victim?"

A little leading, but Dan would let it slide.

"Absolutely. The bite mark on the victim's hand matches the exemplar taken from the defendant after he was arrested."

"Conclusion, doctor?"

"Conrad Sweeney bit the victim's hand. Probably during a struggle."

"Thank you. No more questions."

Dan could see the impact this was having on the jury. Finding the corpse in Sweeney's office was bad. The DNA evidence was bad. But this was worse. If the prosecution could prove Sweeney bit the man's hand, then he must be the killer.

He needed to bury this evidence fast.

Dan heard Sweeney muttering. "As if I would put that sleazebag's hand in my mouth. What do they think I am, a cannibal?"

"If they could make that accusation fly," Dan murmured, "they would leap on it."

Dan walked toward the witness. "Let's cut to the chase, Doctor. Bite-mark evidence has fallen out of favor in most jurisdictions. Some courts won't even permit it. Right?"

"There has been no ruling by the Florida Supreme Court—"

"Please answer the question. Isn't it true that some courts have forbidden bite-mark evidence?"

"In my opinion, the problems experienced by other courts are not due to the nature of the evidence, but the poor quality of the testimony. Sadly, there are some so-called professionals who don't know what they're doing. I, however, have been trained—"

Dan cut him off. He would have to be forceful. This was a smart witness and he was not going down without a fight. "Isn't it true that the Texas Forensic Science Commission, after a six-month investigation, recommended that bite-mark evidence be excluded from all trials due to its inherent unreliability?"

Columbo smiled. "We're not in Texas."

Dan smiled back. "I still want an answer to my question."

Columbo sighed, as if he would have to humor this silly man who knew so much less about everything. "That's true, but—"

"And the reason the commission gave was that bite-mark evidence did not meet the current standards of acceptable forensic science."

"I disagree with their conclusion. I've found bite-mark evidence to be reliable."

"Of course, you used to testify about microscopic hair comparisons, right?"

That slowed Columbo down. "Many years ago…"

"And that type of evidence is completely discredited now, correct? No court in America would allow that in a criminal trial today."

"Science moves forward. Standards change. That doesn't mean—"

"Isn't it true that many people convicted based upon bite-mark evidence have now been released from prison because DNA evidence proved they did not commit the crime?"

"I may have heard—"

"Are you familiar with the case of Steven Mark Chaney?"

Columbo drew in his breath. "Of course."

"Chaney spent twenty-eight years in prison based on bite-mark evidence. DNA later proved he didn't commit the crime and he's been freed. But no one can give him back those twenty-eight years of his life."

"The Innocence Project is always trying to stir up trouble…"

"Wouldn't it be more accurate to say they're always trying to release people who have been wrongfully convicted? By evidence exactly like what you're trying to perpetrate in this case?"

Columbo folded his arms across his chest. "I stand by my testimony."

"Sir, isn't it true that human skin is extremely malleable?"

"I don't know that I'd say 'extremely.'"

"Wound patterns can differ, even between two samples taken from the same person, right?"

"To some degree."

"So when you say these two samples matched, what you're really saying is that they were somewhat similar, right?"

"More than somewhat. They matched."

"To some degree, all adult male teeth patterns are going to match."

"You're not—"

"Isn't it also true that people's dental patterns can change over time?"

"Only in a minority of cases. If there's been an injury, or abnormal growth, or decay, or tooth extraction, or—"

"Is the present case one of those minority of cases?"

Columbo did not answer.

"You don't know. Right?"

"I...haven't performed any comparative analysis of the defendant's teeth over time. I don't have access to his dental history."

Dan pulled a report out of his backpack. "In a study conducted by the Texas Commission, a panel of leading forensic dentists studied photographs of bite wounds and couldn't agree on whether there were any matches. In fact, they couldn't even agree on whether the marks were made by human teeth."

"I think we know the bite mark in this case was made by a human."

"Do we?" Dan took a step closer. "Do you know where the victim's remains were between when Andrus was killed and when he was discovered in that freezer?"

"No...."

"We know the body was dismembered and it wasn't done in my client's office. How do you know it wasn't out in the Everglades, or a forest, or some other place filled with wild animals?"

"I don't think—"

"But you don't know, do you? You can't say with certainty that this bite mark matches my client. You can't even say with certainty that it came from a human. And that's why the prosecution called you to the stand. They have nothing that definitively connects my client to the murder, so they called you up. Too bad they didn't have any microscopic hair evidence. You probably would've been willing to talk about how reliable that was, too. You're an expert-for-hire, and you clearly don't care whether there's any science backing your testimony or not."

"I protest—"

Jazlyn rose, but before she could speak, Judge Smulders banged his gavel. "Mr. Pike, you're out of order."

"I'm sorry. I'm done. I have no more use for this...witness." His voice dropped. "Who didn't witness a thing."

CHAPTER THIRTY-THREE

DAN BROUGHT DINAH A CUP OF EARL GREY TEA. SHE SAT IN THE living room of their office with Maria and Garrett talking about the day's trial.

"How are you feeling?" he asked.

"I'm fine. Stop nursemaiding."

"You're my sister. I'm allowed."

"I'm your girlfriend," Maria said. "Where's my beverage?"

"You hate tea."

"True. Why people want to drink boiled leaves escapes me. But it's a symbolic gesture."

He leaned down and gave her a kiss. "How's that for a symbolic gesture?"

She grinned. "A heck of a lot better than tea."

Dinah sipped her drink. "I heard you kicked butt in court today, little brother."

Dan shrugged. "I'm surprised Jazlyn would resort to bite-mark evidence. She's as familiar with the latest developments in forensic science as I am."

"Do you think...someone is pushing her?" Garrett asked.

"When I was at the prosecutor's office, we were constantly getting nudged by the mayor. Or the governor. Or the feds."

"Jazlyn is used to handling that. No, I think she desperately wants to put Sweeney away."

"And who could blame her for that?" Maria said quietly.

"She sees this as the chance of a lifetime that might not be repeated."

"Meaning she'll do anything to make it stick?" Dinah asked. "Even if it's...underhanded?"

Dan shook his head fiercely. He couldn't believe that. "It wasn't underhanded. Just...ill-advised. And she would normally see that. Her need to get Sweeney behind bars may be clouding her judgment."

"She's still got a case," Maria reminded him. "Even if the jury rejects the bite-mark evidence—there's still the problem that the body parts were found in Sweeney's freezer. And the DNA evidence."

"But they haven't established any real motive. Sure, Sweeney needed cash, but that doesn't mean he'd kill his art dealer."

"Motive will come from the next witness," Maria said. "You've held your own so far. And done the excellent job you always do, even if your client doesn't appreciate it. But Jazlyn has saved her best for last."

She cast an eye toward everyone in the room. "This is where it gets real."

JAZLYN CALLED CLINT DILBERT TO THE WITNESS STAND. MAYBE he imagined it, but Dan thought this was another witness Jazlyn would prefer to avoid but felt she had to call to put Sweeney away.

Dilbert was obviously a bodybuilder. Even in court, he wore a thin muscle shirt and tight slacks. Shaved head. Porn-star mustache. Bleeding crucifix tattoo visible on his left arm and, Dan suspected, a bunch more tattoos he couldn't see.

"Seriously?" Sweeney muttered. "They're going to convict me with Popeye?"

Dan held a finger across his lips.

Jazlyn sketched Dilbert's background briefly. Dan suspected there was not much to brag about. In less than five minutes, she brought the witness to the night in question. "Mr. Dilbert," Jazlyn said, "where were you that night?"

"I was at Beachcombers. Place near the marina I go sometimes. My daughter tends bar there."

"And what did you do on the night in question?"

"Had me a beer, what else? Kicked it back. Soaked some suds. Tried to read a newspaper I found lyin' around, but it just made me mad. It's all fake news from the liberal media."

"Did you see anything unusual?"

"Yeah. Shouting from the booth behind me. I could see them over my shoulder. I mean, most people at Beachcombers are pretty mellow. But these jokers had the opposite vibe. Totally aggro. Beachcombers is a noisy place, but I had no trouble hearing them."

"And who were the people you saw at this...noisy booth?"

Dilbert pointed. "That big guy. The defendant. He was there."

"And the other person?"

"The dead guy."

Jazlyn held up a photograph. "Christopher Andrus?"

"That was him. And there was a third person. A woman. I don't know who she was."

Dan assumed that was Tulip Krakowski, the woman both Carvel and Sweeney mentioned being there. But no one had been able to find her.

"What did they talk about during this...angry meeting?"

"I couldn't hear every single word," Dilbert replied, "but I heard a lot. They talked about some paintings. Bigshot paintings from bigshot painters. I didn't recognize the names and I can't remember them now. But they acted like the stuff was worth a lot of money."

"Was the defendant trying to sell paintings?"

"I don't know. I know he wrote the guy a check."

"You saw the defendant write a check?"

"No, but I found the check after all three of them left. It was on the table, made out to Christopher Andrus and signed by Conrad Sweeney. In thick blue ink."

"Like it was signed with a fountain pen?"

"Yeah. The fancy kind with the shiny tip."

Jazlyn lifted an exhibit. "Your honor, at this time I will direct the court's attention to pre-marked and pre-admitted Exhibit 47, which is a series of handwriting exemplars made using the blue-ink fountain pen found on Conrad Sweeney's desk. As is readily apparent, the pen nib has a pronounced left bent, which gives any writing by the pen a distinctive appearance. Which can be seen in the signature on this check."

Judge Smulders examined the exhibit. "You're saying this check was signed using the same pen the police found on the defendant's desk?"

"Exactly. We also have an affidavit from the department's handwriting expert, which the defense stipulated to prior to trial. The defense might try to claim the signature was forged. But no one could duplicate the distinctive markings made by this pen." She returned her attention to the witness. "What happened next?"

"The fight got worse. Big time. Both shouting at each other. The poor lady cowering, scrunching back into the booth. I couldn't hear most of what they were saying because they both spoke at the same time. I never heard people go at each other like those two did."

"Can you repeat any of what you heard during this disagreement?"

"I know how it ended. The big guy, the defendant, he stood up. He's a large man, as you can see. He slammed his fist on the table and said, loud enough to be heard in the next county—'You will be sorry you crossed me.'" Dilbert drew in his breath. "Then he stomped out of the bar, making the floor shudder like a tyrannosaurus was passing through."

"And the other two?"

"The woman left first. She went out the front door. The other guy waited a while and, when he finally left, he went out the back way."

Sweeney scratched a note on the legal pad on their table. NEVER HAPPENED.

Jazlyn waited a few beats before she continued. "You've said the defendant was angry."

"Yeah."

"And he threatened Andrus."

"Big time. He was mad."

"Mad enough to kill?"

Dan objected but at the same time, Dilbert answered. "Definitely." And no objection would ever make the jury forget that.

CHAPTER THIRTY-FOUR

DAN STARTED WITH THE OBVIOUS. "MR. DILBERT, ARE YOU receiving any benefit in exchange for your testimony today?"

"No."

"Are there now or have there ever been any charges pending against you?"

"No."

"Have you been sentenced, or subjected to any form of punishment or incarceration?"

"No."

He wasn't surprised. Jazlyn was smart. If she'd given Dilbert an immunity deal, she would've brought it out herself rather than let Dan go to town with it.

"You said you couldn't read the newspaper you found. Why?"

"I don't trust reporters. They're all socialists and liars."

He wanted to make sure the jury got this. "What paper were you reading?"

"The local one."

"The *Tampa Bay Times?*"

Dilbert nodded.

"You consider that fake news?"

"It's all controlled by the Deep State. A multinational liberal conspiracy."

Jazlyn rose. "Objection, your honor. This is not relevant."

"I disagree," Dan quickly rejoined. "Goes to the credibility of the witness. Goes to possible prejudice. The jurors have a right to know who they're listening to."

Judge Smulders thought for a moment. "This might be…of interest. I'm going to allow it."

"Your honor," Jazlyn said, "he's trying to use politics to impugn the witness."

"You're the one who put this man on the stand," Dan said quietly.

The judge raised his hand. "I've ruled. Counsel, proceed."

Dan turned back to the witness. "Mr. Dilbert, since you don't read the papers, where are you getting your information about the world? And the press. And…conspiracies."

"From the internet. Like everyone else."

"Are you a follower of QAnon?"

Jazlyn rose again but, before she could speak, the judge cut her off. "I've already ruled."

Jazlyn sat down, incensed.

"I've read QAnon stuff."

"Do you believe it?"

"I believe there are a lot of people trying to steal this country from the real Americans."

Dan cast a glance to the jury box. Especially the three jurors of color. "And who are the real Americans?"

"The one who work hard and don't sit on their butts accepting handouts."

"Did you accept your COVID-19 stimulus check?"

"That's completely different."

"That was a handout."

"That went to everyone. Not just deadbeats."

"Do you consider my client, Conrad Sweeney, a real American?"

"I consider him a rich fat cat. Part of the one percent. Probably hasn't paid taxes in years."

"Is that why you're testifying against him?"

"No." Dilbert's voice was a bit too loud. "I'm here because the lady prosecutor asked me to be here."

Dan had the feeling there was more going on here than he understood. "Tell me more about the conversation you overheard. Did you actually hear my client threaten to murder Mr. Andrus?"

"He told the guy he was going to be sorry he crossed him."

"That sounds like the sort of thing businessmen always say when they can't get the deal they want. 'You'll be sorry.' So what? It's not a threat."

"Mister, I was there. This was a threat. The expression on his face, the fist on the table, it was all sayin' the same thing."

"Did he ever use the word 'kill'?"

"He didn't have to."

"Did he use the word 'murder'? Or any synonym of 'murder'?"

"Believe me—there was murder in this guy's eyes. And sure enough, two blinks later the poor chump is dead."

"You don't know that my client killed him."

"I think I do." He turned, facing the jury. "I saw the expression on his face. I know what it meant. I won't kid you—I've hung around some nasty customers in my time. But I never saw nothing like this before. That man had murder on the brain. I thought he was going to tear the poor guy apart right then and there."

Dilbert paused, then raised his arm and pointed. "That guy murdered Andrus. There's no doubt in my mind."

"You don't know—"

"That man is a killer," Dilbert said, his voice rising. "I am absolutely sure of it. Tell all the lies you want, shyster. That man is a murderer. I guarantee it."

Dan glanced at Maria. She gave him a worried look and he knew exactly what that meant.

She had predicted this was about to get real. And it just did.

CHAPTER THIRTY-FIVE

TULIP OPENED HER EYES.

She could barely see. It was as if she had gauze over her eyes. Everything was hazy. She had no idea where she was.

And she remembered the last time this happened.

Dear God, don't let it be true. Was she still in the desert? Was she still lost and alone and...?

She tried to recall what had happened last. It was like when she fell asleep while reading and the next morning couldn't recall what she'd read. Only worse. Her memory seemed completely blank...

She remembered the wandering. The heat. The thirst. The pain. Her searing skin. Stumbling through the sand, hoping she was traveling south. She remembered trying to be strong and telling herself she would not let them destroy her, but...

Wait.

She was not thirsty. She wasn't starving.

Which could mean only one of two things. She was dead...or someone found her. And took care of her.

She didn't feel great, but she was almost certain she wasn't dead.

The light clarified around her eyes. She detected movement, but she couldn't make out any distinct impressions.

She tried to raise her hand—and was pleasantly surprised to find that her arm responded. She rubbed her eyes.

Her vision sharpened. She could see a wall. And a window.

She was not lying in the sand.

Where was she?

"Nurse. She's awake."

Tulip tried to turn her head in the direction of the sound, but her neck was stiff and didn't immediately comply. Now that her consciousness was returning, she found she hurt in a lot of places. All over, in fact.

She used her hands to feel up and down her body. She was under a sheet, but she could reach beneath it.

She wore a gown. Her arms and legs were intact.

She was in a hospital. And most importantly, she was alive.

She heard footsteps scurrying into the room. A moment later, two faces appeared above her, one black and female, the other white and elderly.

"Can you hear me?" the black woman asked. "Can you hear what I'm saying?"

Her lips were slow to respond. Her jaw cracked as she tried to move it. "I...can."

"I'm your nurse, honey. I knew you'd come back to us. I knew it. I am so glad I stayed in today. My boyfriend wanted to go to the World Poker Championship and see this player called BB Thomas he thinks is all that, but—"

"Where...am I?"

"Sunrise Hospital. You've been in a comatic state. Do you have any idea how long you've been here?"

The elderly woman shot the nurse a harsh glance. Apparently she didn't think that needed to be the lead topic.

"No, how could you know? Doesn't matter. But we're glad

that you are back with us. You came in with no ID. What should we call you?"

"My…friends call me…Tulip."

"Tulip!" The nurse seemed to exude joy. "I love that name. You can call me Karen. I know, Karen is supposed to be a white girl who thinks she's supervising the world, but that's the name my mamma gave me and there's nothing I can do about it now."

"Karen." Tulip tried to smile, but it was difficult. Her lips felt dry, swollen. Chapped. "Thank…you."

"You're welcome, girl, but it wasn't just me. There's been a whole bunch of us looking after you, and they are going to be so jealous that I was the one who was here when you finally came around."

"What…happened?"

Karen tucked in her chin. "We were kinda hoping you could explain that to us."

"I remember…the desert. The heat."

"You'd been out there a long time. A family of campers on their way to Yellowstone found you. Said you were in a bad way, lying in the sand, exposed and muttering stuff they didn't understand. They brought you here and this is where you've been ever since."

"Who…were they? I want to thank them."

"I've got their information. But you're not ready for that. Evelyn, can you page the doctor?"

The other woman nodded and disappeared.

"Let me tell you, girl," Karen continued, "when you came in here, you were a mess. Dehydrated. Skin red as a robin. Sorry to tell you, but you're probably going to be dealing with skin damage for a long time. We'll get a dermatologist to come in and look at you. You had some wounds, too. Were you in some kind of scrape?"

Tulip knitted her brows, trying to force herself to remember. There had been a fight…and a gun. The car keys, his eye—

She winced. She didn't need to remember that. Ever.

"Honey." Karen leaned closer. "Who did this to you? You need to tell us."

"He...can't hurt anyone else. Ever again."

"You're sure?"

"He's dead."

Karen was quiet for a moment. "Well then. Enough said about that. I've been in a few bad scrapes myself. Was it your ex?"

She shook her head slightly. "Much worse." And then, all at once, her eyes widened like balloons. "*St. Petersburg.*"

"Um, excuse me? You lost me there. You're not saying your ex is a saint, are you?"

"That's the city where I'm from. That man brought me here against my will. Tied me up like a steer at a rodeo. He wanted to kill me."

"Why would he do that?"

"I'm not sure." She scooted up a bit. Her neurons were finally firing. In fits and starts, bits and pieces, her memories were returning. "It must've had something to do with that meeting. Because they grabbed me right outside the door. The instant I left the club."

"Why?"

"Kit got himself into trouble. I think maybe they thought I was in on it."

"Kit?"

"This guy I was with. Christopher Andrus."

As soon as she said the name, Karen's face went blank. "You know Christopher Andrus?"

"Yeah. He was working a deal with this big dude, but he didn't trust the guy, so he asked me to come with. Why, do you know him?"

Karen was typing into her phone. "I thought I recognized

that name. This story made national news." She paused. "I got some bad news for you, sweetie."

"What happened? Why did Kit make the news?"

"It wasn't so much what happened as...how it was done."

"What...was done? Is—Is Kit—"

"He's dead." Karen glanced back at her phone. "Christopher Andrus of St. Petersburg, Florida, was murdered. And—"

"What happened to him?"

"It's...not pretty. Someone's on trial for murdering him. A guy named Conrad Sweeney—"

"He's the man at the meeting!" Tulip sat upright. "Should I... do something?"

"Don't make a target of yourself, honey. Someone already came after you once. They might try again. You can't go anywhere now anyway. Not till the doc says so. And that's gonna be several days yet."

"And then?"

"Up to you." Karen straightened. "But if I were you, I wouldn't go anywhere near Florida. People are getting killed out there. And there's no telling who might be next."

THE GOOD FIGHT

CHAPTER THIRTY-SIX

DAN TRUDGED THROUGH THE FRONT DOOR OF THEIR SNELL ISLE office and threw his backpack onto the sofa. "That was depressing."

Maria followed behind. "Did you see the faces on the jurors? They're ready to convict today. Like, right this minute. As soon as possible."

"I saw the face on the judge, too. I think he's stunned we have the temerity to mount a defense."

Maria flopped down in the middle of the sofa. "Problem is, we don't have a defense."

"That's a bit of an exaggeration. We have witnesses…"

"We have absolutely nothing that can undo what the last prosecution witness did."

"Sweeney will dispute everything he said."

"Sweeney will be a horrible witness. I don't care how much time we spend coaching him. He's arrogant. Self-righteous. Thinks he's smarter than everyone else in the room."

Dan flopped down beside her. "It doesn't look good. But something will come up. If we can find an expert who will—"

Maria raised a hand. "Dan, I know you want to talk about the case. You always do. But I need a break."

He smiled and snuggled closer. "I assume that's a euphemism for making out."

She raised her other hand. "Maybe later. Right now, I can barely think straight. I need food."

"As it happens, that's my best thing. Well, other than making out."

He heard Garrett tromping down the stairs. He was wearing a Rays T-shirt. "Hear you had a rough day in court."

"How goes the research? Find anything promising?"

"Maybe. I've been watching and re-watching that surveillance footage so much I'm starting to dream about it. But I think I've found something useful. The footage for—"

Garrett was interrupted by a doorbell.

They looked at one another.

"Are we expecting guests?" Dan asked. After a moment, he walked to the front door. "Shades of déjà vu."

Prudence Hancock. Again.

"Hello, handsome." She gave him a quick onceover, then touched him on the cheek. "When are we going to end all this flirting? I know you want what I've got. And I could use a good sorting out."

Over his shoulder, he saw Maria mouth "Skank."

"I do not want anything you've got. Why are you here?"

She strode past him into the living room. "Are you having a trial postmortem?"

"Of course."

"Then I assume you'll want my input."

"It's...more of a team meeting."

"Then I'm appointing myself to the team."

"That's not how it works."

Prudence sat on the sofa beside Maria. Maria scooted away.

"What have you got to bury Dilbert?"

"Nothing," Dan admitted.

"About what I expected."

Garrett cut in. "I've been researching this extensively, Ms. Hancock, and I've spoken to more than two dozen people who were at Beachcombers that night. Unfortunately, it's a noisy place and although some recall seeing Sweeney there, no one has any idea what was said or whether there was fighting."

"C'mon," Prudence said. "I know the kind of scum that hangs out at that place. I'm sure there's someone who could be... persuaded to remember."

Dan gave her a harsh look. "We don't do that."

"Don't lecture me about your morals. I've seen you use all kinds of courtroom trickery to—"

"When I'm in the courtroom, I have a professional obligation to use all legitimate means to assist my client. That most certainly does not extend to paying bribes."

"I never said anything about bribes. There are many ways of persuading people."

"What are we talking about now? Threats?"

"You're so melodramatic. Just lean on them a bit. People are more flexible than you realize. If you want to win this case —prove it."

"I'll prove it in the courtroom. Without paying bribes."

"So far, you haven't done much."

"Maybe you should represent Sweeney yourself."

"Would that I could. I am—" All at once, her voice broke. She pressed her hand against her forehead. "I'm sorry. I'm just so worried."

Dan and Maria exchanged a look. Was she about to cry again? He preferred the mean and nasty Prudence they'd known for years.

Prudence drew in her breath and composed herself. "I am sick and tired of people trashing Dr. Sweeney. They don't know anything about him. They don't know what he's been through.

They don't know what he's had to overcome to achieve the position he has today. Sure, he's not perfect. He has a lot of flaws." She covered her eyes. "But he doesn't deserve to be executed. For a crime he didn't commit."

"Forgive me for asking," Maria said, "but—why have you stayed with that man so long?"

"I thought—" Prudence took a deep breath, then tried again. "I thought I could help him. Just as he helped me. When I first came to his office as an intern, I didn't know anything. I was on the rebound, broke, drinking too much. He overlooked everything and helped me when no one else would. I'll never forget that." She looked up. "He was having troubles, too. He'd had a bad relationship somewhere in his past that scarred him big time. He'd walled himself off. All business. No personal life. I tried to take on everything possible so he could focus on the big picture—and maybe have a private life again."

"Did it work?"

"No. He'll be a workaholic till the day he dies. I think I've made myself invaluable, but..." She shook her head. "You and Dan have each other. Don't bother denying it. I've seen the two of you together. I think that's nice. I'm sure it was hard to... open the door and let someone in. Sweeney never lets anyone in. If they take away his paintings, his fortune, his freedom—he'll have nothing left."

To Dan's amazement, Maria placed her hand on Prudence's shoulder. "Rest assured that we will do everything possible—everything legal—to see that he's acquitted."

Prudence looked up, wiping her eyes. "Thank you." She swallowed. "And if there's anything I can do to help, just ask."

"We will."

"I mean that. I don't have to sit around like a rock in the gallery. I'm extremely resourceful."

"I know that."

A voice sounded from the staircase. "As long as we're having big revelations, can I add mine?"

Every head in the living room whipped around.

"Jimmy!" Maria shouted.

"In the flesh." He walked down the stairs. "Are you having a team meeting?"

"Yes. We didn't think you'd—"

"Then where's the food?"

Dan grinned. "I can whip up a little pasta in fifteen minutes."

"It can wait. I…have something to tell you."

Maria grabbed his hand. "Does this mean you're back on the team?"

Jimmy hesitated. "It means I know something that might be of use to you. I won't lie—the idea of helping Sweeney makes my stomach turn. But I heard what Prudence said and…she's right. Sweeney is a human being. With rights like everyone else. He might be disgusting beyond belief—" Jimmy looked at Prudence. "Sorry, ma'am."

"No offense taken. Please proceed."

"But he doesn't deserve to die, or to spend the rest of his life in prison for a crime he didn't commit."

Maria continued squeezing Jimmy's hand. "So you're going to help us."

"So despite the fact that I objected to this case in the most strenuous way possible…I can't permit a gross miscarriage of justice. I'm an officer of the court. When I know something crooked is going down, I have to speak up."

"What do you know, Jimmy?"

"I spoke to Shawna recently. She's resigning and moving. But she gave me a lot of useful information about this case."

"Like what?"

"Like…someone is being induced to testify. And the testimony is highly suspect."

Dan tilted his head to one side. "I don't believe Jazlyn would countenance that."

"I don't think Jazlyn knows anything about it," Jimmy replied. "But it's happening, just the same. Someone is getting a secret deal, completely off the books. And if you don't stop it"—he shook his head—"you're going down in flames."

CHAPTER THIRTY-SEVEN

NEXT MORNING, SWEENEY WAS AT THE DEFENSE TABLE WHEN DAN arrived. Prudence hovered behind him. She appeared to have recovered her composure. As he approached, she was adjusting the lie of Sweeney's tie.

Dinah scooted up behind him and placed a manila envelope in his hands. "Consider the man served."

"You did it?"

"Served my first witness subpoena. Signed the affidavit and everything. I feel very important now."

"And it went okay?"

Her smile faded. "A little scary, to be honest. He wasn't happy."

"You'll get used to that. But he'll appear?"

"I think so. We've got a guy watching him."

"Excellent." He laid a hand on her shoulder. "You done good, sis."

She beamed. "I have a great teacher."

Dan turned toward the table. "Everyone ready for the first day of our defense?"

Sweeney wore a blue suit. White shirt and red tie. "Is this where you start to show some balls, Pike?"

"If by that you mean, is this where we go on the offensive, yes."

"I'm not sure you have the guts to be offensive."

"I didn't say I was going to be offensive. I said—"

"If you're going to win anything in life, you have to be willing to make some enemies."

Dan tried to rein in his temper. "What's on your mind?"

"I wonder if…perhaps…your friendship…or whatever it is… with the prosecutor is preventing you from putting up a real fight."

Temper, temper. "I've been fighting—on your behalf—since the trial began."

"You've been making a half-assed effort and we both know it."

Was Sweeney deliberately trying to goad him? Was that the man's strategy—bullying him into action? "Everyone on this team has been working night and day on your case. At considerable personal risk."

Sweeney scoffed. "Talk is cheap. I want to see it on the stage."

Dan turned away. This was only going to enrage him and that would impair his effectiveness. He needed to focus on hacking down the prosecution's considerable mound of incriminating evidence.

JUDGE SMULDERS ENTERED AND BROUGHT THE COURTROOM TO order. "Counsel, does the defense wish to present evidence?"

As if. "We do, your honor. The defense calls Staci Mauney."

When he went looking for a DNA expert, he hadn't intentionally looked for a woman, but he did think Mauney made a nice counterpoint to Deanna Folsom. Younger, hipper, more up-to-date. She didn't come to this field through the backdoor. It had been her focus since school and throughout her professional life. She was in the private sector, not a police department. She worked out of Tallahassee and was considered one of the leading experts in the nation.

Mauney took the stand. Slender. Business-like. No visible jewelry. Poised. Might not be fun on a third date, but exactly what he needed in the courtroom. He established her credentials, her degrees and awards and numerous published articles.

"Dr. Mauney, just to be upfront, are you being compensated for testifying today?"

"For testifying, no, but I will charge my standard fee for DNA analysis, plus travel expenses."

"Thank you. Please tell the jury what you do."

"My office is basically a check on the numerous law enforcement DNA labs around the country. As a result of misinformation and primetime TV, people have come to believe DNA evidence is irrefutable. It isn't. DNA must be interpreted. Errors occur."

"Can you give me an example?"

"Sure. A few years ago in Houston, a local CBS affiliate news station obtained samples of DNA processed by the Houston Police Department Crime Laboratory and sent them out for analysis by independent experts. The results were shocking. The Houston techs were mishandling and misinterpreting even the simplest samples."

"Does this happen a lot?"

"Sadly, yes. Initially, DNA evidence released many innocent people. But now we're seeing people wrongfully convicted by DNA evidence, in some cases due to negligent handling, but in others, as part of a deliberate effort to stack the deck for conviction."

"How hard is that?"

"Not very. Jurors are often baffled by DNA evidence. They

can't read the genetic markers that appear on test strips as stag-gered lines of blue dots. They have to rely on the techs who are testifying."

"Have you written articles on this subject?"

"Many. Like all sciences, forensic science evolves. I believe you spoke earlier about how bite-mark evidence is widely discredited now. That's been around since the Salem witch trials, but few courts will permit it today. Microscopic hair evidence has been entirely discredited. Some experts are questioning ballistics testing. Turns out the supposedly unique markings made on bullets when fired are not nearly so unique as was once believed. Even fingerprints are not as one-of-a-kind as lawyers sometimes suggest. So it is perhaps not surprising that DNA evidence, while potentially useful, is far from infallible."

"Please tell us about the current status of DNA evidence."

"Testing standards have improved," Mauney replied. "The FBI started its CODIS database to store the DNA profiles of arrested and convicted criminals. People heard a lot about DNA on television. One study indicated that if the prosecution had DNA evidence, the jury was thirty-three times more likely to convict. Sometimes prosecutors could get suspects to confess or take a plea if they told them they had DNA evidence. So everyone wanted DNA evidence. One way or the other." She paused. "Too often, defendants and their lawyers can't afford independent verification, or think it will be useless. They've bought into the DNA myth. So sloppy work goes undetected."

Dan glanced at the jury. He had been worried that this might be too high-school-science class for them, but they seemed attentive. "Is that a problem?"

"Of course. Science is only as good as the people applying it. DNA evidence only indicates that one sample is similar to another. If there's no similarity, that's a good indication that the donor should be eliminated as a suspect. But a finding of similarity is not proof of guilt. And of course, similarities can be...exaggerated."

"What do you propose?"

"The best solution would be to send all DNA evidence to independent labs like ours. Perhaps one day we'll be able to automate the process and take people out of the equation. Several experts are working on software that would handle the analysis, but we're not there yet. We need lab techs—reliable ones. People who are not paid by or have any affiliation with law enforcement, so they're free to report their true findings. Did you know that some crime techs are actually given a bonus if their evidence results in a conviction? That's obviously going to bias the analysis. We need a firewall between the scientists and law enforcement."

"Any other problems?"

"DNA analysis is incredibly complex. Remember—we all share 99.9% genes identical to every other person on this planet. But even the variations—we call them alleles— are shared by a smaller percentage of the population. So the DNA analyst has to find the variations that are the least observable part of a sample but still are not completely unique. This is particularly important when looking at a mixture of DNA samples or a split sample. The analyst must interpret whether the observable similarities are sufficient to declare a match. It is not at all cut-and-dried. It's more like an interpretive art. It's more subjective than objective."

"And the consequences of sloppy or biased interpretation?"

"Wrongful conviction. Erin Murphy has written a book detailing dozens of cases where DNA typing went horribly wrong. It's terrifying. It's an affront to the justice system."

Jazlyn rose. "Your honor, while I'm sure the jury is enjoying this opinionated science lesson...are we going to talk about the murder case?"

Dan replied. "I'm going to tie this into the case, your honor. Right now."

The judge nodded. "Please do."

"Dr. Mauney, have you had a chance to examine the DNA evidence in this case?"

"I have."

"Did you draw any conclusions?"

"Yes. I find that while the DNA evidence does not exclude the defendant, it certainly does not prove he committed the crime. And I have many concerns about how the sample was handled. Remember, DNA evidence does not come to court by magic. Context is everything. I detected signs of contamination. That's not surprising given the circumstances—a fleck of skin found on a decapitated head in a freezer. But it mitigates forming a definitive conclusion."

"What else?"

"There's a complete lack of transparency here. I asked Dr. Folsom and her staff for a report describing their procedure. They refused. I asked to interview them. They refused."

Jazlyn rose again. "Objection. Your honor, talking to outsiders is contrary to SPPD policy."

The judge looked back at her. "So the witness' statement is correct."

"Yes, but—"

"Overruled. Please sit down."

Dan continued. "Dr. Mauney, what is meant in the field of DNA forensics by the term 'secondary transfer?'"

"It's simple. The DNA sample moves from one place to another. The skin fleck in question was purportedly found on the head in the freezer. But it could have been planted there."

Jazlyn again. "Objection. This is getting preposterous."

"Is it?" Dan asked. "The two police officers, and numerous others, were in my client's office. Given the enormous rate of human skin shedding, there must be flecks all over the place. Finding one and planting it would not be difficult."

He and Jazlyn started talking at once. Judge Smulders raised his hands to quiet them. "You are all free to make whatever arguments you like in closing. But this is proper defense testimony. Madame Prosecutor, you are overruled."

Jazlyn flung herself into her seat, eyes burning.

Dan couldn't be sure, but he thought he saw a few tiny kernels of doubt in the eyes of the jurors. His work wasn't done. But this was a definite step in the right direction.

CHAPTER THIRTY-EIGHT

AFTER THE BREAK, DAN CALLED HIS NEXT WITNESS. HE WAS GLAD to see Garrett in the gallery. But for him, they wouldn't have this witness at all.

David Norris took giant steps to the witness stand. He was extremely tall and a bit pudgy, probably the natural result of spending too much time staring at screens. Mismatched socks. Bad haircut. Sleepy left eye.

"Mr. Norris, you're a security officer working at the downtown SweeTech office building, correct?"

"That's right." Norris seemed nervous. Probably his first time to testify. He was technically a defense witness, but he didn't want to be here at all, and Dan would have to bear that in mind as he framed his questions. "I've been working there for three years."

"Do you like your job?"

"It's okay."

"Do you know my client, Conrad Sweeney?"

"I've seen him on the video monitors a lot. I've never actually met him."

"Who hired you?"

"That would be Prudence Hancock." He pointed. "I report to her."

"Can you describe your duties?"

"Basically, I watch the computer monitors that display the input from the security cameras positioned throughout the building. I have four screens, but they rotate through the views from twenty-four cameras."

"Is the feed from those cameras recorded?"

"Yes. Everything is digitally stored on a cloud. I'm watching in case something suspicious or dangerous occurs that requires an immediate response."

Like one of Sweeney's many enemies trying to rub him out. "Are the recordings dated?"

"Yes. Each one is automatically encoded with a time-and-date stamp."

"Can those stamps be altered?"

Norris' back stiffened. "If you're suggesting—"

"I'm not suggesting anything. I'm asking if it can be done."

"If you have the coding skills. Metadata can always be altered. Just as an image can be altered. But I've examined the original recording. The images have not been doctored."

Dan wasn't surprised. He'd had them independently verified. The images were true.

"Mr. Norris, a member of the SPPD previously testified that he reviewed your security camera recordings and found one showing my client and the victim, Christopher Andrus, exiting the penthouse-level elevator and entering my client's office. Are you familiar with that recording?"

"Yes. I helped Detective Kakazu find it. Took a while."

"And the images weren't altered?"

"No chance."

"Have you reviewed any of the other footage showing those two men together? Like, from previous occasions?"

Norris' head pulled back. A thin line crossed his brow. "No."

"Do you think there might be some value in that?"

Norris was confused. "I...have not been asked to do that. I allowed the police to access all the recordings, though. I also gave access codes to your researcher."

"Garrett Wainwright. Isn't it true that Christopher Andrus visited my client at his office on numerous previous occasions?"

"I do recall seeing him before."

"Fairly frequent visitor, isn't he?"

"Not so much lately."

Because Sweeney didn't have the cash for expensive luxury items anymore. "So how can we know that the footage purportedly taken shortly before Andrus' death wasn't taken ten years earlier?"

"The recordings are all categorized, filed, and organized. By time and date. Like I said. Metadata."

"You told me that could be altered."

"Only by someone with access to the recordings."

"And you just told me you granted access to the police department. How many people there had access?"

"I don't know."

"Did the District Attorney's office also have access?"

"I...don't know."

"Did the police department grant access to anyone outside the department?"

"I have no way of knowing that."

"Do you even know who inside the police department had access?"

Jazlyn rose to her feet. "Your honor, if counsel is suggesting that anyone in my office tampered with those recordings, I can assure you it is not true. And I am appalled—"

Dan cut in. "I don't have any reason to believe that the district attorney has done anything improper. My point is obvious. Many people had access to those files. And these days, changing metadata doesn't require a super-hacker. A talented high school coder could do it."

"That doesn't prove anyone did."

Dan bowed his head. "Since I haven't heard an actual objection, may I proceed?"

Jazlyn settled into her chair, but her expression left little doubt about her current emotional state.

Dan activated the television monitor near the jury box. "I'm going to play the footage in question so the jury can see what we're talking about. All the footage taken from SweeTech security cameras has been stipulated to by the parties and pre-admitted by agreement." He pushed a button. "This is the footage from the day we're discussing, taken shortly after the alleged meeting at Beachcombers and about twenty hours before the remains were found in the freezer."

Dan watched the footage, though he had seen it a thousand times. Garrett had screened it for him forward and backward, in real-time and slo-mo, full-screen and with selective enlargements.

The elevator doors opened, just barely visible in the lower left part of the screen. Two men emerged, Sweeney first, Andrus trailing in his wake. Both wore somber expressions, but no one looked scared, and Andrus was walking of his own volition. They strolled down the corridor without speaking. Sweeney opened the door to his office and they both went inside. Unfortunately, there were no security cameras inside Sweeney's office, much less his mancave, so there was no footage showing what happened next.

"Mr. Norris, does that appear to be the footage in question?"

"That's it."

"Good. Now let me show you something else."

Dan pushed a few more buttons. A moment later, the screen lit.

The new footage appeared to be the same as what Dan

showed before. Sweeney and Andrus exited the elevator, crossed the corridor, and entered Sweeney's office.

"Looks like the same footage, doesn't it?"

Norris squinted. "You mean it isn't?"

"According to the metadata, this footage is from eighteen months earlier. We only found it because my researcher is relentless."

"Andrus did visit frequently. I'm not surprised you could find similar footage."

"We didn't find similar footage, sir. We found identical footage."

"That's not possible..."

"Did you notice that both men were wearing the same clothes?"

"I believe...the defendant favors white suits."

"And Andrus? Does he wear the same clothes every day?"

"Well..."

"Let me show you something else." Dan froze the frame, then turned the enlargement dial, focusing on a tall ashtray beside the elevator doors. "Note the stubbed cigarette—because the exact same cigarette is in the exact same position in the previous footage. Now look at this." He scrolled down to the opening for trash below the ashtray. "See the newspaper sticking out? Thanks to digital enhancement, I can zoom in on the date. You see?"

Everyone did.

"Eighteen months before. Now I'm going to return to the footage supposedly shot just before the murder." He switched back to the first recording, then focused on the ashtray. "Same newspaper. Same date."

The jury stirred. This had suddenly become interesting.

"I will submit, Mr. Norris, that the footage from eighteen months ago was copied and mislabeled as footage taken shortly before Andrus' death. And the only reason to do that, of course, would be to frame my client by putting Andrus in a place where he never was."

"Objection," Jazlyn said. "Is this cross or closing? He's giving a speech."

"Sustained."

"And furthermore," Jazlyn said, more quietly, "the defendant is the person with the easiest access to the security camera footage. Maybe there was something he didn't want the police to see."

"So he replaced it with incriminating footage certain to get him arrested?" Dan asked.

Jazlyn's jaw tightened. "Maybe the original footage showed him lugging in the body. Or parts of it."

"You can't even prove Andrus was at my client's office on the day in question."

"I can prove part of him was. The part Detective Kakazu found in the freezer."

"This will stop immediately!" Judge Smulders banged his gavel, then rose to his feet, towering over them. "What did I say before about speaking objections, counsel?"

Dan thought it was best to remain quiet. Jazlyn did the same.

"The jury will make its decision based upon the evidence. And nothing else. This bickering will end now. And it will never be repeated. Understood?"

Judge Smulders waited a few moments before continuing. "Do you have anything more, Mr. Pike?"

"I'm afraid I do." He approached the witness. "We can see that at some point prior to the arrival of the police, the original recording was replaced with footage from an earlier visit. Mr. Norris...were you on duty the day the police discovered the body?"

"I've already said I was."

"Is it possible you...left your post for a while?"

"No."

"Got hungry? Fell asleep. Had a date? Forgot to activate the cameras?"

"Absolutely not."

"I think you did. And when news of the murder broke, you realized everyone would want to see that missing footage. So you found some old Andrus footage and substituted it for what was missing because you weren't there."

"That is absolutely untrue."

"I'm sorry to hear that. Because the only other possible explanation is that someone made this substitution as part of a deliberate effort, a conspiracy even, to frame my client."

CHAPTER THIRTY-NINE

DURING A BRIEF RECESS, WHILE DAN CONTEMPLATED HOW BEST to handle the next, all-important witness, Jimmy rushed up behind him. "Found it."

"Fantastic. Did you give copies to Jazlyn?"

"Of course."

Dan took the documents, scanned them, and smiled. "I knew you wouldn't disappoint me."

Jimmy tucked his thumbs inside his cardigan pockets. "If there's a way to work this town, I'm the one who can find it."

"How well I know that." Dan glanced up. "Good to have you back on the team."

"I—never said—"

"Nonetheless." He faced his partner. "I want to apologize."

"You don't have to do that."

"I do. I was arrogant and presumptuous and—"

"You? Daniel Pike?"

He laughed in spite of himself. "But I know this team is stronger with you on it."

"Oh stop. You're the superstar. I'm the weakest link and always have been."

"No." He took Jimmy by both shoulders and looked him straight in the eyes. "You're the heart and soul of this team. And you always have been."

If it was possible, he thought Jimmy might be blushing.

Jimmy found a seat in the gallery and Dan sat beside Maria.

"Nicely done," she said. "But I thought I was the heart and soul of this team."

"You're the spunk and spitfire. And the brains."

"Well played."

After the judge returned, Dan recalled Clint Dilbert, the man who supposedly overheard a heated conversation between Sweeney and the victim at Beachcombers.

Jazlyn rose. "Objection, your honor. This witness has already been on the stand. Opposing counsel had a chance to cross."

"The testimony I plan to elicit breaks new ground," Dan explained. "It's outside the scope of Ms. Prentice's direct. Plus we have new evidence. We have shared copies with opposing counsel. Not that we are obligated to do so. But in the interests of fairness, we did."

Judge Smulders looked at Jazlyn. "True?"

"Yes. But these documents don't reveal anything relevant to this case."

"I strongly disagree," Dan said. "They change everything. As will be readily apparent."

Judge Smulders pondered. "If this testimony is going to change everything, I can hardly forbid it. But I will be paying attention, Mr. Pike. If it starts to sound redundant, or like something that should've been raised earlier, I will shut you down."

"Understood, you honor."

The judge peered into the gallery. "Mr. Dilbert, I believe you've been subpoenaed."

Dilbert rose. "But—I never agreed—"

"Yes, criminal trials are full of surprises. That's what makes them exciting. Please take the stand."

Dilbert grudgingly dragged himself forward.

"Mr. Dilbert, during your previous appearance, you testified that you witnessed an angry conversation between my client and the deceased."

"Already said that."

"And you claimed you came to the police voluntarily."

"Yeah."

"And you said you received no inducements for testimony."

"I got nothin'."

"But that isn't entirely true, is it?"

A hush fell over the courtroom. He had their attention. Now he had to deliver.

"I don't know what you're talking about."

Dan could see Jazlyn preparing to rise. "Let's take your statement apart piece by piece. You didn't volunteer, did you? The police picked you up on a warrant. That warrant is our latest exhibit. Which I've already shared with opposing counsel."

Jazlyn rose. "Your honor, I've never seen this before but, even if it's true, it's irrelevant."

"No, it's keenly relevant," Dan explained. "It's part of a sadly all-too-common law enforcement ruse to disguise the motivations of a witness. They hid this warrant from us."

"Not very well," Jazlyn mumbled.

"They had it expunged from the court records."

Judge Smulders frowned. "If this was expunged, why do you have it? The whole point of expungement is to make it unavailable."

"I have a teammate who knows the records systems inside out. And has friends."

"This is still highly unorthodox. Expunged documents are not meant to be used in any future capacity."

"But it's important to the case, your honor."

Smulders tossed the document down. "Very well. Proceed."

"Mr. Dilbert, is it true that, prior to your testimony, you were brought in by the police? And questioned?"

"Sure, but nothing came of it," Dilbert said. "They released me. It was later that I came back to them with information."

"Of your own free will."

"Right. Because I saw that fight at the bar and, after I read on my phone that the guy got butchered up, I thought it might be important."

Something didn't make sense, but he wasn't nailing it down. "Did the police ask you to follow Sweeney? Or Andrus?"

"Definitely not."

"Then why did you go to Beachcombers?"

"I said this already. My daughter bartends there."

The look in Dilbert's eye triggered something in Dan's brain.

"I go whenever I can," Dilbert continued. "Gives me a chance to catch up with her. Every daddy loves his daughter."

Bingo. Dan stepped closer to the witness. "When you testified before, you emphatically stated that you received nothing of benefit in exchange for your testimony."

"That's true."

"Because *you* didn't get anything. It was your daughter who benefitted. You made a deal to testify in exchange for some benefit to your daughter."

Dilbert did not immediately reply. His eyes darted to someone in the gallery. Undercover cop, perhaps?

"What was it? A drug offense? Was she peddling drugs in the alley behind the bar? I know others have done it before."

Dilbert stuttered, but no words emerged.

"You are under oath, sir. It's one thing to hide the truth. But if you commit actual perjury, you could go to prison for a long time. And any deal you made for your daughter will be revoked."

Still Dilbert didn't speak.

"Was the deal written down? Were charges brought against your daughter and then dropped? Do you think we can't find the paper trail?" Dan came closer, his voice rising. "We found the expunged warrant. We'll uncover this immunity deal, too. And when we do, you'll be looking at a prison sentence. As will your daughter. You won't be able to catch up with her when both of you are behind bars."

Dilbert looked stricken. His eyes darted all over the place.

"The court wants the truth, sir. This is your daughter's last chance."

Jazlyn rose, but Dilbert spoke first. "I was just trying to help Suzie." His voice was high-pitched and strained. "She's my little girl. Any father would do what I did."

Dan exhaled. At long last. "That's no excuse for perjury."

"It's not her first time." Tears rushed to Dilbert's eyes. "She's looking at five years minimum."

Dan checked the faces in the jury. They looked uncomfortable. No one enjoyed seeing someone suffer like this. He decided to go easy. Cruelty wouldn't help Sweeney's case.

"So the arrangement was that if you testified, the charges against your daughter would disappear?"

Dilbert nodded. "And they did."

"Did the police tell you what to say?" He didn't bother eliciting the names. He knew Internal Affairs would be investigating soon.

"No. I knew what they wanted."

"Mr. Dilbert, were you even at the bar that night?"

"Yeah. And I saw Sweeney and Andrus and the woman."

"But there was no fight?"

"No. I think they made an appointment to meet later. But they just talked."

Jazlyn shot up. "Which does not in any way prove the defendant did not commit this murder."

True. But there was no fight, and there was no security

footage showing Andrus going to Sweeney's office. Sweeney was still the top suspect. The body parts were in his freezer. But piece-by-piece, Dan was dismantling the prosecution case.

"Let me also add," Jazlyn said, "that I had no knowledge whatsoever of any deal or arrangement regarding this witness or his daughter."

"And let me also add," Dan said, "that I absolutely believe the district attorney. There may have been some underhanded actions at the SPPD, but I don't believe Ms. Prentice knew about it. I've known her for years, know her to have great integrity, and know that she would never call a witness she thought might be tainted."

Smulders nodded. "I appreciate that counsel." He turned toward the jury box. "I will instruct the members of this jury to disregard the prior testimony of this witness. But then, I suspect you already have."

CHAPTER FORTY

HERNANDEZ SLAMMED HIS FIST DOWN ON THE TINY TABLE IN THE dimly lit motel room. His anger was palpable. He could feel it. And he wanted to make sure his two associates could feel it as well.

"This is intolerable!" he bellowed. He knew he should probably keep his voice down. These walls were thin. The hotel was filled with cockroaches. Not bugs. Human cockroaches, people who would sell their own mothers for a dime bag of low-grade cocaine.

Jose and Santiago sat on the filthy bedspread. They looked worried. Good. They damn well should be. Neither spoke. That was also good. He wanted them cowed. He wanted them humiliated. And desperate to redeem themselves. "Explain yourselves."

Jose looked at his comrade, who looked back at him. "I did as you asked. I eliminated Lombardi. I terrified the sister."

"Not well enough. Her brother continues to work for our enemy. She herself appears in the courtroom assisting. It seems you cannot even frighten a frail woman, Jose. Perhaps you are more a woman than a man."

"You told me not to kill her. You said you didn't want her seriously injured."

"You failed to even frighten her."

"Forgive me, sir, but I can assure you she was frightened. Terrified."

"If you want her killed," Santiago added, "we can make that happen. But I do not believe she will be scared away. Any more than Pike has been."

"So we just let Sweeney slip through our fingers?"

"He is on trial for murder. My contacts say he is likely to be convicted."

"I have read the news reports. One by one, that stupid lawyer has undermined the prosecution witnesses."

"But Sweeney is still the most likely suspect. And when a crime as ugly as this one occurs...jurors see clearly. They want to feel safe. They want to put someone behind bars, whether sufficient proof is there or not."

"That is simply not good enough." Hernandez stood, pacing in the tiny room. "We must end this defense. With finality. Plunge a harpoon into the great white whale."

"The simplest approach would be to eliminate Pike."

"That would create a martyr. And a trial delay. I want Sweeney in prison. Once there, my people on the inside will be able to eliminate him permanently."

Jose swallowed. "Sir...you complain of our inaction...but forbid us to do anything."

Hernandez inhaled deeply. He took a moment, hoping it would give his lieutenants a chance to reflect. And think. And worry. "I have not forbidden you to do *everything*."

"Then what? We can't go after Pike. So you sent us after the one he cares about most."

Hernandez raised a finger. "That is where you erred. You did not go after the one he loves most. There is another. Family ties are strong. But nothing is as strong as passion."

"Do you mean...the former mayor?"

"Of course not. She is dead to him now." He pushed a photograph across the table. "My people tell me that he is now in a relationship with his law partner. Maria Morales."

Santiago nodded. "They do seem...friendly."

"I know this Pike. He is a real man. He will feel a responsibility to protect the woman of his heart. And when he fails...it will devastate him."

Santiago took the photo. "You want me to go after her?"

"Precisely."

"And this time...what are we permitted to do? Simply scare her?"

Hernandez shook his head vehemently. "This time, the gloves are off."

"Meaning...we can hurt her?"

Hernandez smiled. "Meaning you can do anything you want to her. And then kill her."

MARIA WALKED BACK TO HER APARTMENT, TRYING TO STAY IN THE light cast by the intermittent streetlamps. She'd stopped at the corner grocery to pick up a few essentials. There was a brisk chill in the air tonight. She wore a hoodie, the one Dan had given her with the lined pockets. She walked at a steady pace. Still cold, but she'd be home soon.

She was starving. This always happened when they were in a big trial. It was as if everything normal about her life, all habit or routine, disappeared. She had been so busy she forgot to eat. This case was particularly unsettling since, first, they were dealing with a murderer who had dismembered a body and, second, she had to sit next to Conrad Sweeney all day long. She would never get used to that.

She'd picked up some pasta at the grocery and was hoping to

whip up a snack before bedtime. Dan might be the gourmet chef, but she knew how to slap together a darn good meal and she could usually get the job done in about ten minutes. Dan took that long just to chop the vegetables. And fuss about whether he was using kosher salt or pink Himalayan sea salt.

Dan. What the hell was she doing? She still didn't know how to define their relationship. He seemed to like her and was no longer embarrassed to show it in public. He was affectionate. Kind. Considerate.

But he still hadn't invited her back to the boat. Was there something wrong with her? Was he deliberately keeping a distance?

She rounded the corner and headed toward her apartment building.

Or, she worried, was Dan still scarred, devastated, by how the relationship with Camila turned out? How that woman betrayed his trust?

She tried to block that out of her head. They had a case to win. When that was over, she'd sit Dan down in a chair and read him the relationship riot act. Put up or shut up, dude. And if he didn't—

A man leapt out of the shadows. She had no time to identify him, no time to react, no time to do anything. He tackled her and knocked her into an alcove beside the front door of the apartment building, where the Dumpsters were kept. Her head slammed back against something hard and metal, dazing her. A clanging reverberated through her ears.

She knew she had to think fast or it would be too late. What would Dan tell her to do? Scream. Then run. Unfortunately, at the moment, she didn't seem to be able to muster the energy to do either. Weren't security people supposed to be watching her? Where were they?

Then she remembered. She told everyone she was going home for the evening. They thought they were done for the day. Then she made a last-minute decision to go to the grocery.

Alone.

"End of the road for you, lawyer." The man towering over her had a thick Spanish accent.

She started to push herself up off the concrete. He kicked her hard in the chest. Her head slapped back against the Dumpster, making a thunderous sound.

"You're not going anywhere, lady."

"I'll scream."

"Maybe for a second." He reached inside his coat and withdrew a hammer. The flat end glistened in the moonlight. "I have a way of silencing screams. Quickly."

"Is this about the Sweeney case?"

"Doesn't matter." He paused, hammer hovering in the air above her. "The only question is whether I kill you fast, like I did Carvel, or if I have some fun with you first."

A cold chill raced through her body. He was a hundred pounds heavier than her, taller, stronger. And he had a hammer. "You kill me, I won't be any good to you."

He shrugged. "One blow to the spinal column. You will be immobilized below the neck. You might be awake, but unable to resist. Unable to do anything except watch."

"You filthy…disgusting…"

"Stop the sweet talk. You're turning me on."

He squatted down, then grabbed her blouse, tearing it. "The fun begins."

He leaned in closer, smiling, almost drooling.

Maria reached into the lined pocket of her hoodie—and withdrew a taser.

She jammed it into the man's gut. He stiffened, then thrashed spasmodically in midair. After a few seconds, he collapsed on top of her.

She grimaced, then shoved him aside. He started to push

himself up. She jabbed the taser into his side again. And left it there.

He convulsed as if he were having a seizure, but she did not remove the taser. She smelled burning flesh. Blood came out of his ears. But she did not remove the taser.

Only when she feared he might be on the verge of a stroke did she remove the taser. And even then she kept it close and at the ready.

"Filthy son-of-a-bitch," she muttered, wiping her brow. She inhaled deeply, trying to bring her respiration back to a normal rate. For a moment there, when he hovered over her, she had been so scared...

She made a mental note to thank Dan, who had insisted on tasers for every member of the team, and Mr. K, who paid for them.

And her father, who taught her to protect herself, because no man had any right to exercise power over her against her will.

If only all men were like Dad, she thought, and then she jabbed the taser back into her assailant's gut.

While he thrashed on the pavement, she scrambled to her feet and fumbled for her cell phone. "Did you think I was going to go down easy? Then you don't know anything about me. My daddy didn't raise me to be a victim. He raised me to be a fighter."

She kicked him, just for good measure. "Did you think we didn't learn anything after you went after Dinah? Did you think you could push me around because I was female? Newsflash, asshole. Brains beat brawn every time. I am woman, hear me roar."

Someone picked up the other end of the phone line. St. Petersburg Police. "How may I direct your call?"

"Is Detective Kakazu in? I have a crime to report. And I'm certain he'll be interested."

CHAPTER FORTY-ONE

DAN RUSHED INTO THE POLICE STATION. "WHERE'S DETECTIVE Kakazu?"

The woman at the front desk looked up from her computer screen. "You're Pike, right?"

"Right. And my partner is here somewhere. With Kakazu."

She nodded and led him inside.

As soon as he saw Maria, he wrapped her in his arms, swooping her off the ground.

"Whoa." Maria blinked several times, then slowly returned the embrace. "Does this mean you missed me?"

"It means I was worried about you." He placed his hand behind her head. "How are you?"

"I'm okay. A little shaken. But I'll be fine."

"Did he—"

"He didn't do anything. Except scare me. When I saw that hammer...damn. Anyway, I'm fine."

"I thought you went home."

"I did. But I went out again."

"Would you get mad if I said, 'That was really stupid?'"

"Not this time." Pause. "But don't let it happen again."

He pulled back a little, still holding her. "How am I going to keep you safe?"

"I'm a big girl. I don't need—"

"It's obvious I can't let you out of my sight. I think you should come home with me tonight."

She blinked rapidly. "You—do?"

"That taser trick only worked because it was one guy. If there had been more…" He shook his head. "No, you're sticking with me. Agreed?"

"I…could probably live with that."

Kakazu cleared his throat. "I don't want to intrude…"

"What happened, Jake? Who is this bastard?"

"He's not talking. But he's not an American citizen and he has a thick Central American accent. I don't want to jump to any assumptions, but I think he's with the cartel."

"Then he won't be behind bars long."

"We charged him with assault. We can mess around and delay the arraignment a bit, but not forever. We've got forty-eight hours, basically, to get him to talk."

"He won't. He knows his boss will take care of him."

Kakazu nodded. "Unless…he thinks he's safer inside."

"How do you manage that?"

"If we can convince him that he's a dead man once he steps into the outside world, he might be more interested in talking to us. And making a deal for protective custody."

"You'd give him immunity?" Maria said.

"To get this cartel out of St. Petersburg once and for all? Yes. Throw back a minnow to catch the whale." He smiled a little. "C'mon, Maria. You already got your licks in."

Dan's eyes widened. "What's this?"

"The perp wants to charge Maria with assault and battery. But that isn't going to happen. I believe she acted in self-defense. Enthusiastically." He glanced at Dan. "Here's my advice. Don't get this woman mad at you."

"Message received and understood."

"We'll keep working on him," Kakazu said. "He's scared. Scared people make foolish decisions. He had a hammer, which may tie him to the attack on Dinah and the murder of Carvel. If we charge him with first-degree murder, he won't get bail."

"Can you make that stick? Just based on a hammer?"

"I'm hoping it won't be necessary. I don't want to lock him away. I want him to crack. And if he does…" Kakazu paused. "I don't want to be overly optimistic, but…maybe we've finally reached a turning point in our decades-long fight against that disgusting cartel."

"Let's hope," Maria said. "He's probably scared about what could happen to him in prison."

"Actually," Kakazu said, "I think what he's most scared of is you."

***

DAN INSISTED ON TAKING A TAXI BACK TO HIS BOAT, EVEN THOUGH it wasn't that far and he would normally enjoy a brisk walk in the sea salt air. But not tonight. It was pitch black outside, no moon, no stars. The wind was still. And when he thought about what might have happened to Maria…

No. Tonight they would ride.

"We could probably get a continuance," Dan said. "Given… what happened to you."

"Don't even think about it," she replied. "I want this trial over with. Done. Out of my life."

"I'm down with that. We don't have that much more to do."

She closed her eyes. "Sweeney."

"Yeah. You still think we should put him on the stand?"

"We have to. Trials are a form of storytelling. The jury votes for the side that tells the best story. If we don't put Sweeney on the stand, our story has too many unanswered questions. And an anticlimactic conclusion."

"Jazlyn will not cut him any slack. She'll go after everything. The business debts. The money laundering. The porn operation."

"Sweeney can handle it. He's smart. He won't get confused or tripped up. Remember that speech you heard him give when he opened the last Sweeney Shelter? He can be eloquent, if he wants to be. If there's any way to get the jury on his side, he'll find it."

"She'll make him look like a crook."

"But she won't make him look like a murderer. And that's how we succeed."

"In the exoneration of the most vile, disgusting person I've ever known." He snuggled in a little closer. "Do you ever get the feeling that your life has become…completely different than what you thought it was going to be?"

She grinned. "I know, right? Like, every day."

He put his arm around her. "Completely different…and much better."

CHAPTER FORTY-TWO

As Dan strode down the center of the courtroom, he had the weird feeling he was doing a perp walk. He knew all eyes were on him. He spotted several members of the press in the gallery, but far more civilians, people who were there for no reason except to see whether the city's best-known defense lawyer could get the city's best-known criminal off the hook.

He spotted Jamison too. And Prudence, of course. And—

He froze.

There was someone new in the gallery today. Someone he had never seen there before.

Alejandro Hernandez. The reputed leader of the El Salvadoran cartel. He'd never formally met the man, but he recognized him just the same.

Why was he here? Was this some kind of implied threat? Reminding Dan that they might strike at Maria again? Was he threatening the judge? Did he think a courtroom appearance might help his flunky get out on bail?

Or maybe he was trying to warn Sweeney about what might happen if he exposed any cartel secrets on the witness stand.

The two men locked eyes.

He'd be lying if he didn't admit he felt a shiver. Hernandez had caused so much misery in the world. Been responsible for so many broken lives.

And yet, as he stared into those eyes, he saw...

Was this man tired? He was in his eighties. Was it possible he was sick of all this? Or was he worried? Was he was just as scared as the rest of them?

Dan passed through the swinging gate and approached Sweeney. "We need to talk."

Sweeney looked up, unimpressed. "Haven't we been over this chapter and verse? It's isn't rocket surgery, you know. I'll just tell the jury what happened."

"We have company today."

"Yes, I know. Hernandez is trying to spook me. Screw him. He doesn't scare me." He glanced over at Maria. "Hell, he doesn't even scare her."

Prudence leaned over the dividing rail. "Do you want me to drag his wrinkly ass out of here?"

"No!" Dan and Maria said simultaneously.

Sweeney smiled. "Let's not stir up unnecessary trouble, Prudence. He can't do anything to me here."

Prudence sat back. "Believe me, it would be a pleasure."

Sweeney nodded. "Another time."

Dan jabbed his thumb toward the far end of the courtroom. "Let's have a little talk. One last chat before you testify."

Sweeney followed him. The attending marshal watched them carefully but made no attempt to restrain Sweeney. Presumably, he realized that if Sweeney were going to make a break for it, he wouldn't bring his lawyer.

Sweeney started. "I already know what to say."

"I know. I want to talk about your...demeanor."

"You don't want to see my usual effervescent personality on the witness stand?" Sweeney laughed heartily. "You want me to put on a show. You want me to act like a nice person. Smile? Maybe bat away a tear every now and again?"

"Totally wrong."

"What do you want, then?"

"Hard as this is to say...I want you to be yourself."

"Okay, now I'm confused."

"Look." Dan tossed his head toward the jury box. "Those twelve all-important jurors are a lot smarter than people think. The fact that they were chosen randomly doesn't mean they're stupid. Some may be more educated, but few are truly dumb. And almost all jurors try to do the right thing."

"Your faith in humanity is applaudable. And risible."

"No, listen to me. The ones who don't care rarely get on juries. It isn't hard to figure out what responses during jury selection will get you tossed off. The ones who make it through the process want to serve. They want to do their civic duty. And they certainly do not want to put an innocent man behind bars. That's why they pay close attention. That's why they watch the witnesses. And no one gets watched more closely than the defendant. So don't put on a show."

Sweeney pressed his hands against his chest. "You wound me."

"In my experience, jurors are pretty good at differentiating the straight-shooters from the con artists. So don't try to flim-flam them. If they detect a false note even once, they may start disbelieving every word you say."

"Human lie detectors?"

"Kind of, yeah. If even one juror thinks you're dissembling and says so, they might convince the others—and you could go down in flames."

Sweeney pondered a moment. "I hear what you're saying, Pike, but...I am perhaps not renowned for my warm personality."

"And this would be the wrong time to pretend. Just be yourself."

"Warts and all?"

"Exactly. You're never going to convince these jurors that you're a saint, but if you play straight with them, you might at least convince them you're not a murderer."

Sweeney's head bobbed slightly. "That makes sense, actually. Thank you."

Dan shrugged. "Just doing my job."

DAN SPENT ALMOST AN HOUR ESTABLISHING WHO SWEENEY WAS and allowing the jury to know him better. Started as a small businessman. Had a failed business. Had a failed relationship. Redoubled his work commitments afterward. "I focused on what I did well, not what I was obviously completely incompetent at." He forgot about women and discovered a new passion —art. Got into tech at just the right moment. Diversified into many other fields. Became the richest man in the city. Wanted to give back, so he became the most high-profile philanthropist in St. Petersburg.

Dan watched the jury the whole time. Were they buying it? He thought he detected some healthy skepticism, especially when Sweeney talked about his philanthropy. Which convinced him that he needed to be the one to bring up a bit of unpleasantness. Better he tackled it head-on than left it for Jazlyn to wrap around Sweeney's throat like a noose.

"Would you consider the women's shelters to be the crown jewel of your philanthropic efforts?"

"Absolutely. We built fourteen of them. Hundreds of women and mothers were given a safe refuge when they had nowhere else to go."

"Has there been some...unpleasantness associated with those

shelters?"

"Sadly, yes. The police uncovered a pornography operation in the basements. I believe you played a role in the discovery."

"Did you have anything to do with those porn shops?"

Sweeney turned slightly and looked directly at the jury. "Absolutely not. I find the whole situation disgusting. I created those centers to help women, not to abuse them."

"But if not you, then who?"

"I don't know. I'm hoping the police will be able to provide answers someday." Sweeney gazed into the gallery, locking onto Hernandez. "But I understand that a great deal of crime in this town has been linked to a Central American cartel—"

"Objection," Jazlyn said, rising. "The witness is not speaking from personal knowledge. He has no proof of this assertion."

"I believe he already acknowledged that," Dan replied.

"The objection is sustained," Judge Smulders said. "Please stick to what the witness has seen and heard. Without speculation."

He had planted the seed. The jury had to be given some idea who might've been behind the porn scheme. He would just have to apparoach it differntly.

"Earlier, the prosecutor made mention of a Central American cartel. Have you been involved with a cartel?"

"Never. Which is why they're out to get me. And this is not speculation. This is what I know. They want to get into tech. The sex trafficking and organ smuggling businesses are eroding. Tech is the future and they want a piece. That's probably why they targeted my shelters. They tried to put me out of business. It's industrial sabotage."

"What's the current status of the shelters?"

"Prior to my arrest, I was working with the oversight committee to get them up and running again. The police shut them down during their investigation. And I understand why they felt that was necessary. But those shelters were helping people. There was never anything wrong above the ground. I want to see the shelters reopen."

Couldn't do any better than that. Time to get to the heart of the matter. "Sir, did you know Christopher Andrus?"

"I did."

"How did you know him?"

"He was an art dealer and, as I've already explained, I'm an art collector. Or was. He helped me find pieces that were on the market but that, for one reason or another, were not being sold through the traditional channels. Auction houses and such."

"Why would that be?"

"Some sellers wish to avoid the glare of the spotlights. Old families. Old money. They see auctions as undignified. Shabby. And in some cases, people are selling works due to financial problems they don't want the general public to know about."

"Did you buy anything from Andrus?"

"Many times. He knew how to get the best works, and often at bargain prices, due to the distress of the seller and the fact that they needed ready cash in a hurry."

So far, so good. "Sir, we've heard testimony alleging that you met with Andrus at a place called Beachcombers shortly before his death. Is this true?"

"Yes. He and the woman he brought. Tulip Krakowski."

"Was he brokering another painting for you?"

"No. This time, I was the one who was selling. And wished to do so…quietly."

"Can you explain that?"

"I made some unwise investments. It's an axiom of business that you either grow or die. I wanted to grow. But I picked the wrong horse. I invested in a bio-quantum computing venture that ultimately cost almost half a billion dollars. Was supposed to be the next big thing after the next big thing. But it came to nothing. I later learned that some of the investment offering documents had been falsified. The man who promoted the investment is now in prison and there's no way I can get my money back." He paused and, for a brief moment, Dan wondered if he was going to brush away a tear. "Selling one of my paintings was like selling a child. But I had to do it."

"Did you write the check entered into evidence by the prosecution?"

"I did. Andrus said he needed a small sum up front, so I gave it to him. And yes, I used my blue fountain pen."

"Sir, we've heard reports that you became angry during this conversation. Is that true?"

"Absolutely false. I was sad, not angry. Maybe that eavesdropper can't tell the difference. My voice might've risen, but not in anger. In grief."

"Were you having trouble persuading Andrus to sell your paintings?"

"Far from it. He knew what my collection was worth. Even if he only sold half of it, he stood to make a bundle. No, his only concern was the cartel."

He saw Jazlyn straighten, ready to bounce back to her feet if Sweeney crossed the line.

"Can you please explain?"

"Andrus knew the cartel was gunning for me. He was afraid that if he helped me, they might come after him. And if you ask me—they did."

"Objection," Jazlyn said. "Once again the witness is speculating."

Dan turned back to Sweeney without waiting for a ruling. "Do you have any evidence of that assertion?"

"Absolutely. The cartel sent a man to my office to kill me and very nearly succeeded. I got lucky. If I'd been a second slower, it would've been me tumbling out that window."

"Any other evidence?"

"Look how Andrus was killed—it's an obvious mob hit. I'm on trial in the biggest frame of all time. Based on planted evidence. Tainted forensics. A bribed witness. Police who just happened to be there when body parts appeared in my freezer."

"The inner office where the body parts were found had a fingerprint scanner on the door, right? So no one but you could get in."

"That's how it was supposed to work. But it's clear someone either hacked the system or duplicated my fingerprint. I don't know how they did it, but I know it can be done. Since iPhones started using fingerprint ID, apps for overriding fingerprint scanners have been everywhere."

"There's also been talk about a paperweight being used as the murder weapon."

"I doubt that. It's steel, true, but hollow. Swinging that around in a sock and hitting someone's head would've hurt. But I doubt it would kill anyone."

"What happened after the meeting at Beachcombers?"

"Not much. Andrus did not return to the office with me. That security footage was switched. I never saw him again. And I certainly did not kill him. I was as surprised as anyone when..." He swallowed. "When his head rolled out of my ice cream freezer."

"Which obviously led some to believe you committed the murder."

"Look." Sweeney drew himself up, broad shoulders, square chin, earnest expression. "I have not led a blameless life. I will be the first to admit it. I've made mistakes. But that doesn't make me a murderer. I've never taken a life and I hope I never will. But if I did, I wouldn't be stupid enough to leave body parts lying around in a room only I use when I know the police are coming over." His jaw tightened. "This is so obviously a frame I can't believe anyone would be suckered into it. The police have nothing on me. And you know why?"

He looked straight into the jurors' eyes. "Because I did not commit this crime."

CHAPTER FORTY-THREE

DAN KNEW HE WOULD NEVER GET A BETTER EXIT LINE THAN THAT, so he ended his direct. As soon as he stepped back, Jazlyn jumped into the fray with an eagerness—an energy, even—that was intimidating. And more than a little frightening.

Jazlyn's body language sent Sweeney a clear message. I'm not afraid of you. "Mr. Sweeney. Let's talk about the man who tumbled to his death from the window of your penthouse office shortly before your meeting with Andrus."

"Objection." Dan couldn't let this pass without a fight. "We've already addressed this business of dragging in other crimes. Relevance."

"Sweeney raised the incident himself." Jazlyn tried a new argument. "Goes to pattern. The defendant's history of violence and disregard for the sanctity of human life."

Judge Smulders pondered. "I would prefer that the evidence presented concern the crime with which the defendant has been charged. Pattern evidence is problematic at best, and frankly, if you wanted to go down this road, you should've raised the issue at the pretrial."

Jazlyn hung in there. "Your honor, there is substantial evidence—"

"If the evidence is substantial, why haven't you pressed charges? Why isn't he on trial for two murders?"

Exactly what Dan had said during his opening.

Jazlyn persisted. "This is not the first time the other murder has been mentioned. The defendant did it only a few minutes ago."

The judge appeared troubled. He considered. "I will allow you to reference the incident. But I will not allow this to become a cross-examination accusing the defendant of a different crime."

"Understood." Jazlyn returned her attention to Sweeney. "Isn't it true that a man tumbled to his death from the window in your penthouse?"

"Sadly, yes."

"Who was that man?"

"I didn't know him, but the police say his name was Fabian Fuentes. He was an El Salvadoran émigré and is believed to have been involved with the cartel I mentioned."

"You claim you'd never seen him before?"

"True."

"And you weren't in league with his cartel."

"Definitely true."

"And yet somehow Fuentes managed to get into your building and your private offices."

"Yes." Sweeney shifted his weight. "At this point, it's rather clear that my office security needs an upgrade."

"I will submit that he knew how to get in because he'd been there before."

"Incorrect. I believe your office scoured months of security camera footage and never found Fuentes."

"Of course, thanks to your lawyer, we've learned how unreliable that security camera footage is."

"We learned that one substitution has been made. To hurt me, not to help me."

"You say Fuentes tried to kill you."

"And I had bruises to prove it. I visited my personal physician immediately after the incident. I believe he has records and photographs."

"But somehow you, an overweight man in his mid-fifties, were able to overcome a trained assassin from a Central American cartel."

"I didn't get where I am today by being weak. I never quit, and I never give in. But the truth is, I got lucky. He fired once and missed. We wrestled for a long time and I managed to knock away his gun. He lost his balance. I took advantage. The struggle went on for what seemed like an eternity. But I managed to prevail. I tackled him and knocked him into the window. That glass is reinforced and I didn't think it would break. But it did. The bullet had weakened it."

"So you tossed him out the window to his death."

"It was self-defense. Which is why you haven't charged me."

"If you never worked with the cartel, they would have no reason to kill you."

"Wrong. It was my complete refusal to help them that put me on their hit list."

"I have another theory. I think they were angry about the video-porn operation in the basements of your shelters."

"As I've said, I knew nothing about that."

"I think the cartel knew nothing about it. And when they learned their partner-in-crime was running a high-risk but highly profitable operation and not giving them a cut, they were angry. When the operation was exposed, they were even angrier. You ceased being an asset and became a serious liability."

Dan was impressed. He'd had similar thoughts himself. But

Jazlyn managed to piece it together without the assistance of his client.

"You're wrong," Sweeney said, maintaining impressive calm. "I had nothing to do with the cartel or the pornography. And I have to point out, once again, that you have not charged me with any crime relating to the cartel or the video-porn. Which proves you have no evidence."

"Where there's smoke, there's fire."

"No. Where there's smoke, there's a desperate prosecutor trying to make her name by persecuting a prominent citizen. But you don't have the evidence to back up your offensive insinuations. Not on this trumped-up murder charge or any of the rest of it."

Dan and Maria exchanged a look. Sweeney was doing fine, but he wished his client wouldn't bait Jazlyn. He didn't need to make her angrier than she already was.

Jazlyn strode right up to the witness stand, laying one arm on the rail. "Mr. Sweeney...what happened to your power tools?"

Sweeney appeared surprised. Perhaps it was the abrupt change of subject. Dan had no idea what she was talking about.

"My...power tools?"

"You're a bit of a handyman, aren't you? An amateur carpenter? I read that in a magazine article about you."

Sweeney shrugged. "I like to tinker in my spare time. Which I have little of. I have a workshop in the parking garage beneath my office building."

"What do you do there?"

"I've made chairs. Small tables. It's a retreat and a release. Gives me a chance to work with my hands, to build something tangible. Reminds me of the work I used to do when I was younger, before tech became my life."

"What equipment do you have in your little workshop?"

"The usual. Screwdrivers and pliers and such."

"A table saw?"

"Yes."

"A rather large one, in fact."

"I like to work with high-quality woods."

"Hand saws?"

"Certainly."

"Knives?"

"A few."

"Lathes? Electric planers? Plastic tarps?"

"I use the tarps to protect my works-in-progress."

"So this is a fully equipped workshop. The perfect thing for making a cabinet."

"Yes."

"Or dismembering a body."

The sudden silence felt as if all the air had been sucked out of the courtroom.

"That's...absurd." Sweeney's tongue seemed thick and slow. "I would never—"

"That's been the big mystery in this case. Not who did it. That was obvious from the start. But how was the body dismembered? Where? Why is there no blood in your office? Those were unanswered questions—until we discovered your little workshop. I hear the big cartels have workshops just like that. For the same purpose."

"Objection," Dan said, just to interrupt the flow. "This is pure speculation."

The judge shook his head. "Overruled. Counsel may proceed."

"Why didn't you tell the police about your workshop, Mr. Sweeney?"

"They didn't ask."

"You didn't think it was relevant?"

"I still don't think it's relevant."

"You know, the interesting thing about that workshop is

that, even after we learned about it—from a third party, not you
—we couldn't get in. It was locked up tight. So the police
obtained a warrant and forced their way in. But by the time they
got inside, it had been swept clean. Looked brand-new. Like it
had been scrubbed and disinfected for an inspection by a five-
star general." She leaned closer. "Or the police lab techs."

"This is—this is—nonsense," Sweeney sputtered. Dan could
see juror eyes narrowing.

"I also checked with the man in charge of waste disposal at
your building," Jazlyn continued. "He hauls off the trash for the
entire building every morning bright and early. You know what
he said?"

Sweeney's lips thinned. "I'm sure I don't."

"He says you were at the office uncommonly early, the day
after your last meeting with Andrus. In fact, he thought you'd
stayed at the building all night. Your clothes were wrinkled
and...you had an odd smell about you. And you asked to borrow
his truck."

"Your honor," Dan said, "I object. This is hearsay. If Ms.
Prentice has this custodian, put him on the stand."

The judge disagreed. "This is cross. She can ask the question.
If the witness believes the statement is untrue, he's free to
say so."

"Why did you want the truck, Mr. Sweeney?" Jazlyn asked.

"I—I don't—"

"I do in fact have the custodian in the courthouse and I can
call him if necessary. And I have his sworn affidavit. Would you
like to see it?"

Sweeney pushed back in his chair. "If you must know, I was
delivering some furniture I'd made for...a friend of mine."

Dan's eyebrow arched. Sweeney had a friend? He looked
back at Prudence. She didn't appear to know anything about it
either.

"I needed the truck to deliver a little desk and chair set I'd made. And yes, after it was delivered, I cleaned the workshop. That had been a big project and the place was a mess."

"So you disinfected the floor and walls?"

Sweeney looked downward. "I'm...a bit of a germophobe."

Jazlyn looked as if she were about to laugh out loud. "I will submit, Mr. Sweeney, that you took apart Christopher Andrus' body in that workshop using tarps to contain the splatter of blood and flesh. Then you hauled off most of the body, viscera and all, to some undisclosed location. Then you scoured the workshop before the police could search."

"This is a complete fantasy," Sweeney said. He sounded shaken. His voice had a discernible tremor. "A total fabrication. Facts rearranged to fit your fantasy scenario."

"The only remaining mystery is why you kept the head and hands." Jazlyn paused. "Mr. Sweeney, isn't it traditional in organized crime outfits for an assassin to bring the head and hands to the crime boss as proof of death? Or for a rival organization to send the head to an enemy as a warning?"

"I—I wouldn't—"

"I will submit that the meeting at Beachcombers wasn't about selling paintings. You were on mob business. You and Andrus both laundered money for the cartel. Something went sour and your Central American masters wanted Andrus eliminated. You agreed to do the dirty deed for them. You told him some lie to get him back to your office, then you killed him."

"That's absurd! Why would I—"

"You need money. Desperately. What better way to get cash under the table than to execute a mob hit?"

The stir in the courtroom swelled. Several jurors' eyes widened. It was all starting to make a crazy sort of sense...

"The security camera footage is irrelevant," Jazlyn continued. "I don't know if you took him back to your office. I don't care when your DNA fell onto the body parts. But you met with Andrus. Fought with him. And killed him. Brutally. Dismembered his body in your sadistic little workshop, then saved the head and hands so you could collect your payment. What you didn't count on was Detective Kakazu finding them before you could get them to the head of the cartel."

Speaking of…

Dan whipped his head around. Hernandez was no longer in the courtroom.

"That is not true!" Sweeney raised his voice. The jury stared at him, expressions of disgust all too easy to read. "None of this is true. None of it!"

"It's the only explanation that makes sense," Jazlyn said, turning away. "And the jury knows it just as well as I do."

CHAPTER FORTY-FOUR

DAN AND MARIA HUDDLED IN THE DELIBERATION ROOM, TRYING to determine what they could possibly do next. Soon they would have to tell the judge whether they were resting the defense case. They didn't want to end on such a disastrous, incriminating note. But the only way to extend the trial would be to call another witness. And who would that be?

Dinah entered bearing coffee.

Maria grabbed one. "My hero."

Dan tucked his chin. "I thought I was your hero."

"You're my snuggle-bunny. It's not the same."

"But I want to be your hero."

"Get a Starbucks account." She sighed. "Or win this damn case."

"I watched the jurors during Jazlyn's cross," Dinah said. "I don't want to be the bearer of glum tidings, but they were buying it."

"Of course they were buying it," Dan replied. "It made sense. I still don't think Sweeney committed this murder—but Jazlyn told the more compelling story."

"I was surprised Sweeney didn't do a better job of defending himself."

"I know. At times it almost seemed as if he was...holding back. And since when did Sweeney ever hold anything back? He always comes on strong, firing with everything he's got." Dan pressed his hand against his forehead. "I watched the jury, too. They're ready to convict."

Dinah shoved a coffee cup into his hands. "Take. Drink. It may not be as gloomy as all that." She grabbed a coffee for herself. "Garrett found Tulip Krakowski."

Dan sat up straight. "What? When did this happen?"

"A few hours ago. While you were in court. Garrett is bringing her over now and grilling her as he drives. Truth is, she called us. She's been in a hospital, but she heard about the trial. She was the woman at the Beachcombers meeting and she's willing to testify."

"If she can tell the jury the meeting was about paintings and not a cartel hit, that would help. If she can confirm that Sweeney never got angry and in fact needed Andrus to sell paintings, it would be even better."

Dinah glanced at her phone. "Garrett is outside parking."

Dan pushed to his feet. "Maria, call Jazlyn and get to the judge's chambers. Tell him we need more time to prep a last-minute witness. Jazlyn won't like it but, given the circumstances, I think Smulders will let it in. I'm going down to meet Ms. Krakowski."

Dinah's eyes brightened. "You think we still have a chance?"

Dan tilted his head uncertainly. "I think this is the last chance we're going to get."

TULIP KRAKOWSKI WAS A TINY WOMAN WHO, AS IT TURNED OUT, had a huge reserve of strength. When she testified about overcoming the cartel assassin trying to kill her, it was hard not to admire her. But when she told the jury about her ordeal afterward, wandering in the desert, hungry, thirsty, lost—she had the jury hanging on every word.

"Deep down, I didn't think I was going to make it," Tulip said. "But I kept trying. And somehow I managed to survive. I believe it was for a reason. I think I was meant to be here. To tell what really happened."

Dan couldn't have chosen the words better himself. He'd had precious little time to prep her, but he was already impressed by the job she was doing. Despite only recently being released from the hospital, she looked strong. Confident. Underweight, understandably. Light brown hair. Dimple on the right cheek.

"How do you feel? Mentally and physically."

"Fine. The doctors gave me a clean bill of health. And before I left, Vegas PD had a police psychiatrist named Susan Pulaski check me out. Wonderful woman. Said she admired my perseverance and saw no problem with me testifying."

"Do you have any idea who the man who tried to kill you was?"

"He didn't share his name with me and he didn't have any ID on him. The cops still haven't found his body. Personally, I hope it's been picked apart by vultures. But he did speak with a Spanish accent. Which fits, all things considered."

Dan knew what she meant, and he thought the jury did too. The cartel. Always the cartel.

"Let's return to the meeting at Beachcombers. The jury has heard several different accounts of what happened. You were there, right?"

"Yes."

"Why?"

"I came with Kit. I was sort of his apprentice. I know, everyone assumed we were an item, but that just shows how gendered and stereotypical the world is. Kit was married, gay, and not remotely interested in me. But I was more than happy to learn from him. Whether I approved of everything he did or not, he had built a successful life over a long period of time in the art world, and there are not many people who can say that. He was living my dream."

"So you...followed Andrus around?"

"Basically, yeah."

"How did that work out?"

"I learned the ropes but, unfortunately, I learned much more."

"Please explain."

"Kit did more than merely traffic in art of dubious provenance. I know some have speculated that Sweeney was the cartel's money launderer—but they're wrong."

Every juror straightened. Their eyes were riveted to the witness.

"It was Andrus. He sold paintings that had been...liberated by the cartel. He laundered money for the cartel. He was the funnel. Not Sweeney, at least not at the time of this meeting. Sweeney didn't have enough business. But Kit did. I mean, how could anyone verify how much someone paid for a painting, or how much vig they gave the dealer? He'd launder the cartel's cash, then get it back to them by overpaying for something that was worthless or didn't even exist."

The jury was listening. And absorbing. But were they believing?

"Was there anything more to this operation?"

"Yes." Tulip drew in her breath, obviously hesitant to proceed. "Kit got overconfident. He thought he'd discovered a way to skim a percentage of the laundered funds for himself—more than his agreed cut. He underestimated the cartel—a fatal error. The cartel has no patience for people who steal from them. Even though he was useful to them, once they realized he was cheating them—they put out a hit. Alejandro Hernandez himself came to Florida to see that the job got done. Kit's days were numbered and he knew it. He tried to get me to help hide him, but what could I do? I reluctantly agreed to come to this meeting so he would have a witness. He wanted money up front from Sweeney so he could disappear. I wanted nothing to do with any of it." She paused. "As it turned out, attending that meeting was a deadly mistake. I think they concluded Kit and I were working together. So the hit on him was extended to me."

"Did you get any indication that Sweeney was going to carry out that hit?"

"No chance. He needed Kit. Badly."

"One witness said there was a big fight at the Beachcombers meeting."

"I didn't see that. They argued a little, mostly over money, but there was no shouting. Both of these guys were too savvy to put on a show in public. And too desperate. They both needed to find a solution to their problems."

"What did they argue about?"

"Kit didn't want to do anything that would anger the cartel even more. He just needed some major cash so he could get out of town. I think Sweeney suspected as much, but he was desperate too. He wrote the check, but it wasn't nearly enough for what he was asking."

"Did you say anything during this meeting?"

"Very little. I got the distinct feeling we were being watched, and I don't mean by that loser in the next booth. I mean the cartel. Somehow, they found out about the meeting. I got out of there as quickly as I could—but as it turned out, not quickly enough."

"What happened afterward?"

"I got kidnapped and shipped to Vegas to be murdered."

"Did the cartel also kill Andrus?"

"Objection," Jazlyn said. "How could she possibly know? She was abducted and unconscious."

"I can ask her if she knows," Dan replied.

The judge nodded. "Overruled. I will allow the witness to draw reasonable inferences based upon her knowledge of the parties and the situation."

Tulip answered. "I don't know for sure what happened to Kit. But I know the cartel wanted him dead. It's obvious to me that they used the body parts to frame Sweeney."

"Why not just kill Sweeney?"

"They tried that. Didn't work. He's too smart, too well-protected. So they tried something else. Kill Kit, mutilate him, stash body parts in Sweeney's freezer—that would guarantee he'd get the death penalty."

"Objection," Jazlyn said. "This is pure speculation."

"Based upon experience," the judge said. "The jury understands that the witness is theorizing based upon her knowledge of the people involved. Overruled."

Dan continued. "Did you ever see anything that suggested my client killed Andrus?"

"No. Sweeney needed Kit. Kit had served Sweeney well for years. Sweeney was devoted to him."

Devoted. Devoted.

Something was tugging at the corners of Dan's brain. Tulip's story made sense and miraculously turned Sweeney into a victim rather than a murderer. But something about this still bothered him...

Paintings. Laundering. Cash flow...

No, that wasn't it. Something else.

Failure. Passion. Focus.

Somewhere in his head, a critical synapse snapped into place. He was getting warmer...

Intern. Devotion. Devotion. I would do anything...

Oh my God. Oh my God.

That was it.

And now, finally, everything made sense.

"Mr. Pike?" The judge was staring at him.

He realized he'd fallen silent too long. "Your honor, I have no more questions for this witness."

Jazlyn rose. "No cross."

He wasn't surprised. Tulip was obviously telling the truth, and a lengthy cross would only reinforce everything she had said.

Judge Smulders peered down at him. "I assume the defense rests?"

"Actually, no, your honor. We have one more witness to call."

"What purpose—"

"Sorry. But this case is not quite over yet." He whirled around and gazed into the gallery. "The defense calls Prudence Hancock."

CHAPTER FORTY-FIVE

"Objection," Jazlyn said, rising to her feet. "What is this about?"

"This is about," Dan replied, more quietly than usual, "finding out what really happened. Which means we need to talk to someone who actually knows what really happened."

Jazlyn didn't wait for the judge to express his thoughts. "Your honor, Ms. Hancock works for the defendant. She's obviously biased."

"Which I'm sure you will bring out on cross. That hardly means she can't testify."

"She's not on his witness list."

Judge Smulders gave Dan a stern look. "Is that true?"

"Yes." He took a step toward the judge, his eyebrows knitted together. "And I wish I had a fancy excuse, like fraud or newly discovered evidence. But I don't. I can't say we just learned about her, like our last witness. The truth is…I just figured it all out. I should've understood sooner, but I didn't."

"If this woman is not on the list—"

"The jury will never learn what happened unless this witness tells them." His voice was almost pleading. "Don't let my client go to prison because I was so dense. Please. I'm begging you. Isn't learning the truth what matters most?"

The judge cleared his throat. "Madame Prosecutor, did you know about this witness?"

"I knew she existed," Jazlyn said. "I didn't have any reason to believe she knew anything relevant to the murder."

"Did you interview her before trial?"

"Of course. She works closely with the defendant."

"Then I'm going to allow this. There's no ambush here. At best there was a minor procedural problem—"

"Your honor, I—"

Judge Smulders cut Jazlyn off with a wave of his hand. "The defense is not even required to submit a witness list. It's a courtesy, nothing more. I've afforded both sides great leniency during this trial, and that includes you, Ms. Prentice. Because what matters most is not our procedural rules but that the jury gets the information it needs to make a fully informed decision. Defense counsel assures me this witness is important and I trust him, so I'm going to allow it. Your exception is noted."

Jazlyn retreated. Unless Dan misread her, she wasn't that upset. She'd made the objection her job required.

It was just possible that she, like he, had begun to realize that there was more to this case than anyone imagined.

"I object too." This time it came from Prudence herself. She stood in the gallery, just behind the rail. "I've had no notice that I might be called. I don't know anything about this."

The judge tilted his head. "But you are in the courtroom. I'm afraid you're subject to the jurisdiction of the court."

"And if I refuse?"

"Then the sheriff will be happy to escort you to a cell till you change your mind."

She glared at Dan, her eyes like daggers. "This is a farce. More of Pike's trademark courtroom trickery." She pushed through the gate and headed for the stand. "Let's get this joke over with."

In due time. "Your honor," Dan said, "may I have one minute before we begin?"

The judge nodded.

Dan turned to face the gallery—but Sweeney grabbed his hand. "*I* object," he said.

"Sorry. You don't get to do that."

"You work for me."

"And I am acting in your best interests."

"I will not see Prudence subjected to your needling and questioning and—"

"Actually, I'm hoping she'll do most of the talking."

"She has been a loyal employee and I do not want to see her turned into a scapegoat."

"Neither do I."

"I'm telling you—"

He laid a hand on Sweeney's shoulder and suddenly realized it was the first time he had ever deliberately touched the man. "Trust me."

While Prudence settled in, Dan stepped outside the courtroom and called Garrett. It only took a minute to explain what he wanted.

He returned to the courtroom. "Please state your full name."

"Prudence Chastity Hancock."

"And what do you do for a living?"

"I've worked for Conrad Sweeney for the last nineteen, almost twenty years."

"How did you come to be in his employ?"

"I was his intern, originally. When his business was much smaller than it is today, though still successful. I've had the pleasure of watching him turn a successful business into an empire. I've had the privilege of helping him make more donations and perform more charitable work than anyone else in this city. In the history of this city."

"What's your official position?"

She thought for a moment. "I don't know."

"Do you have a title?"

She glanced at Sweeney, then back at Dan. "If so, I don't know what it is."

"You just do what my client tells you to do."

"That's about it."

"In fact, I once heard you say you'd do *anything* for him."

"Look, if you're going to try to accuse me—"

"I'm not going to accuse you of anything." Yet. "I just want the jury to have all the facts. You are aware that my client has been having financial problems, right?"

"Of course. I'm intimately involved in his business. I've helped execute loans and redirect cash."

"You're aware that SweeTech does not have the cash flow it once did."

"Yes."

"You're aware of the porn operations discovered in the basements of the so-called Sweeney Shelters."

"Me and everyone else in the city. But he had nothing—"

"Please just answer the question."

"Yes."

"Has this discovery affected my client's income?"

"Horribly. No one will do business with him, including people Sweeney raised up from nothing. He can't even get people to take a meeting anymore."

"Except Christopher Andrus."

Prudence sighed.

"You knew Andrus."

"I've been involved in many of the art deals. I help Dr. Sweeney with everything."

"And on some occasions, you've acted as his personal security guard."

"It has been my honor to keep him safe. I stay in shape, exercise regularly. I'm trained in several martial arts. I like extreme sports—as I know you do."

"You're my client's all-around all-purpose go-to, aren't you? Were you present when Fabian Fuentes came by to kill him?"

For the first time, she hesitated. "I...No. Wish I had been."

"Aren't you supposed to protect him? Keep him safe? You seem more likely to defeat a cartel hitman than my client."

"As I said, I wish I had been there. My goal is to serve Dr. Sweeney in whatever way I can."

"Your loyalty seems to go...beyond the typical employer-employee relationship."

"We're not lovers, if that's what you're hinting at. Our relationship is strictly professional."

"Yes," Dan said quietly. "That I believe."

"Your honor," Jazlyn said, "I'm trying to be patient, but how is this relevant?"

"I will tie this up immediately," Dan promised. He turned back to the witness. "You had access to my client's office, didn't you?"

"I couldn't get into his little art-cave, if that's what you mean."

"We'll get to that in a minute. I mean the building. The penthouse suite. You had keys, right?"

"Of course. How else could I keep him safe?"

"You had access to his desk?"

She shrugged. "Sure."

"Which means you could access that paperweight. The one the medical examiner speculated could have been the murder weapon."

"I could. But I didn't."

"I believe you. I don't think that was the murder weapon.

But the point is, you had access to virtually everything my client did."

"Except the hidden room. That required a fingerprint ID."

"But you know as well as I do that those scanners can be fooled. Prints can be lifted. Reproduced. Copied. You had access to his office, where his fingerprints were literally all over the place."

"I wouldn't begin to know how—"

"But I recall that you have been in the gallery during some of my previous trials. My teammate Garrett Wainwright found a guy who can take a latent fingerprint and transfer it to the tip of a specially designed glove. These are normally used to fool the fingerprint scanners on iPhones—but they could just as easily be used on the scanner in Sweeney's office. To get inside the private office when my client wasn't around."

Out the corner of his eye, he saw several jurors leaning forward. This was getting interesting.

"I don't know anything about that," Prudence said.

"I saw Colin Baxter, the glove man himself, in the courtroom a few days ago."

"Do you think I'm stupid enough to meet someone like that in a crowded courtroom?"

"No. I think you probably met him someplace secluded nearby, and then he got curious and visited the courtroom. Till you shooed him away."

"You're wrong."

"Did you have access to the woodworking shop on the garage level of my client's office building?"

"I hate that place. Can't stand all that macho, 'Look at me, I made a cabinet' stuff. Give me Ikea any day."

"But you had access, right? Keys?"

"I have master keys. I can open any door in the building."

"And your primary mission in life is to protect my client."

"Yesss…"

"And you've said you would do anything for him."

"I wouldn't murder for him, if that's what you're getting at."

"Even if you knew it would help him?"

"No."

"Even if you knew he'd be...grateful?"

"No."

Dan got right up in her face. "Even if he asked you to do it?"

"He didn't ask me to do it. He didn't want Andrus killed. He needed Andrus."

"Did he need you?"

That threw her for a moment. "He depended on me."

"Did he appreciate you?"

Her jaw tightened. "I would like to think so. Especially after I —" She stopped short.

Dan locked eyes with her. "Especially after you saved his life?"

Prudence leaned back, as if trying to get away. Behind him, Dan saw Sweeney cover his face with his hand.

"I don't know what you're talking about."

"I think you do. Something about this case has always bothered me. Well, more than one thing. My client keeps saying he overpowered Fuentes and I keep thinking...nah. He'd put up a decent fight. But beat a cartel assassin? I can't see that happening." Dan leaned in closer. "But I bet you could mop the floor with him."

Jazlyn rose. "Your honor, relevance. He's talking about a completely different—"

The judge waved her down. "Shush. Overruled."

"I'm right, aren't I?" Dan continued. "Sweeney would've been the one who went out that window but for you, the physically fit, extreme-sports, martial arts expert. You saved his life." He paused. "And even then, he wasn't interested in you. Not in the way that you wanted."

Prudence glared back at him. Then she looked at Sweeney, sitting at the defense table, a sad expression in his eyes.

"It's going to come out, Prudence. Just tell the truth. You don't just admire Dr. Sweeney. You love him. Right?"

Several tense moments passed. And then she gave in to it. "I have loved that man since the first day I walked into his office. He's always kept me around. By his side. But to use me. Not to love me."

"He paid you well. He made you his top assistant."

"Yes. Assistant." Tears welled up in Prudence's eyes. "I didn't want to be an assistant. I wanted to be his partner. I don't care about the ring. Marriage is meaningless. I wanted him to value me. To understand that I had been with him all along, at every critical juncture. SweeTech was as much my success as his. But no. He kept me around—like a faithful puppy dog. A favorite pet." Her voice choked. "Not like someone he loved."

Dan glanced behind him. Maria's lips were parted, gaping. Sweeney pressed his hand against his forehead. And Jazlyn looked like she'd been struck by a bolt of lightning.

"You wanted him to love you?"

"We could have been so happy. We didn't need all the business deals and paintings and cartels. He still had enough money to lead a normal life. He has cash stashed in offshore bank accounts. We could've gone to Fiji and lived like royalty. Together. Forever."

"So," Dan said quietly, "even after you saved his life, he still didn't love you. You realized that all your devotion was for nothing, that you would never be appreciated. That he would never take you into his arms—"

"You heard what he said on the witness stand. Idiot. One bad relationship and he decides to swear off women. I think he's still pining for her, even after all this time. Still pining for his stupid Alice."

Dan's head jerked up. Sweeney's ex was named Alice?

Just like Dan's mother.

"So when you finally realized it was never going to happen, he would never appreciate you, never love you...you plotted your revenge."

"No..." Prudence said, looking down, shaking her head. "No..."

"You're the only person who has access to everything. Fingerprints. The woodshop. Skin flecks all over Sweeney's office. Andrus. The cartel found Tulip but they couldn't find him. Because you'd already dealt with him. In a way that was certain to be blamed on the man who scorned you."

"No..." She continued shaking her head. "No...not...not..."

"If there is anyone in this story who's tough enough to dismember a human body, it's you. You disposed of the rest but kept the hands and head so Andrus could be identified. You put them in that freezer, probably right before the police arrived. My client, having no idea what was in there, brazenly invited the cops in and Detective Kakazu opened the freezer. As you anticipated. Then you asked me to represent Sweeney, which you probably thought would make you the least likely suspect. And it did. For a while. I remember your exact words when you came to my office. 'Dr. Sweeney did not commit this murder. I know that for a fact.'" He paused. "You weren't kidding."

"I gave him everything..." Prudence was murmuring more than talking now. "But he doesn't care...He doesn't care about me..."

"Doesn't he though?" Dan turned slightly toward his client. "I think he's suspected you were behind this for some time. But he never said anything. Even when it looked like he was going down. He did that for you, Prudence."

"You're wrong." She drew her head up, sniffing, wiping her eyes. "You're wrong and you can't prove anything. I should have left that man years ago. The biggest mistake I ever made—"

"The biggest mistake you ever made," Dan said, "was telling

me, back when you visited our office, that you had one of those doorbell cameras installed at your home. That device automatically records everything on your front porch. My techie teammate, Garrett, has been hacking into your system. He's got the footage from the day of the Beachcombers meeting. The cartel couldn't find Andrus because he went to your house after the meeting. With you. And never left alive." His voice grew louder. "How did you lure him over? Private art deal? Under-the-table cash? Sex? Doesn't matter. You never had any intention of doing anything for him. Except killing him. Did he go down easily? Or did you have to bite him first? And then chop him up like butcher's meat."

"That's a lie!" Prudence screamed.

"Is it? Garrett just texted the video footage to me." He pulled his phone out of his pocket. "Let's all take a look."

"*Noooo!*" Prudence leapt out of the witness stand. She flung herself at him, knocking Dan down. His phone skittered across the floor, glass smashed.

All at once, the courtroom descended into chaos. People cried out and leapt from their seats. The jurors were closest to the action, but it was hard to get out of the box. They tripped over each other, adding to the chaos. The judge pounded his gavel furiously but no one was listening.

And Prudence sunk her fingernails into Dan's throat.

He grabbed her arms, but she had a lock on him and he couldn't break it. Those strong gym-girl arms were hard to dislodge.

He saw Maria leap to her feet, Sweeney right behind her. The marshal in the courtroom followed.

"Ma'am, step away!" the marshal cried.

Prudence did not reply. Dan felt the life draining out of him, but thought it best not to struggle. Let the marshal handle it. That was his job.

"Lady, last warning. Step away."

Prudence did not release her grip. The marshal flipped the safety strap on his holster and pulled out his gun. "Lady—"

And at that moment, Prudence pounced. She sprang like a tiger, wrapping herself around the marshal's waist and propelling him backward. He slammed into the judge's bench. The judge ducked and disappeared from sight.

The room filled with panicked screams. People pushed and shoved to get out of the seats.

Dan scrambled to his feet. And when he did, he saw Prudence staring him down.

With the marshal's gun in her hand.

"Get down on the floor! Now!" She waved the gun in the air, threatening everyone in the courtroom.

In the rear, a few people made for the back door. "Touch that door and you're dead!" Prudence shouted.

They backed off.

"Same for the back door, judge. No one's going to chambers. No one's going anywhere."

She strode across the courtroom, passing Maria but making a point of shoving Sweeney aside. "I'm not your little bitch anymore."

She spun around in circles, pointing the gun at everyone in sight. "I'm not anyone's little bitch anymore!" She fired a bullet into the ceiling. The crowd screamed and cowered.

"You think you're so smart, Pike. Well, guess what? I am not going to prison for this. I've given up too much already. I'm not doing time for you, or Sweeney, or this screwed-up system. I don't care if I have to shoot everyone in this courtroom. I'm getting out of here. And if anyone tries to stop me, I'll kill you and rip you apart with my teeth. Just like I killed Andrus."

CHAPTER FORTY-SIX

GARRETT RACED UP THE STAIRS TO THE SECOND FLOOR OF THE courthouse taking the steps three at a time. He sped round the corner and ran toward Judge Smulders' courtroom.

Jimmy was already outside. With four armed sheriffs.

"How'd you get here so fast?" Garrett said, gasping for air.

"Shawna called me when she heard the first shot. I was downstairs getting coffee."

"My phone alert said there was a hostage situation. What the hell is going on?"

"We're not sure. The sheriffs are still gathering information."

"But Dan is in there?"

Jimmy nodded grimly. "And Maria. And Jazlyn."

One of the officers, a tall African American, nodded at Garrett. "You work with Pike, too?"

"I sure do. What's happening?"

"All we know for sure is that the marshal was overpowered. And someone got his gun. A woman."

Garrett looked puzzled. "A woman overpowered—"

Jimmy jumped in. "Prudence."

"Oh." That was believable. "Why?"

"Looks like she's the one who murdered Andrus. And she isn't eager for a lethal injection. So she's holding the entire courtroom hostage—lawyers, spectators, judge, marshal. Everyone."

Garrett pressed his hand against his temple. He'd heard some crazy stuff since he joined this team, but this might be the most insane development yet. "I assume you're assembling some kind of response. Like, an army."

The sheriff shook his head. "We could go in now, just the four of us. We could probably take her out. But not before she killed some of her hostages."

"There must be something you can do."

"Headquarters is assembling a hostage-response team. People trained to deal with situations like this."

"And till then?"

"We wait and see what happens."

THREE HOURS LATER, DAN AND MARIA HUDDLED IN THE JURY BOX, the one place in a courtroom where he had never sat. Interesting view. But at the moment, his attention was focused on a woman who blamed him for her current desperate situation. And she was holding a loaded gun.

What had happened? He'd never liked Prudence. She'd always seemed edgy and aggressive and dangerous. But not insane. It was as if something inside her head snapped in the blink of an eye. Like she'd been teetering on the brink for a long time—and now she'd gone over the edge.

And he was the one who made it happen. He was responsible for everything, including this hostage scenario.

Which couldn't possibly end without someone dying.

Prudence had barricaded both doors and herded everyone in the gallery against one wall, while Dan and the other lawyers and the judge—plus Sweeney—gathered in the jury box. She seemed to almost enjoy ordering people about, pointing the gun in their faces.

She aimed at a middle-aged Latinx juror who appeared terrified. Bullying was unnecessary to keep her in line. Prudence was doing it anyway.

"You didn't believe me when I was on the stand, did you?" Prudence held the gun to the woman's nose. "You thought I was lying."

The woman stuttered but said nothing coherent.

"Answer me!" Prudence demanded.

"I—I—I believed you. When you talked about...about...your boss. Never appreciated you. Wouldn't love you. I've been in... in...something like that." Her eyes lowered. "I know how much it hurts."

Prudence swung the gun around and clubbed the woman on the side of the face. People screamed. Dan rose to his feet, only to feel Maria clutching his hand, yanking at him.

"You can't help her," Maria whispered. "Not now. No heroics."

"You know nothing about it," Prudence spat back at the woman now lying on the ground. She swerved around and faced the jury box. "Do you want to be next, Pike?" She pointed the gun at him.

Dan bit down on his lower lip. If she fired, the bullet could go anywhere. Maria. Jazlyn. Smulders.

He lowered himself into his chair.

"Good." Prudence snarled. "You know this is all your fault, right, Pike?"

"Yes. I know."

"Remember that when the blood starts to flow."

He wrapped an arm around Maria, hugging her tight.

Prudence started pacing again. Her cell phone buzzed and she took it out and shouted some more.

"Got a plan yet, Dan?" Maria whispered.

"I think it's best to leave this to the professionals."

"What professionals?"

He nodded toward Prudence. "She's been talking to some-one. I'm betting that's a hostage negotiator. Maybe an FBI tactical commander. They're trying to get us out safely without anyone being harmed."

"Good luck with that," Maria murmured. "Prudence looks like she's about to completely flip out. And take the rest of us with her."

"They have a routine. Trust, contain, reconcile, resolve. Right now, they're trying to gain Prudence's trust and to contain the potential damage. But Prudence keeps hanging up on them. Which probably impedes negotiations."

"What do you think she wants?"

"I thought I heard the word 'helicopter.'"

"What, an escape copter to Fiji? That's never going to happen."

"I know. But I'm not sure the lady with the gun does."

"She must realize there's no escape. She's sunk."

"And going to prison. For murder. Which is what worries me."

"What do you mean?"

"I bet I can answer that." Jazlyn stood beside them. "Mind if I join you?"

Dan looked up eagerly. "Please do."

She took the chair beside them. "Prudence killed someone and hacked him to bits. That's a death penalty offense, no question. So how much worse can it get if she knocks off a few hostages?"

Dan felt a hollow in his chest. "She has nothing more to lose."

"Exactly. Look at her."

Prudence was patrolling the room, waving the gun, acting

increasingly desperate. She huddled the people in the gallery together, kicking them and shouting at them.

"Maintaining control has to be a strain," Jazlyn said. "Even for her. How long before she realizes it would be simpler to just kill everyone?"

"Probably not long." He looked up. "I'm sorry. I—"

"No," Jazlyn said. "I'm the one who needs to apologize."

"You don't—"

"I'll admit, when I learned you were representing Sweeney, I was appalled. You and I have dreamed about putting him in prison, but when the opportunity finally presented itself, who stood in the way? My friend and colleague. The man who knew better than anyone else how dangerous Sweeney is."

"I had reasons..."

"Yeah. Like the fact that he wasn't guilty. So you stuck to your principles. How many people would've had the strength of character to do that under those circumstances? Not many." She turned, a crooked smile on her face. "And you were right. I'm sorry I've been giving you the cold shoulder. I'm proud to know you. I'm proud you're my friend."

"Likewise," he replied.

"Can I get in on this lovefest?" Maria asked. "Because I feel the same way."

"Definitely," Jazlyn said. "If we get out of here, let's throw a party. We've earned it."

"No joke," Dan muttered. "I feel like I could—" His voice broke off. "Oh no."

He had been watching Prudence while they talked. But now he detected something else. Movement behind the back row of seats.

Someone was creeping around back there.

He did a quick inventory of the hostages.

The marshal was missing.

He was making his move.

Prudence was still screaming. "Did you think you were going to put me away?" She laughed, loud and unnaturally. "Tables are turned now, huh?"

The juror on the other side of her gun stuttered. "W—W—We just want to go home."

"But you were ready to have me killed." She pressed her gun into the man's face. "So why should I treat you any differently?"

"Please don't hurt me. I—I have a wife. Children."

"Is that bragging?"

"No." He held up his hands, as if they might somehow stop a bullet. "No, I—"

"You have everything I wanted but never got. Thanks for the reminder, loser. If they don't find me an escape route, you'll be the first hostage I sacrifice."

He tried to scoot away. "Please, no!"

"In fact, why wait? Why not just do it now? Maybe if I take out a few hostages, they'll start taking me seriously."

"*Please!*" the man cried.

"I'll tell your kids you died screaming, you pansy." She raised the gun and aimed it at his face. "I'm looking forward to seeing your brains splattered against—"

Out of nowhere, the marshal threw himself at her. Dan assumed the man thought it couldn't wait, but he was too far away. He fell short, a few feet away from her.

Prudence whirled and fired.

Everyone screamed. Cried. Shouted. Pushed themselves against the wall, trying to get as far away from her as possible.

Except for the marshal. He lay on the floor. In a pool of his own blood.

CHAPTER FORTY-SEVEN

GARRETT HUDDLED OUTSIDE THE COURTROOM DOOR, TRYING TO stay out of the way while getting some idea what the law enforcement plan might be.

He couldn't help but notice that more armed officers were appearing regularly. But so far, no one had done anything.

They set up a negotiation center in one of the deliberation rooms. He'd seen a woman he knew named Meredith Burnside enter. Back when he was in the prosecutors' office, she was considered the leading hostage negotiator in the state. If anyone could contain the impending explosion, she could. But that was no guarantee of success.

If this turned into a bloodbath, Prudence could take out many hostages before she went down. Including Dan. And Maria. And Jazlyn.

Dinah had heard the news as soon as she got out of class and came running up the stairs. Garrett suggested that she return to the office but she ignored him. "That's my brother in there. I'm staying put." He didn't like it, but he couldn't argue with her.

He spotted a senior police officer he'd known for decades,

Sam Evans, who passed close enough that Garrett felt justified asking a question. "Can you give me an update?"

Evans glanced over his shoulder. "I'm not supposed to talk to civilians."

"Our friends are in there." He tilted his head toward Dinah. "And her brother."

Evans frowned. "We're trying to negotiate with the woman. But she's completely off the rails. Won't listen to reason. They think she's had a complete breakdown. Which makes it difficult to arrange any kind of rational compromise."

"What does she want?"

"Out. Away. Doesn't want to be executed. Which, you know, who could blame her, but she's going about it the wrong way."

"Is there any chance she could actually escape?"

He craned his neck. "She's asking for a copter."

"To do what? Land on the courthouse lawn?"

"Basically, yeah. One pilot. She'll reveal her destination when she's safely in the bird."

"Any chance of success?"

"Not that I can see. We've posted snipers all around the building. Even if she surrounds herself with hostages, I doubt she could make it to the copter. Even if she did, they'd track it. It can't fly forever. Eventually she'll have to land. And as soon as she steps out—" He pointed a finger like a gun. "Blam."

"So she's dead already."

"If she doesn't surrender. The problem is..." He glanced at Dinah, then lowered his voice. "How many innocents could she kill before we kill her?"

Dan glanced at his watch. Four hours had passed since Prudence took hostages. Everyone was tired and dripping with sweat. She'd spent the whole time pacing, alternately shouting on her phone and shouting at hostages. The courtroom was a powder keg. One he very much feared was about to blow.

Jazlyn's hands were covered with blood. She'd been attending to the wounded marshal, trying to prevent him from bleeding out. He'd heard Prudence shouting about the wounded man to the negotiator, but so far, she hadn't allowed a medical team inside.

Jazlyn wiped her hands on her jacket. "The judge told me there was a first aid kit behind the bench. That was a godsend. I put pressure, then a bandage on the wound. I don't think the bullet hit any major organs. I've slowed the bleeding...but still."

Dan nodded. "He can't last forever. Not without medical attention."

"He's in pain. I think he's gone into shock. Eventually, the pain and the blood loss will cause him to lose consciousness. And after that..."

"Right."

"I'm returning to my patient," Jazlyn said.

"I'll go with," Maria said. "I probably can't help. But at least I can be moral support."

"Much appreciated."

The last thing Dan wanted was Maria in the gallery, where Prudence spent most of her time. But she wasn't any safer with him. Prudence had constantly taunted him, threatened him. If she decided to take out a hostage, he would be at the top of the list.

To his surprise, Sweeney plopped into the vacated seat beside him. "Got any thoughts?"

"On how we get out alive? No. You knew how upset Prudence was. Didn't you see this coming?"

"Did I foresee that Prudence would lose her mind and take the courtroom hostage? No, sorry, I didn't."

"She's a proactive woman. Not one to take anything lying down. She won't go out without a fight." He turned. "You must've suspected Prudence was the killer. That's why you were holding back when Jazlyn crossed you. Why didn't you say something?"

Sweeney sighed heavily. "Prudence has been with me for many years. She knows about...my operations. She's seen the books. The real books, not the ones we send to lawyers and auditors."

"She can prove you worked with the cartel. She could put you away for life."

Sweeney gave a small nod. "I never thought she would. I was...aware of her attachment to me. Used that to keep myself safe. But you seem to have blown that. Just like you've blown so many other things in my life."

"If you're waiting for an apology...it will be a long wait."

Sweeney almost chuckled. "That was a bluff, right? In court, I mean. With Prudence. You didn't really have any doorbell-cam footage."

"Garrett was working on it. But he hadn't had enough time. And I would've had a hard time getting hacked security footage admitted into evidence. And I didn't know for certain she killed Andrus at her home. I'm surprised Prudence didn't see through me."

"Clearly she is not at her best at the moment."

A long silence fell between them. Dan watched Prudence pace back and forth. She seemed to become more agitated with each step. How long before she started killing people?

This was probably not the time, but he decided to go there anyway. "So your former flame's name was Alice?"

"I'm surprised you haven't figured it out. You got everything else, eventually. But you've always had a blind spot when it comes to your mother, haven't you?" Sweeney drew in another deep breath and, for once, Dan thought he detected a tiny ounce of regret. "Yes, I knew your mother. Long before she knew your father. Or Fisher. She threw me over. Said I would never amount to anything."

Dan felt a catch in his throat. "Guess you showed her."

"Depends on how you look at it. Your father ended up in prison because he killed Fisher to protect your mother. And I'm..." His head fell. "Dying. In more ways than one."

"I was right, though. You were the other person in the cop car. With Fisher. During the gang shootout. When Fisher was killed."

Sweeney sighed. "I did promise you answers if you won my case. Which you kinda sorta did." He stretched his legs out, propping them up on the rail. "I was going to kill the bastard myself. I knew he'd threatened Alice. Sure, she didn't want me. But I still loved her and I wanted to protect her. Your father beat me to it." He looked up reflectively. "He was a good man, Ethan. And you, Daniel Pike, are just like him. Too damn much like him, in fact."

Down in the gallery, Dan heard Maria speak. "This man has lost consciousness." She was talking about the marshal. "He's dying."

Prudence spun on her. "He brought it on himself. That's what happens to people who get in my way." She waved the gun back and forth, so wildly she could potentially hit anyone or anything. "That's what will happen to all of you if you try anything."

"But he's dying," Maria said, her eyes wide and pleading.

Prudence swung the gun around. "And you will too if you don't shut the hell up."

Without even thinking about it, Dan rose from his chair.

"Pike," Sweeney said. "What are you doing?"

Slowly, Dan walked out of the jury box and started toward the gallery.

"Pike. Don't be a fool."

Dan kept walking.

He'd waited long enough. These people had suffered long enough. Hostage negotiation was not working. And Prudence had directly threatened Maria.

He'd caused this mess. And now, by God, he was going to end it, one way or another.

"Prudence," he said, softly, evenly, not insistently. "Give it up."

She laughed in his face. "Just like that? Because the great almighty Dan Pike says so?"

"You can't get away. You know that as well as I do."

"Just watch me."

"There is no realistic scenario that allows you to escape. They're not going to give you a copter. And even if they did, you wouldn't get far. They'd track you. You'd have to come out eventually."

"If they try that, I'll take everyone in sight down with me."

"Which will not improve your situation in the slightest." He took another tentative step forward. "Give it up."

"You must be joking."

"I'm not." He held out his hands. "This game is over. Give me the gun and let these people go home."

"Stay back." She raised the gun to eye level. "Do you think I won't shoot you? I'd rather see you go down than anyone here."

"Really? Are you angry at me?"

"Yes! And him." She swung round toward Sweeney. "That fat bastard who led me on all these years. Let me be his devoted slave while he took advantage of me year after year."

Dan shook his head. "It's not him, either. That's not who you're mad at." He paused. "You're mad at yourself."

Prudence made a dismissive sputtering noise. "Spare me your amateur psychiatry."

"You've wasted years serving someone who didn't deserve you. But you don't have to throw good years after bad. Make a fresh start. Build a better life."

"Where? Behind bars?"

"It's been done before. Gandhi. Mandela—"

"Maybe you haven't noticed, Pike, but I don't give a damn about world peace."

"I was thinking more of your inner peace." He took another tentative step forward. "Please. Give it up, Prudence."

"I will shoot you, Pike." She stiffened her outstretched arm, but that only made it wobble more. "I will."

"You won't." He kept walking. "You've got the goods on Sweeney. You can put him behind bars—for a crime he actually committed. Justice will be done." He looked at her with his most earnest expression. "No one needs to die."

"Except me." Prudence appeared to be losing some of her steel. "They'll give me the death penalty."

"Turn state's evidence. Tell them what you know. Lead them to the documents, the offshore bank accounts. If you can give the cops the goods on your boss and the cartel—"

"And I can," she interrupted.

"Perfect. Then you can make a deal. They won't let you walk, but you can get the death penalty off the table."

"I'll be in prison for the rest of my life."

"Maybe." He allowed himself a small smile. "Depends on how good your lawyer is."

Her left eye twitched. "Is that an offer?"

"Yes. The case against Sweeney ended the instant you confessed, so I no longer represent him. I can represent you. If that's what you want."

Her arms slowly lowered. "And...And you would do that?"

"I would."

"That's a real offer?"

"That's a promise."

"And you could get me off?"

"No. But I can get you the best deal you could ever possibly get. And this ordeal will be over." He took another step. They were barely two feet apart. "Let this end, Prudence. Let this marshal get the attention he needs before you have another death on your hands."

Her arm dropped. "All I ever wanted was to be loved." The ice had broken. The anger was gone. Tears streamed from her eyes. "Is that so much to ask? I just wanted someone to love me."

"You're not the first person to let their heart get in the way of their head." He stepped forward and took the gun from her. "And sadly, you won't be the last."

CHAPTER FORTY-EIGHT

DETECTIVE KAKAZU STORMED INTO BEACHCOMBERS. HE DIDN'T normally like to attract a lot of attention when he did his work. But just this once, he didn't care. Sergeant Pemberton trailed behind him.

"You got the warrant?" Kakazu asked.

"Ready to serve." Pemberton smiled. "This will be a pleasure. You think we should do it in here? He may have...friends."

Kakazu passed through the bar, scanning for his quarry. "I'm not letting this slimy fish slip through my fingers. He knows how to disappear. If he leaves the country, he'll be out of my reach."

Kakazu arrived at a booth near the rear. "Alejandro Hernandez?"

The elderly man looked up. He sat opposite a much younger man. "Who wishes to know?"

"I'll take that as a yes. You're under arrest."

Hernandez laughed. "You have nothing on me."

Kakazu yanked the man up by the collar. His younger associate started to rise, but Hernandez waved him down. "That may have been true yesterday. But not today. Prudence

Hancock has delivered a treasure trove of fascinating information. And your former underling, Santiago, has turned state's
evidence. He's testifying against you. And what he has to say
will put you away permanently."

"Then he is a dead man."

"Don't think so. We'll hide him. Protect him."

"We will find him."

"You will not do anything, because you will be behind bars.
And if you think you'll run your cartel from prison, forget it.
Santiago has named names. Your cartel is finished."

"We will see."

"Indeed we will." Kakazu snapped the cuffs over Hernandez'
wrists. "Come to think of it," he added, "let's take your friend,
too."

Jose slid out of the booth and raced toward the front door.

"Should I chase him?" Pemberton asked.

"Don't bother. Let the boys outside do it."

"This is a farce," Hernandez bellowed. "I demand to see my
lawyer."

"In time." Kakazu noticed the crowd gathering. "And tell
your associates to stand down. I left many officers outside. If
you start a riot, people will get hurt. Starting with you."

Hernandez spat in his face. "Fool. I will be out in an hour."

"Not this time. We're charging you with sex trafficking,
organ smuggling, conspiracy, incitement to riot, incitement to
murder, murder-for-hire, and about a dozen other charges.
There is no judge on earth stupid enough to put you back on the
street. No one you can bribe. No one you can threaten. You're
going to jail."

Hernandez snarled and struggled, but Kakazu held him
tight.

"I have friends on the inside, you stupid policeman. Many
friends."

"Thanks for the reminder." Kakazu whipped out another

pair of cuffs and, without warning, snapped them across Sergeant Pemberton's wrists.

"What the hell?"

"Don't even start. You're the mole. Sweeney's little plaything. Probably working for the cartel as well. Did you think we would never figure it out?"

Pemberton clenched his teeth together. "I don't know what you're talking about."

"I guess you inherited Sweeney's sense of invulnerability. Except now he's going down for the count. And so are you."

"You can't make this stick."

"I can. Dan was suspicious of you the first time he met you. And I became suspicious when we visited SweeTech and you knew the way from the elevator to the office, though you said you'd never been there before. I totally baited you in the lab when we discovered who the body parts in the freezer belonged to. I kept Andrus' name out of the media for twenty-four hours, but you leaked it to Sweeney. There was no other way he could have known."

"You're just guessing. You have no real proof."

"We'll see." Kakazu swerved Pemberton around and pushed him toward the door right behind Hernandez. "Face it, Pemberton, you're looking at a long prison stay. And," he added, "I hear they don't much like cops in there. I hope whatever Sweeney gave you was worth it. Because the rest of your life is going to be a living hell."

CHAPTER FORTY-NINE

DAN HURRIED OUT OF THE COURTROOM BACK TO HIS CAR. HE didn't want to be late. They were planning a celebration at the office. Food. Drink. Gloomhaven. And a big surprise for Maria.

He was halfway down the sidewalk when he was approached by a man he did not recognize. About thirty years older than he was, give or take few years. Small man. Still trim for his age. Thin white hair at the top. Casual dress. "Excuse me. Daniel Pike?"

Dan paused. He wasn't normally suspicious of strangers, but given all he'd been through lately, it was hard not to be. "Do I know you?"

"We've never met. Though I would be honored to shake your hand." He extended his own.

Dan hesitated. Something about the man was familiar. "And you are..."

"My name is Benjamin J. Kincaid. My friends call me Ben."

"I know that voice." Dan's eyes widened like balloons. *"You're Mr. K!"* He almost dropped his backpack.

Ben laughed. "Guilty as charged. K for Kincaid."

"But—But—I can't believe it. You really exist."

"And I decided it was time we met in person. What better location than a courthouse?"

"Why now?"

"That's a good question. And a bit of a long story."

"I've got time. Why don't you get in my car? Come back to the office. Your office, really, since you're paying the bills. Meet the whole gang—"

Ben raised his hands. "I can't do that. And I'm going to have to ask you to keep this conversation confidential."

"But—why?"

Ben relaxed, leaned against Dan's car. "I'm a lawyer, too."

"We always guessed as much, but—"

"I live in Oklahoma. Had a good career. Still pop up in the courtroom every now and again."

"You must've made a fortune at it."

"Not really. I had a bad habit of representing people who needed help but couldn't pay their bills."

Dan grinned. "You were the original last chance lawyer."

"I guess I was at that. Anyway, to cut to the chase, my father was the one who made a fortune. I mean billions. He was a physician, but most of his wealth came from a cardiac surgical device he invented, magnified by some extremely wise investments. Turned out his invention didn't work as well as he thought, but he made millions before that was discovered."

"And he left the wealth to you."

"No. He cut me out of his will."

"Ouch. Sorry."

"Don't be. We never saw eye to eye on anything. When he died, the money went to my mother. But now she's passed, and everything has gone to me and my sister Julia, who is…keeping a low profile. She asked me to manage the money, so I do. But it's far more than our families will ever need. So I decided to make some investments of my own."

"You started the Last Chance Lawyer firm!"

"Exactly. So law could be practiced the way it should be, without billable hours and meritless cases taken for financial reasons while deserving clients are ignored because they aren't rich. What I like to think every lawyer wants to do but can't." He paused. "For you, I made it possible."

"Why have you stayed in the shadows?"

"I thought it was best. I didn't want conspiracy theories rising up about how I'm using big money to promote my socialist agenda. And I didn't want my family in the line of fire."

"Why me? Why St. Petersburg?"

"You think you're the only one? Dan, I've got Last Chance Lawyer firms all over the country. I believe lawyers can and should be a force for good, and you've proven me correct time and time again. Defending the unpopular. Freeing the innocent."

"Our firm is only one of many?"

"But the best of the lot. The first time we talked I said I'd had my eye on you for some time. Sure, you had a tarnished rep, but I was convinced that if I stepped in and made it possible for you to have the kind of practice you wanted, you'd pay it forward a thousand times over. And I was right."

Dan felt as if he'd been struck by lightning. "I—I literally don't know what to say. I feel like I'm meeting my...my surrogate father."

"I'm okay with that. You would make any father proud."

A thousand thoughts raced through Dan's brain. He had so many questions he didn't know where to begin. "Why are you revealing yourself to me now?"

Ben cleared his throat. "Because of the way you handled this last case I gave you. Representing the man you despised most. You've always had a passion for justice. And I liked that. That's important to me. But I wanted to put your feet in the fire and see how committed to your ideals you really were."

"You were testing me."

"And you passed with flying colors. I know how hard it was

for you. I once had to represent a white supremacist. Toughest case I ever tackled. But I did it because it was the right thing to do and an innocent man was saved." Ben handed Dan a small briefcase. "Take this. I know, you prefer backpack to briefcase. But I'm the older model."

"What is it?"

"The schematics for my entire operation. All the Last Chance Lawyer firms. You see, Dan—I'd be honored if you would take over the reins."

"You're joking."

"I'm not getting any younger, and my wife Christina wants to travel more. She's still never seen France and she's getting cranky about it. Our daughters are old enough that we can take more time for ourselves. And I think it's time. I owe Christina that much. Much more actually." He smiled. "But if I'm going on an extended vacation, someone else needs to have their hands on the tiller."

"You mean—I'd be the new Mr. K?"

"No, dude, that's my name. You can be Mr. P."

Dan pressed his hand against his forehead. "I feel like...like I'm Charlie Bucket and Willy Wonka just offered me the choco-late factory."

"I want you to feel that way. It's a lot of work. Finding the right cases. Screening the clients. But it's also rewarding. When it turns out right. Like it always has with you."

"Could I still handle some cases myself?"

"If you've got time. It would be a crime if I deprived the world of your legal talents."

"Can I—Can I have some time to think about it?"

"Sure. Take a day. Then I'm going to start booking flights. Because I can already tell you're going to do it."

"Can I talk to Maria about it?"

"Of course. Keep her close and treat her well. She's perfect for you. I should know. Remember, I chose her even before I chose you. And I arranged for the two of you to meet."

"You're sure about this?"

"My wife is. And she understands people better than I ever will."

Dan thumbed through the file. "Man. You have a lot of these firms."

"And we could afford more. I don't want you to just maintain. I want you to expand. I want you to create a shining example of what legal practice could and should be. Who knows? Maybe it will catch on."

Dan swallowed. "This is a big responsibility."

"But you're up to it." He placed his hand on Dan's shoulder. "Who knows? Maybe one day every lawyer will be a Last Chance Lawyer."

CHAPTER FIFTY

As soon as Dan stepped through the front door, he was attacked—by a small girl.

"Esperanza!" Dan beamed. This was the girl who had launched his career with the Last Chance Lawyers. The one he saved from deportation and who Jazlyn later adopted. Seemed appropriate. She'd been there at the last major turning point in his life, and she was here now, at what appeared to be the next one.

"Hey, Uncle Dan. Thank you for saving my mommy."

He shrugged. "I didn't...really..."

"The hell you didn't." Jazlyn strode up and kissed him on the cheek. "You saved us all."

"Okay," Maria said, jumping between them. "That's enough of that. No more fraternization."

Jazlyn laughed. "No worries. He's all yours. I'm too busy being the DA and a mommy. I have no personal life."

Maria shrugged. "Personal lives are overrated."

"Hey," Dan said, "what does that mean?"

"Nothing, nothing. What took you so long?"

"I got an offer that you are not going to believe."

"What a tease you are. Spill."

"In a minute." He spotted Jake Kakazu standing with a woman he didn't know. "Jake. I'm so glad you could come."

"Least I could do for the man who has almost emptied my cold case file. We've arrested Hernandez. Almost two dozen of his operatives. And by the way, the police mole was exactly who you thought it was."

"And Sweeney?"

"Turned himself in, believe it or not. I thought he'd try to skip to Argentina as soon as he was released from the murder charge. But he knew the game was over."

"I think what happened with Prudence hit him hard. I'm probably wrong, but...it's just possible he's an actual human being. With feelings and everything. And of course...his remaining days are numbered. Perhaps he decided he didn't want to spend them running and hiding."

Maria nodded. "Any word on Tulip?"

"Mr. K has agreed to cover her ongoing medical expenses. She's going to need a lot of skin care. And she may have other health complications from her ordeal. Get this—Bernard Jamison has offered to give her the art internship she didn't get from Andrus. For a fee, of course. Tulip is very excited about it."

Kakazu glanced at the woman standing behind him. "Oh, where are my manners? Dan, this is Teresa Crosswaite. She's a lab tech. She's the one who ID'd Andrus."

Dan arched an eyebrow. "So glad you could come to our celebration."

"Glad to be here," she said. "I hear you're a gourmet chef. I've been trying to improve Jake's palate. For all his upper-class education, he eats like a five-year-old."

"I'm sure you can turn him around."

Dinah raced up clutching a small card. "I got an A. I got an A!"

"Um, context, Dinah."

"In my legal assistant class. I just took the final. And I passed. I can get licensed and everything."

"Glad to hear it. Since we've been treating you like a legal assistant for weeks. You're going to be a valuable asset to the firm. Our best ever legal assistant."

Dinah made a snorting noise. "Forget that. I'm going to law school next."

Kakazu grinned. "Better look out, Dan. I think she's gunning for your job."

"Funny you should say that. It's just possible there's…going to be a vacancy soon."

Maria gave him a sharp look. "Does this relate to your surprise?"

"Oh no. That's something different. I went house shopping today."

Maria blinked several times rapidly. "House…shopping?"

"Yeah. And I think I found a humdinger. Not far from here. On Snell Isle. We could walk to work. Together."

"Together?" She continued blinking. "You mean…this place would be for…?"

"If you approve. I told the Realtor I'd talk to you first and then—"

Maria wrapped her arms around his neck. "I approve." She kissed him long and hard.

Dinah jumped up and down. "My best friend and my brother. This is perfect."

Esperanza ran up and wrapped her small arms around both of them. "I'm going to have an aunt!"

Everyone laughed. Jazlyn was the first to ask a sober question, several moments later. "Does this new house come with… any jewelry?"

"I don't care," Maria said, before Dan could answer. "As long as we're together."

A harsh noise emerged from the kitchen. Jimmy and Garrett

entered tooting on kazoos. And carrying large platters over their heads.

"I know, Dan," Jimmy said. "you probably planned to cook. But I had a different idea."

"We decided," Garrett added, "that just this once, we'd prepare the food."

Dan's lips parted. "I am impressed. That is so thoughtful."

"You deserve a night off," Jimmy replied. "Tonight, we just want you to relax."

"We've got a wide array of dishes," Garrett said. "Plenty for everyone."

They lowered the platters and Dan scanned them. Soup, sandwiches, salads...

"Wait a minute. Is this takeout from Panera Bread?"

Jimmy jabbed him in the side. "We said we prepared food. We didn't say we cooked."

Dan nodded. "Probably just as well."

Kakazu cut in. "Okay, one last thing before this celebration disintegrates into a total lovefest. I've been working on a little project at the police department. Ever since the Sweeney defamation suit. Since you uncovered the truth about...you know. Your father."

Dan's expression fell. "I'm not sure this is the time..."

"Bear with me a minute, please. Dinah, you're included. I know you and Dan had different fathers but I also know Ethan cared about you very much. He sacrificed everything to make sure you were safe." Kakazu turned back to Dan. "I know your dad lost his badge when he was arrested, but most of the officers and I think he was a hero. It took some work but...we got all the bad stuff expunged from his record. Ethan Pike is now listed as retired in good standing. And I got this." Kakazu reached into his jacket and withdrew a small black box. "This is your dad's badge. Reinstated. Most officers here in Sunshine

City take their badge with them when they retire. I want you to have your father's."

Dan found it hard to speak, so he didn't say anything. Maria squeezed his arm tightly.

"Thank you," he managed finally.

"The honor is mine," Kakazu said. He stiffened, then offered a formal salute. "This is for Ethan Pike. That man was a hero. Just like his son."

Late that night, after the party ended, Dan fulfilled a promise he had made to Dinah long before.

"I'm sorry we didn't get to this sooner."

"It's okay. You've been a little busy."

"True." He trudged through the cemetery, shining a flashlight till he found the headstone. "I took you to visit our mother at the home. But I've never brought you here."

He shined a light on the tombstone. ETHAN NATHANIEL PIKE.

"He was a great man," Dinah said softly.

"And he loved you very much. And Mom." Dan paused. "And me."

Dinah put her arm around him.

"My father used to talk about keeping the faith. And boy did he ever. Justice for everyone, that was his credo. As a police officer, he tried to make sure everyone was treated fairly."

"The same thing you've done. As a lawyer."

"I suppose. But Dad made the ultimate sacrifice for you and Mom. He was so brave. Braver than anyone I've ever known."

He reached into his coat pocket and withdrew the badge, then spread it open and gently laid it on the grave.

"I know how much this would've meant to you, Dad. So I

wanted to make sure you saw it. One way or the other. Clean record. All honors restored. And you had a lot of honor."

He wiped his eyes, then reached back and took Dinah's hand.

"I guess this story has come full circle, Dad. Your sacrifice was not in vain. You showed me how to build a life worth living." He inhaled deeply, fighting back the tears. "I kept the faith, Dad. And it was all because of you."

SNEAK PREVIEW OF SPLITSVILLE

William Bernhardt's next legal thriller, *Spiltsville*, will be released May 18, 2021. And who will be the lead character? Reread Chapter 21 of this book and see if you can figure it out.

Here's a sneak preview of *Splitsville*:

His wife was the easiest to kill. His daughter was the hardest.

But they were all dead now, and soon to be buried in a mass grave beneath the terrace. One wife. Five children. Two dogs.

Darien stirred the wet concrete in the wheelbarrow. Once he finished disposing of the bodies, he would disappear and no one would ever know what happened to any of them. No one but him.

The remains would be discovered, eventually. Busybodies or relatives would break into the home. Someone might notice that part of the terrace had been resurfaced. In time, someone would start digging. But by then he would have a new life elsewhere, with a new name, a new path, and a very different calling.

His true destiny began today.

It didn't have to happen like this. She forced his hand. How much was a man expected to tolerate, and for how long? The perpetual whining. The endless self-martyrdom. The woman was so busy playing her own violin that she couldn't hear a word he said. He had tried to help her. Again and again. But she wouldn't listen. She always found some trivial fault to complain about. Ignoring all he did for her. For all of them. Resenting him when she should appreciate him. When she should worship him.

You are so charming, she said. Everyone thinks you're wonderful. They have no idea what you really are.

That part was true. They had no idea...and neither did she.

She rallied the children around her, using them as a shield and a ransom. She isolated him, distanced them from him. She would win the battle by winning the children, or so she thought. The offspring became the spoils of war.

She left him no choice.

She didn't think he was serious, not at first. But when he raised the shovel over her head, she realized how wrong she had been. He would never forget the expression on her face, the change wrought in an eyeblink when she understood how disastrously she had miscalculated.

Blood gushed from her head. With the second blow, hot red tendrils splashed across the terrace. Each swing of the shovel spread more splatters across the ceiling, his face, his hands. Black blood puddled on the barbeque.

Then he heard Abigail scream.

His second daughter, usually at her mother's side, was the first to see what he had done. Her voice was an earsplitting siren that shattered his already jangled nerves. Until then, he had options. He could've stopped it before the cancer spread to the children. But after that, he had no choice. The story would not end until all the plot threads were sewn together.

One by one the children ran out of the house, panicked, terrified. And one by one he knocked them down like targets in a shooting gallery. Grit. Bone. Blood. At one point, his hands were so slick he could barely grip the shovel. But he managed to finish the job.

Strangely, he did not feel sick afterward. He did not collapse. He did not vomit. If anything, he felt elated, surging with the natural high produced by a job well done.

Now he could work in peace, stirring the concrete and digging the grave. Afterward, he would have to clean the whole area. That would be time-consuming—but he had all the time in the world. No one could see him. No visitors were expected. He worked all night long, sometimes humming to himself. He knew the first day of his new life had arrived.

A sailing expedition might be the thing to clear his head and, after that, a change of venue. Happily, he had always maintained an escape hatch. Money. Transportation. Safe house. All waiting.

Once the grave was finished, he returned to the pile of bodies. His wife should enter first, with her sad minions piled on top. They could be attached to her apron strings for eternity and—

Wait. Something was different. Something had changed.

It took him several moments to realize what it was.

Someone was gone.

He rummaged through the pile, shoving bodies aside and taking a blood-stained inventory.

Two were missing. His oldest daughter and his youngest. The toddler. Annalise. The baby of the family.

Perhaps his job was incomplete. Perhaps he did not see as clearly as he thought.

They could not have been gone long. And where could they go on foot this early in the morning, injured and alone? He had purposefully bought a home far from prying neighbors. He had time.

He grabbed his shovel and started running.

Elizabeth didn't know what had happened or what she could do about it. All she knew was that somehow, miraculously, she was still alive. Like an abrupt burst of light in the darkness, her consciousness had returned. She felt stunned, disoriented. What was happening? Why had Father tried to kill her? She felt sticky with blood, and the stench surrounding her was intense, sickening. This, she realized, must be what death smells like.

Her mother and siblings lay beside her, bloody and still—except one. She saw her baby sister, Annalise, stir slightly. She was alive. But that would end if her father noticed. Somehow, Elizabeth had to get both of them out of here without him noticing.

She tried to be quiet. Father was busy shoveling and didn't seem aware of what was happening behind him. He was lost in his own private world. She would take advantage of that.

The night was pitch black, but maybe that was to her advantage. It would be hard for him to see them in this inky darkness. Or so she hoped.

Their estate was almost a mile from any other homes, but if she could get Annalise into the nearest neighborhood, surely someone would come to their rescue.

She had to move quickly. Once Annalise was fully conscious, she would probably not remain silent or still. She couldn't possibly comprehend what was happening. Annalise would be even more horrified than she was.

Quietly, she rose to her feet, scooped up her sister, and raced out of the backyard.

She ran track one year in grade school. She didn't last long because she wasn't very good, but she learned a few things. Don't look back. Point your toes straight ahead. She couldn't swing her arms because she was carrying a little girl who seemed to weigh nothing at first and seemed to weigh two tons now. Every part of her ached, but she ignored that and focused on the road, the destination. She was Annalise's only hope of survival.

She could imagine what she must look like. She could feel blood on her mouth, caked and smeared. The flat side of the shovel had struck her on the head, knocking her to the ground. How had she survived? She didn't know, but it didn't matter. She had a job to do.

She was not going down without a fight. She would fight for herself and her beautiful baby sister.

Tears flowed from her eyes with such intensity that they soaked the collar of her shirt. Waves of grief rippled through her. She saw what Father did to the others. Mother didn't have a face anymore. He almost decapitated her. And then he started on Abigail, and Chris, and Donny. Maybe he was tired by the time he got to her. Maybe he was too far removed from reality to notice that he hadn't killed her. Maybe—

She felt Annalise stir in her arms. "Lizzie?"

She *was* alive. And awake. "You're okay, sis. You're fine."

"Why...are you carrying me?"

It was hard to talk and run at the same time. "Can't explain now."

"Daddy...hit me."

"I know, honey. He hit all of us."

"Why?"

"I don't know. Something...isn't right." She tried to keep her voice flat, to mask the terror she felt.

"Where we going?"

"Someplace safe."

"Is Mommy dead?"

She bit her lip. "I don't know. We just need to get somewhere safe."

She saw the gates at the entrance to Forest Glen, just as the sun's corona crept over the horizon.

She could do this. She knew she could. She—

"Elizabeth! Come back this very minute!"

Her body seized up. It was him. He was not far behind them and closing fast.

She knew her track coach wouldn't approve, but she glanced over her shoulder.

He was swinging the shovel.

A shudder raced through her, like razor blades slicing her into pieces.

She knew she couldn't outrace him, not with Annalise in her arms. But if she could just make it to the first house, the one on the corner...

The house had a small open window on one side. Was someone awake? Did they like the night air? She couldn't be sure.

"Sister," she whispered, "I love you with all my heart."

"Lizzie...what...?"

Elizabeth ran up to the house and shoved Annalise through the window. She heard a crash as her sister landed somewhere on the other side.

"You idiot!" Father grabbed her hair and jerked her down to the ground. Pain electrified her head. He twisted her around at an excruciating angle, dropped the shovel, then grabbed her by the throat with his left hand, choking her.

His fingernails scraped her face. She tried to kick him, to grab his wrist, but she wasn't strong or quick enough. She felt his right thumb pressing against her eye.

Another wave of pain pulsed through her. It felt as if her eyeball was pressed against the back of her brain.

"Do you know what you've done?"

Yes, she thought, I know. I've made it impossible for you to eliminate my entire family. You can't get through that window and you can't ring the bell without starting a conversation you don't want to have.

Even as she felt her consciousness fading, she smiled. No matter what happens next, there will always be a dangling thread. You will always be looking over your shoulder. You will always wonder if this is the day your past comes back to destroy you.

Her last thought was a happy one. My baby sister. Annalise.

She'll be the one who delivers the justice you deserve.

Kenzi stared at the woman on the witness stand, trying not to blink, gape, or otherwise betray her thoughts. Possibly everyone in the courtroom needed an extra moment to digest what the witness had just said.

"I'm sorry. I'm not sure we all got that. Could you please repeat your last statement?"

The witness appeared peeved. "I don't know how I could say it any more plainly. I got inseminated in the bathroom at Dick's Drive-In."

Kenzi glanced around the courtroom. Judge Cornwall, an African-American man in his mid-fifties, was nodding, obviously trying to maintain his judicial poker face. Even opposing counsel seemed to be struggling to remain composed.

Why could she never have a normal case?

Because in divorce court, nothing was ever normal...

DAN'S RECIPES

THERE ARE MANY WAYS TO WHIP UP A TASTY BUDDHA BOWL, BUT this is one of Dan's favorites. And if you don't like tofu, just omit that part of the recipe.

INGREDIENTS (FOR FOUR SERVINGS):
    Tofu, pressed and cubed (16 0z. block)
    Chickpeas, drained and dried (15 oz. can)
    Brussel sprouts, trimmed, outer leaves removed (1 lb.)
    Large apple, cored (1)
    Medium red onion, cut into wedges (1)
    Maple syrup (2 tbsp.)
    Thyme (3-4 sprigs)
    Cornstarch (2 tsp.)
    Garlic powder (2 tsp.)
    Onion powder (1 tsp.)
    Paprika (2 tsp.)
    plus sea salt, black pepper, and olive oil

. . .

INSTRUCTIONS:

1) Preheat the oven to 400 degrees. Cut the brussel sprouts in half. Add sprouts, onions, and apples to a foil-lined, greased baking sheet.

2) Mix some olive oil, maple syrup, salt and pepper to taste, and drizzle it over the sprouts combo. Toss till completely coated. Turn the sprouts cut side down. Add the thyme. Bake for 35 minutes.

3) If you want tofu, add the tofu and chickpeas to opposite sides of a lined baking sheet. Sprinkle them with garlic powder, onion powder, paprika, sea salt, and pepper. Add the cornstarch ONLY to the tofu.

4) When the oven has only 20 minutes left, add the tofu/chickpea baking sheet. When the oven has 10 minutes left, flip over the tofu and stir the chickpeas, then return the baking sheet to the oven.

A tahini dressing is perfect with this, and kale chips make a great side dish.

ABOUT THE AUTHOR

William Bernhardt is the author of over fifty books, including *The Last Chance Lawyer* (#1 National Bestseller), the historical novels *Challengers of the Dust* and *Nemesis*, two books of poetry, and the Red Sneaker books on writing. In addition, Bernhardt founded the Red Sneaker Writers Center to mentor aspiring authors. The Center hosts an annual conference (WriterCon), small-group seminars, a newsletter, and a bi-weekly podcast. He is also the owner of Balkan Press, which publishes poetry and fiction as well as the literary journal *Conclave*.

Bernhardt has received the Southern Writers Guild's Gold Medal Award, the Royden B. Davis Distinguished Author Award (University of Pennsylvania) and the H. Louise Cobb Distinguished Author Award (Oklahoma State), which is given "in recognition of an outstanding body of work that has profoundly influenced the way in which we understand ourselves and American society at large." In 2019, he received the Arrell Gibson Lifetime Achievement Award from the Oklahoma Center for the Book.

In addition Bernhardt has written plays, a musical (book and score), humor, children stories, biography, and puzzles. He has edited two anthologies (*Legal Briefs* and *Natural Suspect*) as fundraisers for The Nature Conservancy and the Children's Legal Defense Fund. In his spare time, he has enjoyed surfing, digging for dinosaurs, trekking through the Himalayas, paragliding, scuba diving, caving, zip-lining over the canopy of the Costa Rican rain forest, and jumping out of an airplane at 10,000 feet.

In 2017, when Bernhardt delivered the keynote address at the San Francisco Writers Conference, chairman Michael Larsen noted that in addition to penning novels, Bernhardt can "write a sonnet, play a sonata, plant a garden, try a lawsuit, teach a class, cook a gourmet meal, beat you at Scrabble, and work the *New York Times* crossword in under five minutes."

ALSO BY WILLIAM BERNHARDT

The Daniel Pike Novels

The Last Chance Lawyer

Court of Killers

Trial by Blood

Twisted Justice

Judge and Jury

Final Verdict

The Ben Kincaid Novels

Primary Justice

Blind Justice

Deadly Justice

Perfect Justice

Cruel Justice

Naked Justice

Extreme Justice

Dark Justice

Silent Justice

Murder One

Criminal Intent

Death Row

Hate Crime

Capitol Murder

Capitol Threat

Capitol Conspiracy

Capitol Offense

Capitol Betrayal

Justice Returns

Other Novels

Challengers of the Dust

The Game Master

Nemesis: The Final Case of Eliot Ness

Dark Eye

Strip Search

Double Jeopardy

The Midnight Before Christmas

Final Round

The Code of Buddyhood

The Red Sneaker Series on Writing

Story Structure: The Key to Successful Fiction

Creating Character: Bringing Your Story to Life

Perfecting Plot: Charting the Hero's Journey

Dynamic Dialogue: Letting Your Story Speak

Sizzling Style: Every Word Matters

Powerful Premise: Writing the Irresistible

Excellent Editing: The Writing Process

Thinking Theme: The Heart of the Matter

What Writers Need to Know: Essential Topics

Dazzling Description: Painting the Perfect Picture

The Fundamentals of Fiction (video series)

Poetry

The White Bird

The Ocean's Edge

For Young Readers
Shine
Princess Alice and the Dreadful Dragon
Equal Justice: The Courage of Ada Sipuel
The Black Sentry

Edited by William Bernhardt
Legal Briefs: Short Stories by Today's Best Thriller Writers
Natural Suspect: A Collaborative Novel of Suspense

Made in the USA
Columbia, SC
01 August 2021